LOSING
CONTROL

LOSING CONTROL

BOOK 1 OF THE KERR CHRONICLES

JEN FREDERICK

Text copyright © 2015 Jen Frederick

Published by Montlake Romance, Seattle
www.apub.com

Amazon, the Amazon logo, and Montlake Romance are trademarks of Amazon.com, Inc., or its affiliates.

ISBN-13: 9781503944107
ISBN-10: 1503944107

Cover design by Shasti O'Leary-Soudant

Printed in the United States of America

Dedicated to my dear husband
For making sure we ate and had a clean house, fresh
clothes, gas in the car, lights in the house, hot water,
and every other necessity in life that I can't remember to
take care of while in the middle of a book.
I'd never be able to cope without you.

If you prick us, do we not bleed?
if you tickle us, do we not laugh?
if you poison us, do we not die?
and if you wrong us, shall we not revenge?

—William Shakespeare,
The Merchant of Venice, 3.1

CHAPTER 1

Click.

Cancer nurses have kind eyes. Kindness must be their superpower. How else could they continue to smile when most of the time they are treating people who are dying? Because while there is all this talk about survivors, everyone knows cancer is a death sentence. It takes longer to kill some people. And, of course, the good ones like my mother, Sophie Corielli, go down too swiftly.

Click.

Today even the softhearted cancer nurses can only summon up pity smiles for Mom and me as Dr. Chen clears his throat to deliver the dire news.

Click.

Throat cough.

"I'm sorry, Sophie," he begins.

My mom squeezes my hand, the one she's held since we sat down. It's the only thing keeping me from ripping the New York Memorial Hospital pen out of his hands so I don't have to hear the goddamn *click* again. A nurse swishes by, her soft shoes' sweep on the marble adding slightly different vibrato.

Click.

Throat cough.

Shuffle.

It's a bad Broadway musical beat where the disease is the conductor. It's the disease—the mutating, killing cells—that directs the players. Today the tone is somber.

The last time we saw Dr. Chen, we were all high-fiving each other. Even the looming medical bills couldn't diminish the happiness we'd felt when he gave us the all clear three years ago.

"Your MCL is back, and, not surprisingly, it's aggressive. We'll need to start an immediate round of chemo. Last time we didn't need to do stem cell treatment, but I think we'll have to now, and we should do it right away."

I stare wide-eyed ahead because I don't want to see the fear that is in Mom's eyes at this news. Or maybe I'm hiding from my fear. The first time we were told she had a rare, often undiagnosed cancer called mantle cell lymphoma, she was an endless well of optimism, and for three years, I'd been convinced right along with her.

But while I've inherited her light-brown hair and her green eyes, I've always been more pragmatic—which she tells me I got from Dad. I wouldn't know. He died when I was three. My memories of him are dim and incomplete. For twenty-two years, it has been my mother and me.

The Corielli girls. Indestructible. Not brought low by men, disability, or disease.

As Dr. Chen explains about more treatment, including the eight-hour chemo drips Mom will have to endure and the likelihood she isn't going to be able to work for the next two months, my hand starts to get squeezed as if she is attempting to make lemonade out of my fingers.

In my peripheral vision, I see the skin draw tightly around her skull. Even optimism can't hide the deep lines illness has drawn on her skin, aging her far past her forty-seven years of life. Her face is closed down, her gaze fixed at some point over Dr. Chen's shoulder.

My own mind is preoccupied with our ugly financial picture. We're still trying to dig our way out of the medical bill black hole we found ourselves in the last go-around. The spot I'm worrying in my cheek may ache for days, but that's better than having a meltdown over the unfairness of the universe. A lament I'm sure sounds too often in these rooms.

It's not that I don't have options. I do. It's that I had been able to successfully avoid those options in the past, choosing an honest struggle with debt over a more lucrative under-the-table career. My foolish pride isn't going to provide food or medicine. I take a swallow, pushing down the grief and anger, and pulling up my resolve.

"We'll see you tomorrow." Dr. Chen wraps it up, and we all stand. "I'll have Donna call in the prescriptions. Take the steroid and the anti-nausea before tomorrow. And remember," he shakes a finger at my mom, "don't forget to eat."

"Thank you, Dr. Chen." Mom gives him a wan smile and takes the checkout sheet. As she walks out, he grabs my arm.

"Tiny," he says in a low voice, "a minute?"

"Sure, Dr. Chen." My fingers clench the strap of my sling backpack as I brace myself for more unpleasantness.

"I saw on the nurse's notes that you're living in a fifth-floor walkup?"

I nod. "Mom and I moved in together when she was sick and the midtown apartment didn't make sense for the both of us."

Clearly not understood by Dr. Chen was that we could no longer afford the midtown apartment with its lobby and elevator access to the upper floors. He had to know that many of his bills from three years ago, during my mother's first bout with cancer, were still unpaid. Medical bills are astronomical even if you have insurance but if you didn't, they were crippling. Every little luxury had to be excised, so Mom lives with me in a tiny one-bedroom apartment that has no doorman and no elevator and sits over a greasy-spoon restaurant.

He shakes his head and frowns. "She's never going to be able to make it up a flight of stairs, let alone five flights, after her chemo treatments. You really need to do something about your living arrangements."

I laugh but it's a hollow, ugly sound because nothing about today is funny. "I'll get right on that."

"I know times are tough for you and Sophie, but I'm serious." He shifts on his feet and clicks his pen a couple of times. "Maybe you can talk to public housing assistance. I don't know how that works, but perhaps there's some kind of exigent circumstances clause. I'm giving you a handicapped worksheet for Sophie. Use it."

There's no point in telling Dr. Chen we're broke. From the look of his Hermès tie and his hand-stitched Italian loafers, he'd think that meant shopping at Macy's and carrying your own bags instead of having Barney's deliver your purchases to Ralph, your doorman.

"I'll go down to the City Housing Authority tomorrow," I promise and tuck the doctor's handicapped note into my backpack.

"She'll beat this," Dr. Chen says and pats me on the back. "Don't let her get down. You need to be the voice of optimism at all times. Mental well-being is as important as physical well-being."

◆ ◆ ◆

We catch the bus because the subway stop is too far away. Mom is swaying and looks exhausted even though she doesn't start treatment until Monday. The mere thought of IV drips, surgery for ports, and long needles constantly stuck into your most painful places is crushing. I want to pick her up and carry her the short distance to the bus stop, but I know better.

"We should cancel our trip to Vermont," she says as we ascend the three stairs onto the bus.

"If you want." I'm not sure if she really doesn't want to go or is saying that for my sake. Our stilted interaction pains me. It's as if the cancer is now eroding our ability to communicate as well as killing her healthy cells. Already she is withdrawing. Her arms are folded against her sides, her lips are pressed flat and thin, and tension is visible in every line of her frame.

"It doesn't make sense to go. We'll need the money." Her voice is curt and final.

"I never liked Vermont anyway."

No one in her right mind is against taking a tour of a world famous ice cream factory. But we aren't in our right minds any longer. We're straining hard, trying to keep the tide of disappointment and despair from flooding our minds and bodies. Or at least I am. I sit up straighter because if Mom needs me to be the shield for her, I will. I'd take every last drop of her cancer inside me if I could.

I can't help but make more comparisons to last time. Three years ago, when we made this same ride after similar news, she was fierce and determined. "I'm going to kick cancer's ass," she told me. The only time I saw her cry was when her hair started falling out.

Today she has no pithy fight words nor does her expression show anything but defeat. My heart stutters, and Dr. Chen's words follow each ragged beat.

Mental well-being is as important as physical well-being.

"We'll go when you feel better." I pull her against me and try to avoid the sharp ache of anxiety at how frail she feels already. "I'll let you eat all the ice cream you want."

It's not a very good joke, but usually she'd give me a little poke in the side to acknowledge my effort.

To my dismay, she turns her face into my shoulder to muffle a big, watery sob. Sunny Sophie has no happy thoughts today. Tears prick my own eyes, and I close them tight in an effort to try to keep all the worry and fear inside me. I get as close as the scooped seats of the bus allow and hold her trembling body for blocks, the cacophony of passengers getting on and off covering the choked sobs of my mother.

Cancer survivor.

Cancer sufferer.

"What did Dr. Chen say to you?" she finally asks, breaking away from my embrace. She wipes her face with a tissue and looks out the window, avoiding my eyes.

"He, ah . . ." I clear my throat because my feelings are blocking my ability to speak. "He said we needed to move. That you'd have a hard time with the stairs."

When she says nothing, I continue. "I'm going down to the Housing Authority tomorrow. Dr. Chen wrote me out a note that will help us get into a building with an elevator—exigent circumstances."

There's another muffled sob and I can see in the window reflection that she's pressing her fist against her mouth. The other passengers are beginning to notice and look away, not wanting to catch whatever grief we're not handling well.

"We make too much money," she finally chokes out.

"What's that?"

Her head swings toward me, and in her gaze I see guilt. Lots of guilt.

"I already looked. Because I worked this year, we make too much to get public assistance and not enough to move." She presses her lips together but they tremble with the effort.

"When did you . . ." I trail off. If she looked, then she must have had some inkling she was sick again. "When did you know?" I ask accusatorily.

"A couple of months ago," she admits.

"A couple of months?" I screech, bringing curious glances our way. I lower my voice to a hiss. "You've been sick for a couple of months, and this is the first time you've gone to a doctor?"

"I hoped it would go away," she says defensively. "The last thing we need is more medical bills."

Hearing this makes me crazy angry, and I know that it is not the right emotion to be expressing right now, so it's my turn to avoid her eyes. If I open my mouth now, I'm bound to say something I regret.

"I'm sorry, Tiny." Tears flood her eyes, and she begins to weep again.

The sound and sight of her grief destroys my anger. *Be her shield.* I gather her close, ignoring her struggles to push me away. "No worries, Mommy," I whisper. "We're going to be all right."

She says nothing but continues to cry, and no matter how hard I hug her, her tears won't quit. By the time we arrive at our stop, she seems to have run out of water and all that is left are dry, shaking heaves. I help her off the bus, trying to shut out the pitying glances that are cast our way as we exit.

By the time we walk the half block to our apartment complex, she's already breathing heavily. As I unlock the exterior door, she stares at the staircase as if it is some giant mountain, too big for a mortal to ascend. The stairs between each level are split in half so that there are six stairs and then a square landing and then six more to reach the next floor. That's sixty in total that we walk twice every day. Sixty stairs that must look like Mount Everest to my mom.

"Come on," I encourage. "We'll take it a few at a time."

She smiles wanly and takes my hand. We walk up to the first landing and she's leaning heavily against me. The next twelve steps are taken with determination, a spark of the Mom of old. But at the midpoint between the second and third floors, she collapses and I barely react quickly enough to keep her from tumbling backwards.

Heart racing, I sit my butt on the edge of the second floor landing and pull her against me. She's trembling and crying.

"I can't make it, Tiny," she sobs out. "I'm not going to make it."

I pretend she's only talking about the stairs. *Only the stairs.* My eyes are wet too, but I'm going to get her upstairs to the apartment. And when she's lying down and resting, I'm going to make a phone call. I crouch in front of her. "Climb on," I order.

"No, Tiny," she protests, but after a moment she realizes that there are no options for her—I'm not leaving her here in the stairwell. Her slim fingers curl around my shoulders, and I begin the laborious task of carrying my five-foot-six, one-hundred-and-forty-pound mom up the last three flights of stairs. I've never been more grateful than at this moment that I'm a bicycle messenger because if it weren't for the fact that I bike dozens of miles a day, I never would have made it to the fifth floor.

By the time I reach our apartment, my thighs are burning and I'm gasping for air like I'm on the last mile of a marathon. "See, easy peasy," I tease her when I'm able to catch my breath, but it's not enough to generate a smile. She looks defeated and stumbles into the bedroom to collapse.

She's asleep before I can tug off my shoes and get her a glass of water. After setting the full glass by her nightstand, I pull out my phone and dial up a number.

"Hey, it's me, Tiny. You still need someone to do that special job of yours?"

CHAPTER 2

When dispatch calls at seven the next morning to ask if I'll cover for a sick courier, I say yes before Sandra can finish her request. It's either bike around in the sunshine earning time-and-a-half or watch my mother stare out the window at the large brick wall across the alley.

"I'll stay if you'd like." Given that I have my bike shorts on and my helmet on the table, we both know the offer isn't genuine. She waves her hand at me, doesn't even turn around. Sucking in my lips and all the things I'd like to say, I grab my helmet and pull my bike down off the wall.

At the sound of my bike wheels hitting the floor, she rouses enough to say good-bye. "Be safe, dear."

"I will." It's enough to make me smile as I carry my bike down the five flights of stairs.

Then it's the rush of riding. If my thighs aren't burning, I'm not going fast enough. The wind whistles as I speed down Second Avenue toward the offices of Neil's in the Flatiron District. On a Saturday morning, there's very little traffic to avoid. The four-mile ride takes less than fifteen minutes, and I'm inside the second floor of the building where Neil's is located and sticking the packages in my pack before most people could have hailed a taxi. It would have been ten minutes, but there were cops out and I had to obey a few traffic signals.

Saturday's a day for residential deliveries—clothes and small goods for rich, lazy people who can afford a special delivery.

"This one's fragile. Goes to Wiggin' Out over near Columbus Circle." Sandra, our dispatcher, is a mass of curled black hair and heavy eyeliner. She's got a Puerto Rican background and her skin is a gorgeous warm brown year-round without the use of artificial tanners. I think Neil, the owner, has a thing for her. Whenever I've been in the office, he stares at her overlong until she sighs audibly and picks up the phone to make a personal call to her boyfriend.

Even though she's not technically allowed personal calls, this routine can be observed regularly. No one knows if she actually has a boyfriend or if she's calling a friend and faking it. I'm uncertain whom I'm supposed to feel sorry for—Sandra having her boss lusting after her or Neil having unrequited feelings for Sandra. Both make me uncomfortable, and I try to make my visits to the office as brief as possible.

"This box is like paper." I squeeze it and the sides nearly collapse.

"Hey, I said it was fragile." She reaches over the desk to slap at me.

"Aren't they all?" I roll my eyes but hold the box gingerly as I leave.

Neil's is a specialty delivery service. We specialize in the confidential, discreet, and fragile package delivery. Packages are delivered swiftly but not at the breakneck pace seen on television. This doesn't mean I move slowly. I use my brain as much as my legs. Biking can be like playing a game of chess. You have to anticipate the other players' moves before they execute them. Is the car at ten o'clock going to open its door in the next twenty seconds? How long will the bus stop before it pulls out into traffic? Can I squeeze through these two cars and make the corner before the light turns?

Neil pays us hourly rather than by commission because he thinks it reduces his accident insurance premiums. If we aren't required to go so fast and make so many deliveries at one time, we won't get doored as often. Doored is when a car door suddenly opens and either strikes you directly or causes you to lay down your bike. Or, in the case of my ex, sends you into the windshield. He only needed twelve stitches after that one.

The best thing Colin Carpenter gave me during our on-again, off-again relationship was a tip for Neil's Courier Service. Or "Neil's," as it is known. He was biking, and I was looking for a new job because waiting tables wasn't as easy as I thought it was going to be. While it was simple to remember everyone's order, and I had no problem delivering the food, I couldn't write an order fast enough because of my damn dyslexia. The restaurant owner was a decent woman and tried to accommodate me, but it was hell for the back of the house. I got the boot after only two weeks.

Colin was delivering something to the shop next door and nearly ran me over. We exchanged numbers, and then later that night we exchanged bodily fluids, and I started delivering the next day. I'd borrowed a bike from a friend of his until I splurged and bought my current machine, a single speed Nature Boy that could accommodate larger tires for winter riding.

Colin left after a few months because he didn't like dating one person and I didn't like being part of the crowd. He got a job that paid commission and kept him out of my hair. But once you sleep with someone, it's awfully convenient to keep doing it even when you both know it's bad for you. I kicked the Colin habit for good when my mom got the all clear from her first bout with MCL. We were getting rid of all the bad stuff in our lives at that point, and Colin was one of the unhealthy items I took to the trash.

I hadn't been able to install something better. Men in the city aren't known for their fidelity or their staying power. At least the men I've met. But I'm twenty-five, so there's still lots of time, I figure. Right now there are more important things for me to think about—like how I'm ever going to get enough money to pay for first and last months' rent and pass a credit check for an apartment with an elevator.

The phone call I made last night was the first step toward solving that problem, so long as I didn't mind doing things that could get me fifteen years of incarceration if I got caught. At least I'd get free room and board in jail.

I brood all morning long, and I'm not in the mood to have one of the last of my morning deliveries delayed. When I see the sign in the window that says, "Be back in 15 minutes," I let out a little scream of frustration and kick the doorframe.

"Bad morning?"

The question comes from a rich, deep voice to my right. Some stupid actor. The notes of his voice are perfectly modulated, as if he spent years perfecting the tone and depth to reach the biggest audience.

"Yeah, what's it to you?" I challenge, because I'm not in the mood to be chatted up by some wannabe in an Off-Off-Broadway production who wants to try out some new lines on a messenger girl.

My sneering gaze melts right off my face when it lands on the owner of the voice. Dark-haired and dark-eyed, the stranger gives me a slow smile as I take him in. He's tall, much taller than my five-foot-four frame. My eyes have to trek upward to see the entire package.

And there's so much to appreciate—from his trim waist to the wide shoulders encased in a gray wool suit coat that fits him so well I wonder if he was sewn into it. Tiny stitches on the lapel mark its expensive provenance. A darkly tanned neck gives way to a firm chin and lush lips.

"Bee stung" is the description that I've heard used to describe the same look on supermodels. Those lips are about the only soft thing on his face. Those lips and a hollow on the side of his face that appears when those plush lips curve upward. The divot is too shallow and wide to be termed a dimple, but it's just as devastating.

One hand is stuck in a pocket and his jacket is pushed behind the hand to reveal a flat stomach. No desk paunch on this guy. There's an intense sexual aura about him. The nonchalant stance, the dark gaze, the lush lips are all an invitation to rip the buttons of his snowy-white shirt apart and see exactly what lies underneath all of those fabrics.

In the guise of giving my chin a scratch, I stick a thumb under my jaw to make sure my mouth is closed. This guy? He can practice lines with me all he wants.

His half-smile widens knowingly. "Kind of a beautiful day to be kicking doors down."

It's obvious he's well acquainted with his effect on women. Too bad I can't sneak a picture for my mom. A verbal description is not going to do him justice.

"If I can't deliver my packages, then I won't have time left to enjoy said beautiful day." I lift the Wiggin' Out delivery to show him.

He nods and pushes away from the post he's leaning against. "I'm in complete agreement. I say we blow our responsibilities off and head to the park."

He bends his arm and pulls up his suit jacket sleeve to reveal a thick watch with exposed gears. It looks expensive too. He's too well put together to be an actor, and they don't wear suits unless they're on stage or being interviewed by a late night show host. His attire is more suited to the downtown financial district, where pin-tucked lapels and ice-blue ties covered in tiny white dots paired with white linen shirts are deemed normal. This guy's outfit says investor, not poor actor.

"Are you lost?" My mouth opens before my good sense can catch up.

"It's the suit, right?" He flips up the end of his tie and gives me a roguish grin. What is it that Pam from *Archer* says? Oh right, *You could drown a toddler in my panties right now.*

"It's the suit," I confirm.

"Not lost," he says, "But if I was, would you have lent me a hand?" He lifts his own hand, palm up, as if to gesture for me to take it. I follow the thick line of his arm and am surprised at how capable that hand looks. Strong. Like it could hold you up if you stumbled. Not the hand of an investor. I want to grab it and clutch it to my chest. Because I'm not able to pigeonhole him, he's all the more fascinating. I step closer.

"Yes," I say—because who wouldn't? Random tourists would walk out of expensive Broadway shows if he announced that he needed help.

My immediate answer is rewarded with an even deeper smile. It's kind of magical. My bad mood, the worry about my mother, the stress over our lack of money all melts away like ice cream on the sidewalk on a sunny day. I want to stand here and bask in the warmth of this handsome stranger's smile. We grin at each other as if we're both happy to be sharing a moment. His hand is still upward, still waiting for me to take it. I lift my own hand slowly and reach toward him, already anticipating that it will be dry but warm, solid but not hurtful. He doesn't move—not an inch—somehow knowing that I can be easily startled away.

"Where will you take me?" I ask, hand hovering over his.

"Anywhere you want to go." His response is delivered in a low, husky tone as if he's imagining an intimate moment. It's a tone you hear on the beach at the end of a long day spent lazing in the sun and rubbing lotion over your lover. It's the sound you hear when an invitation is issued to come to bed—and not to sleep.

There is something between us. My eyes widen and I feel the pull, the inexorable pull of the universe drawing me closer. I couldn't have stopped my feet if I wanted to. And the closer I get to him, the more I realize that he feels it too.

We aren't strangers. Somewhere, at some point, we must have made a connection and we're now recognizing it again in this lifetime.

"Hello there," he says softly, as if we hadn't spoken moments before. He isn't saying hello to me. He is acknowledging that there is something special between us.

I'm inches from him, and he's bending toward me. He's going to kiss me right here in the street and strangely, wonderfully, weirdly I want to be kissed. New York strangers don't kiss on the street in broad daylight. We don't even make eye contact willingly. We fold up our bodies into tight, compact containers on subways and buses so we can avoid accidental touching.

Yet here I am walking straight into the arms of a guy I would never dream of dating. He's too rich, too polished, too posh for me.

My kind are the worker bees. This guy directs the bees from up high in the clouds. Yet he wants me. I can see it in his eyes, in the way that they've darkened with appreciation and even desire.

"I want—"

"I'll take that package." A body muscles swiftly between the stranger and me, breaking our connection. A petite woman with striking red hair plucks the box out of my hands and turns to the stranger. "Ian, why don't you hold this?" Turning back to me, she asks, "Do you have anything for me to sign?"

I nod and jerkily pull up the app on my smartphone. As she scribbles her name down with her finger, I meet Ian's gaze over her bent head. It's like he's never looked away from me. As if everything he wants is right before him.

Ian. I like it. I like *him.* Would it be so terrible to take him up on his invitation? To go over to Central Park, take my shoes off, and hold his hand as we walk down one of the wide sidewalks and suck in the fresh spring air? Wouldn't it be absolutely lovely to check all my problems at the gate of the park and walk inside? We could stroll to the lake and he'd place those lush lips over mine and I could feel how truly soft they were.

We'd kiss for a long time, and then he'd take me to dinner where we wouldn't eat a thing because we would be too busy talking and laughing and *falling in love.*

The woman takes the package and goes inside the shop, leaving the two of us alone.

"Is this your last delivery?" he asks. "The invitation to the park is still open, now that you've divested yourself of your responsibilities."

"No." My one word comes out with real regret because I'm staring down lost opportunity. I can't go to the park. I can't forget my responsibilities.

I'm her shield.

"I'm not a fan of that word." He steps toward me, but the owner of the wig shop has broken the spell. And a good thing too, because I don't have time for this man who whips up uncommon wants inside me. I know all too well that sick mothers and men don't go together. All my energy should be focused on my mother and this minor god is too big of a distraction. Still, even knowing all that, I can't look away from him.

I hold up my hand to stop him. "Don't."

Before he can say another word, I get on my bike as fast as I can and pedal away without a backward glance. There's a sour taste in my mouth because another time, I would have followed him anywhere.

CHAPTER 3

"Sign this." Malcolm slides me a piece of paper with lots of words on it. It will take me five years to decipher all the words and he knows it—the punk.

"I'm not signing anything. Give me the package, and I'll deliver it." I grab for the empty, dull yellow envelope that presumably is the container for these papers my stepbrother wants delivered. For the past four weeks, I've transported small packages for him all over the city and several boroughs. I don't know what's inside these packages and I hope to keep it that way. Plausible deniability and all that. "By the way, the actor guy that took the big package the other morning looked like he was going to shiv me. Maybe you oughta tell your customers that you have a new delivery girl."

He smirks. "Move a little faster. Isn't that what sets you apart? Your speed? *Double Rush? Triple Rush?* I was watching that show on the Travel Channel. I think your ex started working there."

"Wouldn't surprise me. We both know Colin is an attention whore." Everyone has a reality television show these days, including bike couriers. While I wouldn't be a fan of my life on display, and I certainly wouldn't want to work for the barking, Ritalin-addicted dispatchers that Colin works for, I'd do just about anything for money—which is why I haven't gotten out of my chair and left Malcolm Hedder's apartment in Queens. "I move fast on the bike, but I'm not so sure how nimble I'll be against some dude with a knife."

"Guess you'll have to learn." He smirks and taps the pen on the page near a straight line. I suppose that's where I'm supposed to sign. I can't believe we lived in the same house for four years and didn't kill each other. Back then, we were teenagers trying to cope with the fallout of his father's infidelity and my mother's poor choice in partners. Not every blended family turns into the Brady Bunch.

Since Malcolm graduated from high school, though, I haven't seen much of him. Mom kept up with him, and I'd hear about him through her. He tried trade school, auto repair I think, and then left it. About two years ago, he contacted me to ask if I wanted to do some side deliveries for him, but I turned him down because I was rightly suspicious of what kinds of packages I'd be shuttling around the city.

A couple of months ago, he'd contacted me again and said he had a high-paying specialty job, but his vague descriptions didn't interest me.

And now? Now I've been delivering packages for Malcolm for four weeks. And it's been a shitty four weeks. The last good memory I have is meeting Ian, the Suit, outside the wig shop. Since then it's been holding my mother's head as she pukes after an eight-hour chemo session and trying to force-feed food down her throat during the intervening days because Dr. Chen chastised us both about her iron levels last week.

It's been spending every minute of every day worrying about her, and then trying to be cheerful when I'm home because she seems to have lost her smile. She talks about how she's so done with treatment and being sick. Her eyes are often red and swollen, as if she's spent the whole day crying.

More red meat. More spinach. More beans. About all she can handle are blended shakes. At least the strawberries do a pretty good job of hiding the spinach taste, but I can't turn a steak into a drink for her.

The last four weeks have been nothing but pain and stress compounded by my illicit activities for Malcolm. Delivering Malcolm's packages late at night and in between my regular duties throughout the day, my nerves are stretched thinner than a bike spoke, wondering if—no, *when*—I'm going to get caught.

I don't know what's in the small manila envelopes, and I don't want to know. Nothing good, that's for sure, because I'm getting paid way too much money delivering these packages. I actually have dummy packages in my pack to make it look like I'm not running around delivering drugs.

What else can be in these parcels? It's not like my stepbrother is a lawyer and produces a bunch of paperwork every day. This is the first time he's handed me something even remotely legal-like. I watch the sheaf of papers as if it's a live snake and will jump up and bite my fingers if I get too close.

"Drug dealers have NDAs now?"

"If I'm a drug dealer, I guess that makes you a drug mule," he says softly, but not so softly that everyone in the living room can't hear. His friends, two of them totally blazed, giggle like schoolgirls. "We're going to exchange signatures. Want my help? Sign it, Tiny, or we're done."

His voice never wavers, which signals the seriousness of his intent.

When I called him four weeks ago, after Mom had collapsed on the stairs, he'd said the special project was filled but that he'd help me out with first and last months' rent and pay me enough to afford a handicap-accessible building so long as I agreed to deliver for him, no questions asked, for a year. I said yes.

But whoever was slated to fill the special project role washed out and he asked me again, telling me that I'd either do the special project or I couldn't deliver for him at all.

I gnaw on the side of my mouth for two seconds and then give an internal *fuck it*. There's no real debate. I need the money, and I'm willing to do anything for it. If Malcolm doesn't give me first and last months' rent, there's no way I can move Mom into the new apartment. The sooner I get her out of the dingy one-bedroom with all those stairs, the better it will be. Right now she's like a prisoner because she can't leave without me. And she hates that I have to carry her up the stairs after each chemo treatment. I've convinced myself that she'll cheer up and return to her old happy self if only I can get us into a different apartment.

No, there's no room for debate, morals, or ethics.

"And if I sign this, then you'll help me get the new apartment?"

"Sure," he says easily.

I'm not sure I believe him entirely. There's a lot left unsaid, but I've no other options. I scrawl a few shapes on the line. I wonder if I can even be held to a contract I haven't read. After shoving the papers inside the envelope Malcolm provides, I head for the door.

"Bring this back with his signature and I'll sign whatever damn thing you want," Malcolm says.

As I wait for the elevator, I hear his companion call, "She can work off the debt in my bed."

"She'd have to service a train of guys to work off the debt she's going to owe me," he says flatly. And he's not lying.

The delivery address for the papers I've signed is in the Meatpacking District. I always hate riding down there because cobblestones are everywhere, which is hell for a girl on a bike. Plus, the numbers for some of these buildings are obscured because the more hidden the place is, the more people want to find it. I wonder how that works if there's a need for emergency services.

After biking up and down Hudson Street a few times, I finally spot the building. The front features a corrugated metal garage door that's completely pristine. Not a hint of graffiti, which is odd down here where everything but the glass windows has been tagged by some juvenile miscreant. I lean my bike up against the big metal door and look for a buzzer. There isn't one. I don't even see a side door. I bang on the metal door a few times.

At eight in the morning, no one down here is even awake. People down here don't start their day until eleven in the morning because that's the soonest they can drag their hungover asses out of bed. The life of the moneyed New York City crowd is exactly as the songs say—party all night and sleep all day. And if you want to be part of the crowd, you follow the same hours.

"Hey, delivery for . . ." I pause and look at the envelope. There are letters there, but I can't make them out. "Delivery," I yell again.

"In the back," a male voice from above says, and it scares the bejeezus out of me. I jump and yelp like a dog whose foot's been trampled. In the corner of the black frame of the garage door is a tiny camera and holes, which, I guess, have a speaker behind them. It's so minuscule that only if you were looking really hard could you see it. I stare at the camera for a long time, wondering who the hell is behind it. Is he staring at me?

"In the back," he repeats, his tone a tad deeper and tinged with barely suppressed humor. I guess he is watching me stare. "Number 14001."

His voice sounds familiar, but maybe it's because it sounds throaty and sexy and I'd *like* it to be familiar. I still dream about the man in the Theater District. *Ian.* Knowing his name makes my fantasy life a bit richer. I hop on my bike and cycle down the long block, take a left, and then I spot the alley. It's big enough for one car or truck. I stop halfway in the middle of the block.

The building looms high and has at least three stories. It's all brick on the first floor with another shiny, corrugated metal garage door, but this time there's a tall, thin black door to the right with the number 14001 in stainless steel in the center. I lean my bike against the door and tilt my head back to look up. The second and third floors are full of windows, and despite the fact that there are buildings behind me, and tall ones at that, I can still see rays of sunlight shooting in through the windows. The place must be gorgeous inside.

When I get closer I notice the door is ajar, which makes me nervous. Who leaves their door ajar in the city? Stupid people, that's who—or dangerous ones. I push the door open, half expecting it to creak like a door to a haunted house, but it swings open like the hinges were oiled two minutes ago. The door leads into a narrow hallway that runs the length of the building. There's exterior light from somewhere and I realize that it's from a narrow channel in the ceiling that must lead to the roof. Clever design. I wonder if the roof is entirely glass or if the light is from multiple skylights. This is a rich person's place. Only rich people can bring exterior light to a brick building surrounded by taller structures.

There are stairs with a glass balustrade that point out my path like a giant arrow. Unless my guy appears in the hallway like a David Blaine trick, I'm guessing I should head up the stairs. Gingerly, I take my first step, and when no sirens blast out I figure I'm safe enough. I run up the flight of stairs and at the top, I see one giant—and I mean giant—space.

"You can set it on the table," the voice from the street speaker calls out. I venture farther into the huge, open space. A sleek, modern kitchen like those I've drooled over in home magazines appears to my left and in front of it a long oval walnut table is surrounded by clear acrylic chairs. To my right is a living room filled with cowhide and leather furniture and a big, plush rug in deep red. Beyond the living room is a wall of mirrors and in front of it stands a . . . superhero.

I mean, it's like walking into Bruce Wayne's fuck pad or something and seeing him do a pre-rescue workout. The owner of the voice is doing biceps curls and wearing gym shorts that appear to be in danger of falling down his slim hips with every movement.

He has ridges and planes and jutting protuberances that I've not seen outside a movie theatre. And many of those muscles were fake CGI creations, I learned later. I almost shed a few tears hearing that sad news. He grunts and the shorts slide down a centimeter more. I can't see his face clearly because the distance between me and the mirrors is too great in this cavernous room.

I jerk myself out of my tween fantasy and set the manila envelope on the table and pull out the contract. "I'll need you to sign before I can go."

Bruce drops his weight and palms a towel with almost the same motion. Superhero reflexes to go with the superhero body. Nice. Too bad he's a criminal because I'm not delivering tourist trinkets at the prices Malcolm is paying me. As Bruce draws near, I fumble and nearly drop the ten-pages-thick contract that contains my nearly illegible signature. Bruce is none other than the guy from the Theater District.

"I'd like to think you regret saying no to me, but somehow I'm guessing this is a coincidence." He raises an inquiring eyebrow. "But a good one."

For a moment I forget why I'm here. My fantasies are going to be in high-definition now. I don't even bother to hide how my gaze eats him up. And by his smile it's evident he's enjoying being on display. He certainly doesn't make an effort to hide his bare chest with the towel. No, he stands there, arms at his sides, hands relaxed, feet shoulder width apart. It's an invitation, and I utilize it.

He's cut, ripped, jacked to shit. Up close I can count the indented squares below his pectorals that look so much like polished marble. He's got a sparse sprinkling of chest hair and a dark line that bisects his tight abs, disappearing into his low-slung shorts. I stare at the bottom of the line far too long and suck in the side of my lower lip to keep myself from drooling.

Wrapping around the sides of his abdomen and jutting out from his hips are those *things* that no girl knows the word for—only that they make her feel stupid and hot. They are handles, I guess, to hold on to while you're riding him or giving him a blow job. Or maybe they're made for licking. All I know is that they are a big turn-on and I feel like they're beckoning me to touch them to see if they're real. I wonder how he'd react if I bent over and just licked him like a lollipop.

He's engaged in his own perusal, but I'm looking no different than I was the last time he saw me. My light-brown hair is in a tight braid, although there are many strands that have escaped due to pulling my helmet off and on. I'm wearing my Lycra crop pants and Dri-FIT long-sleeve T-shirt. I look like shit, but his gaze—when I finally meet it—is appreciative.

He rubs the towel through the dark, rich pelt on his head, and then slowly rubs it over his face, then his chest, and finally his abs. My eyes track every movement. His body looks like something that was computer generated. It is hard and powerful and he's so close that I can smell him, a musky clean sweat that fires every neuron. Not every man in a suit looks this good when he strips off the wool and linen. This is the body of a fireman or athlete, not that of a banker.

"You don't have time for a walk in the park. You spend your Saturdays working. Do you do anything but deliver packages?" He finally moves, waking me out of the fantasy dream state where I'm measuring the hardness of his chest with my tongue.

"Not these days," I admit. Mention of my *job* brings my attention back like the hard return of a rubber band. It's almost painful to leave fantasy land. "Here, I need your signature, and I'll be out of your hair."

"I didn't realize I ordered something to be delivered by Neil's," he says, looking pointedly at the logo emblazoned on my shirt and ignoring the papers.

"It's not from Neil's," I say, and then stop because I remember exactly what I'm doing here. This Ian is my special project and since he's working with Malcolm . . . I let that thought die along with all my lust. Bitter disappointment is a sour flavor.

"I find I can't sign anything right now. Hurt my wrist doing curls." He twists his perfectly normal, uninjured right wrist.

Shaking my head, I try to shove the papers at him again, but he remains disinterested. He tosses them to the side without even looking and walks toward the kitchen. Pulling open a glass refrigerator door, he grabs a bottle of water and gestures toward the contents, asking if I want anything. I shake my head no but I follow him. I can't help it. The tractor beam of attraction just tows me right along.

"Your wrist looked fine when I came in."

"Watching me?" He raises his eyebrow again. "Did I have good form?"

I don't want to flirt with him. Or rather, I do but know that I shouldn't. Not only is he involved with some kind of shady business, but until my mom is feeling better, there's no room in my life for anything but work and her.

"Yes. You have a very nice body, but it's a dime a dozen."

"Is that right?" He's amused and not the slightest bit irritated.

Confidence oozes out of his every pore. He knows exactly how women respond to him and he rightly assumes I'm no different, but I'm trying.

"The city is awash with hard bodies. It's more trendy than ever to be fit now. In fact, I heard a news report that young men are having body issues because of the push toward the well-defined abs. You're a bad influence."

He finds this response even funnier and his face cracks into a wide, bone-melting grin. The hollow in his cheek is back and it's got a superpower all of its own. I kind of hate myself for being weak-kneed at the sight of it—at the fact that my own lips are curling up in response. Tonight when I get home I'm going to force myself to watch Spike TV so I can learn to hate men again. Or I'll spend five minutes with my stepbrother. That will do it.

"Just a word of caution, because I don't really care but the next customer might: Messengers are supposed to be invisible." He winks so I know it's not a real insult.

"Sorry, I didn't bring my invisibility cloak, Bruce Wayne."

"Batman, huh?" He leans even closer, so close that his breath tickles my hair. Right above my forehead, he whispers, "One thing you should never do is issue a challenge to a guy like me. I always like to win. Always." Then he draws back and leaves me in a quivering state of Jell-O.

"Always?" I don't even know why I'm asking. It's like poking a tiger with a stick.

"There was that one sad time when I was eleven, I asked my neighbor to my middle school dance. She was seventeen."

"Did she go?"

"Sadly, she turned me down, but it didn't stop me from pursuing her. I tend to be more determined than most."

He made that sound like a threat and a promise at the same time.

"I'm guessing you caught her eventually." That's where these stories of conquest usually end.

"By the time Cass expressed a return affection, I was in the process of moving and not prepared for a long distance relationship, so our childhood love remains unconsummated."

"I can see you are real broken up about it."

He winks. "If I were, would you tend to my broken heart?"

"If cures for the broken heart can be delivered, then I'm your girl," I quip.

"I'm sure I can keep you busy for a long time," he murmurs.

It's hard, but I manage to keep my whimpers soundless. He drains his glass of water and then strides toward the front hall where he'd tossed the papers earlier. I scurry behind him.

"You didn't tell me your name the last time we met."

"Victoria Corielli."

"Victoria." He says my name, testing it on his tongue, holding the syllables inside his mouth for a moment as if he's savoring a fine wine. Everything about him is so sexual. *God.* "What did you bring me?"

"I don't know exactly. A contract," I answer.

"Let's find out." He picks up the envelope and shakes out the papers. It doesn't take but a second for those eyes to lose their warmth and good humor. He looks me up and down, measuring me and apparently, from the cold contempt in his eyes, finding me lacking.

It's completely unfair that he's viewing *me* with disdain because I deliver packages for Malcolm. *This* guy is the one who must want me to do something illegal for him. And by the look of his apartment, he's under no financial distress. His isn't a desperate need-driven business relationship like mine is. I'm the one that should be filled with scorn.

"Had no idea Malcolm had such great taste. Thought he was a little too lowbrow. Were you delivering wigs the other day or something else?" His words are even, but I can sense that he's angry with me. His eyes are accusatory, as if I've betrayed him somehow.

"It's none of your business but, yes, it was wigs," I say as calmly as possible when I'm seething inside.

He tosses the contract to the side. "Why, Victoria? What problems do you have that you need the money from working with Malcolm? Is delivering packages not good enough for you? You like to drink, smoke, gamble, what?"

I gape at him, openmouthed. "What the hell are you talking about? And what right do you have to question me? *You* are the one that is working with Malcolm. All I do is deliver shit."

Hands on his hips, he starts circling me. "Like yourself? You're the package today, sweetheart, and you delivered yourself right to my door. You look shiny and fresh, unlike the other 'packages.' So how much?"

"How much what?" I don't have the faintest clue what he's talking about right now. I pick up the contract and shove it toward him. "Sign and I'm gone."

A muscle in his jaw is getting a workout and the forest green of his eyes looks cloudy. An urge to tell him my whole story, to make him understand, overwhelms me, but I shut it down because this rich jerk who can live in this entire building by himself in one of the richest neighborhoods in Manhattan is judging me.

"What makes you a good fit for this project?" He leans a hip against the table and crosses his arms. The motion emphasizes his muscular arms and my lust flares up again. Stupid body.

"Isn't it a little late to be assessing my 'fit'? I thought Malcolm arranged everything with you."

"The last three 'packages' Malcolm sent weren't suitable and while you're definitely a step up from those others, I'm not entirely convinced he's got the right goods."

I can only stare as he describes me as a product. God, what an asshole. Good thing I figured this out before I took his hand and followed him straight to bed. Assholes truly are a dime a dozen in the city. I could go out right now and run into a handful before I cleared Gansevoort and hit Hudson Street.

"Malcolm asked me to do a special project. He had me sign that—" I nod toward the table. "And I did. Nothing in there can be legal, so I don't know what Malcolm and you've cooked up, but I can't be held to it. I. Deliver. Things." I enunciate each word so he can't mistake their meaning. "You want something delivered, I'm your girl. Anything else, you'll have to go elsewhere."

His hands drop away from his waistband; he stands there for a long moment and studies me. What he is looking for or what he sees is completely lost on me. With a shake of his head, he picks up a pen and scribbles something on one of the pages. "Didn't you read the contract?"

"I can't read, asshole."

He looks at me with bemusement. "Illiterate?"

"Learning disability."

I watch for his expression to change from interest to pity but he only nods thoughtfully.

"Contract says you are a work for hire—a contract laborer—and that you can't say anything about working for me to anyone. Could you do that?"

"Fine. What do you need delivered? I'm a messenger. Put me to work." I throw out my arms.

He swallows a laugh, and then he puts everything back into the envelope and hands it to me. "Thanks, but no thanks. Tell Malcolm you're a dear, but I really can't work with someone like you."

I take it, but I don't want to. Malcolm won't help me if I don't get Ian to agree to this—whatever *this* is.

"Malcolm told me not to come back without your agreement."

"It's not happening. I'm sorry." He sounds regretful, but if I go back to Malcolm without doing whatever it is I'm supposed to do, maybe I *will* have to service a train of men. I love my mom but there have to be options here. I just need to know what they are.

"What is it that you want me to do? Obviously I'm willing to get my hands dirty." I try to keep the desperation out of my voice.

"Are you now?"

"I'm working for Malcolm, aren't I?"

"Touché." He places a palm on the top of my head and pushes the tendrils of my hair back, as if he wants to see what I look like without helmet hair. I want to squirm under his inspection, but I force myself to stay still.

"Do you have a good memory?"

I nod. I have a fucking great memory. It's how I am able to be a bike messenger. Someone tells me the address once and I've got it. I may not be able to read a book, but I can decipher numbers and most letters with time and I can remember anything anyone has ever told me. My worry starts to ease. You don't need to have a good memory for work on your back.

"Can you pretend to be someone else?"

"Yes." This all sounds like something I can do.

His hand drops from the top of my head down to the back of my neck where I'm sure he can feel the tension, pulled tight. I don't know why I argued with him before, challenged him. He's right. Messengers are like children—to be seen and not heard. I open my mouth to apologize but before I can say the words, he forces my fingers to close around the documents.

"I'm sorry, Victoria."

"OK." I can't spend another minute here and retain any dignity—not that I have a lot of it left, but since it's such a precious commodity, I want to keep what I have.

I try very hard to keep my steps even as I walk out of there despite wanting to run. I take each step down the stairs slowly and behind me I can feel his eyes all over my back, my ass, everywhere. This time it is *his* regret that weighs me down as I ride back to Queens.

CHAPTER 4

The breeze from the East River stinks as I bike across the Queensboro Bridge. But it feels good, and I still have the scent from Bruce Wayne lingering in my nose. I know that's kind of illogical—that it's not really his scent, only a memory of it—but it's still there and I suck it in, holding my breath as if I can swallow it and make it part of me.

Then it hits me that I'm mooning over a guy who insulted me, apologized, and is involved in some fashion with my criminal-ass stepbrother. If anything belongs in the East River, it's Malcolm and all his associates.

But shit, I don't even have the right to be mad about this because I'm benefiting from all the illegal crap he's involved with. Deciding I need to drown my thoughts, I crank up AWOLNATION and let the heavy metal guitar riffs occupy my attention as I bike the fifteen miles to the apartment.

I punch the button next to Malcolm's name and he buzzes me up. This fourteen-story building is slightly run-down and in a not-so-great neighborhood, but you have to be where your customers are, says Malcolm. Given the number of times I have made deliveries to individuals living in apartments overlooking Central Park, I think he should move his offices into the city. But then I'm not part of the executive team. I'm merely the delivery girl.

"No go." I slap the package into his chest when he opens the door. A quick glance inside the room reveals that his flunkies are gone. I turn to leave but he grabs my shirt and drags me inside.

"Not so fast. What do you mean, 'no go'?"

"He said he couldn't work with me, but he did write something on the papers."

Malcolm keeps one hand on my shirt and drops the contract out onto the table with the other. Picking up the signature page, he curses. "Fuck you."

"Hey," I protest, finally wiggling out of his grip. "I delivered it. That was my only job. You're the one who made the deal."

He turns the contract to me and holds the paper up two inches from my eyes. "See this? Even you can read this. I know it."

Like I told Bruce Wayne, I have a learning disability, but I'm not illiterate. I can read some, but it takes me a while, so I avoid it whenever possible.

"So he wrote 'Fuck you.' I assume that's a message for you and not me." But I'm dying inside because I know this means that Malcolm won't help me. I wonder if he'll even allow me to deliver for him.

He mashes the paper in my face a little too hard to be a joke. "Goddammit. I gave you one fucking job and you managed to fuck it up. It's a wonder you could get a job even delivering packages, you stupid fuck."

When I say I'm not ashamed of my learning disability, it doesn't mean I'm immune to insults. Malcolm's words sting badly, but I cover that pain by pretending he hurt my nose. He tosses the papers aside, and they flutter to the ground.

I don't use Google because stuff is even harder to read on the computer than on paper. The letters don't just swim on the page, they leap at me in 3-D, and it's a real headache trying to figure out what their correct order is. Since I have a decent paying job, I've given up on trying to learn how to read. The only reason I even have a smartphone is that dispatch uses it to convey instructions, orally, to me.

I have a good memory, can read most street signs with practice, and can locate the majority of businesses by landmarks. I watch television, everything from comedies to documentaries, but I'm not a reader and never will be. I refuse to be ashamed about this, but I'm not dumb, which is the quality most people associate with the inability to read.

"I couldn't force him to sign it," I protest.

"Goddammit!" Stomping off into one of the two bedrooms, he releases a few more curses and then yells at me. "Don't fucking leave. I've got another delivery for you."

"Jesus. Fine." Because I'm well acquainted with Malcolm's hair-trigger temper being expressed primarily through slammed doors and shouts but no real violence, I take the opportunity to rifle through his refrigerator, which is surprisingly well stocked for a bachelor's. He has cold pizza, cold Chinese food, and sandwich makings. "Can I have the leftover shrimp fried rice?" I yell.

He mumbles something that I assume is agreement. After the contents of the box are heated, I unhook the sides and lay the cardboard flat on the table. Malcolm and I discovered the magic of the Chinese takeout box when we were teens and have never eaten leftovers any other way.

He must have heard the completion ding of the microwave because he stomps out of the bedroom he uses as an office. Jerking out a drawer and grabbing another fork, he huffs onto a stool next to me and starts eating the leftovers. It's like we are twelve and fourteen again, back before testosterone overtook Malcolm and turned him into an asshole.

Before then he was a Skylanders-playing, Pokémon-loving goofball. Somewhere around the end of fifteen, on the cusp of sixteen, he left it all behind to become this woman-hating, amoral jerk. Twelve years later, he's perfected what he started—only now he's a criminal, woman-hating, amoral jerk. I wonder idly whether Malcolm fits the profile of a sociopath.

"How's Sophie?"

"She's . . ." I start to say "fine," but she's not and I don't know why I would pretend with him. "She's hanging in there." I push the food around.

"I can get Sophie some good weed. I've got a nice shipment in," he offers. At my raised eyebrows, he shrugs. "I don't hate her. Not anymore, I guess."

Malcolm's dad left his mom for my mom. If I'm objective, I can understand his dislike for us. But who the hell is rational when it comes to someone you love? Not me and not Malcolm either. Neither of us pays much attention to Mitch Hedder anymore. He walked out on my mom when I was sixteen and Malcolm was eighteen. The old man is a shiftless piece of work who inveigles his way into women's lives and then ruins them.

I guess Malcolm thinks relationships are for suckers. He might be right. I've never been able to keep a man in my life.

"I found a place, but I need a cosigner for the apartment application. The on-the-books money I make isn't enough to convince the landlord I can make rent, and I won't make rent without the job."

"Should've thought of that before you left Kerr's, Tiny."

I shift uncomfortably on my stool. I don't want to go back to see Ian and not for any reasons associated with Malcolm's situation. Ian Kerr is a danger to me. The only way I will stay safe is to maintain distance. In a city this big, with our massive economic differences, that should be pretty easy so long as my mother's health doesn't rest on a return visit.

"Sophie's pretty sick," I tell him. "She wants to stop the chemo and just . . ." I can't say it. These last four weeks have been rough. "I need that money, Malcolm. If we had an elevator and she could go outside for a few minutes, it would make all the difference in the world."

"Get Kerr to sign the papers then."

"He said you've sent three others to him and he's turned them away."

"Did he?" He shovels more food into his mouth.

I'm getting frustrated. "What is the big deal?"

"Don't know," Malcolm mumbles around some food. "But I figure if I had his signature on something, I could blackmail him in the future."

"Jesus, Malcolm." I hiss an indrawn breath. "What the hell? That sounds like a quick way to get yourself dumped in the East River."

"Back at ya, sis. You're a fucking hypocrite. You're always busting my chops like working for me is totally beneath you, but you sure like the dough." He pushes me another padded envelope and a wad of cash wrapped in a rubber band.

"It's for my mom," I protest.

"Please, save your situational morality for someone else. We all got mommy problems." Malcolm scoffs bitterly. "Get Kerr's signature and I'll get you any damn apartment you want."

There's nothing else for me to say. I choke down the rest of the food even though I'm not hungry anymore. Returning to Ian's place after he wrote "Fuck you" on the papers seems like a lost cause.

Malcolm's other packages need to be delivered to the Upper East Side, and it'll take me a while to get there. I pause for a moment to appreciate that my last delivery for Malcolm is close to home. He's not always bad, I guess.

I drop off the package at a million-dollar townhouse two blocks off Fifth Avenue near the Guggenheim. The guy who accepts it comes out with mussed hair and lipstick all over his collar. I didn't even know that happened in real life. Thought it was an old wives' tale, used to scare men away from cheating on their partners—although from the looks of this guy, not an effective one. He empties the package right in front of me, shaking out a vial containing six pills and a sleeve of condoms. Ecstasy. I shake my head. Talk about stupid fucks. You start having sex on Ecstasy and it's hard to back off.

"Tell Malcolm thanks," the customer says.

"Will do."

He slips me a ten-dollar bill and winks. "You ever get bored, come on back and try these out with me. I'm always up for new blood."

I try to keep my lip from curling because this is one of Malcolm's customers, and I'm being paid to overlook lewd come-ons along with the illegality of the packages.

"Thanks, but I'm taken," I lie. "My boyfriend's kind of a Neanderthal." I glance furtively around as if I'm being followed. "He doesn't even like when I talk to other dick."

The customer leans out and looks around as well and then, after a moment of indecision, scurries back into his townhouse and shuts the door.

I head home. My feet feel more leaden the closer I get to my apartment. Every day, I dread coming home. Seeing her in pain is excruciating, but there's always the possibility that the good-bye kiss I received that morning was the last one I'll ever get.

When I walk into the apartment, there's no sound but the soft snores of my mom and I breathe a sigh of relief as I set my bike down in the hallway. Then I feel guilty. I should want Mom to be awake so that we can talk about how our days went and what we're going to do this weekend. Monday's her chemo day, so by Saturday, she's usually up on her feet and ready for an outing.

I'm thinking we should go to the Central Park Zoo and eat some ice cream. I duck into the bedroom and see that she's fast asleep, a book spread across her chest. Quietly, I tiptoe over to her and lift the book off her chest. I tuck a bookmark into the page to save her place and then flick off the lamp. Leaning down, I give her a kiss.

The role reversal is striking. At twenty-five, I'm tucking my mom into bed and kissing her sleeping forehead. My throat tightens as I think about this bed being empty and me being alone in the world. Not yet though, I tell myself. She's still with me.

I set aside the worry of the apartment situation and just try to hug that thought close.

CHAPTER 5

On my lunch break, I find myself in SoHo. I meant to go straight to Hudson to Ian's place, but as I biked down Eighth Avenue my front wheel ended up in SoHo, in front of my favorite block of shops. In one store, the Bondoir, they sell handmade lace lingerie, the likes of which I will never be able to own. Next to it is Urban Adventures, where they sell the Dutch road bike I would sell my left arm to ride, although I'm not sure my arm would cover even the front tire.

I should be back at Ian's place instead of here, one neighborhood over, mooning over stuff I won't ever be able to afford. Every day that Mom is stuck in that damn apartment, she retreats deeper into herself. This morning she refused to get out of bed. But I can't come up with a reason why he should hire me because I don't even know what the stupid project is—other than that it requires a good memory and pretending to be someone else.

Do I need to dress up in a clown suit? Deliver a singing telegram? I'll do almost anything. This morning was full of bad behavior. In addition to avoidance, I played a game of dodge with the cars. My mother would kill me if she knew I spent fifteen minutes seeing how many intersections I could beat the lights. Maybe I'll tell her when I get home just to see if I can rile her up.

Hey Mom, almost got doored by three cars, and I lane split between a Mercedes and Bentley today, and I almost took the mirror off of three cabs. Saw my life flash before my eyes and . . .

God, what a shithead idea this is. To tell my cancer-stricken mother that I intentionally rode like a reckless fool down Manhattan? If she didn't haul off and slap me, I'd be disappointed.

Rubbing a hand over my eyes, I try to calm myself. The stuff in the window looks gorgeous—all lace and silk. One of the ladies on the *Real Housewives of New York* name-dropped it, and now every time I'm down here, I stare at the goods through the floor-to-ceiling plate glass windows. Don't know why I torture myself like this; I couldn't have afforded even a thong from this place when I *didn't* have medical bills piling up like a plowed snowbank, but I like to look. Nothing wrong with looking.

I swing my bike helmet by its strap, and I'm so wrapped up in my shopping lust that I don't even notice there's someone beside me until his shadow looms over me.

"You have good taste."

"Oh my god." I hold my hand to my swiftly beating heart. It's Ian. I'd recognize that smell, that voice anywhere. Today his superhero abs are covered in a light-gray T-shirt and jeans. He has some heavy brown boots on his feet and a big watch on his wrist. His brown hair is rumpled, like he just rolled out of bed. I bite down on my molars to keep from leaning forward and sniffing him.

"What are you doing here, stalker?" I sound shrill.

He's amused. Again. Goddammit. Maybe his amused face is his pissed-off face. Or maybe he has only one expression. I don't really know. I'm not like a body language expert. I'm a bike courier. I refuse to refer to myself as a drug mule.

"I'm here to buy a gift. Want to help me pick it out? I usually give the sales associate a tip, but that money can be yours." His hand is on the door and I'm tempted.

"How much?" I'm swallowing back bile at the thought of some woman in his life getting lingerie picked out by him, but he's offering me two things I want: time with him and money. I wonder if the gift is for the redheaded wig shop owner. Jealousy is a terrible taste.

He looks inside for a minute and then back at me. "Twenty percent of the gross receipts."

Holy crap. Twenty percent of just one item could pay for dinner for a week if I was careful. I push down the jealousy and grab hold of opportunity. I gesture for him to open the door. "After you."

A sales associate comes over before the door shuts behind us. She was probably watching the whole thing play out in front of the plate glass windows. "Can I help you?" She looks from him to me and back again, unsure of who she should suck up to.

"No thanks," he says. Then he gives her that glorious smile, and she almost takes a step back under the power of it. It's obvious he uses it as a weapon. He's too knowing. I don't like that about him at all. Knowing, arrogant, and engaged in criminal activities. All bad qualities.

"Pick anything you think she'd like." He waves expansively at the walls. Bras and bralettes are hanging in a multitude of spring colors. All made of lace. There's a ramp that leads downward to another section. I head back there just to get away from all the sales associates.

"What's she like?"

"Hmm?" He sounds distracted, and I realize it's because he's looking at my ass. I clear my throat. So he's knowing, arrogant, and unfaithful. He grins at me unrepentantly, and I mentally slot him right next to Malcolm in the jerk column. No wonder they are going to do business with each other.

"B cup," he says, narrowing his eyes slightly.

"I asked what she is like, not her size."

"Don't you need to know her size?" His eyebrow is raised and it makes me feel stupid, which I hate.

"Do you want my help or do you just want to argue?" I snap.

His grin gets wider, if that was even possible, and his eyes are twinkling. Or it could just be the glint of the sun through the windows because eyes can't really twinkle or dance. I move farther into the store so that I can get out of the sunlight, which is apparently so bright it's causing me to see things. He follows me closely, as if he's my loyal Labrador. As if.

"I want both," he whispers behind me. When I whirl on him, he reels off a bunch of things in rapid fire. "I want colorful things, very sexy things, and also a few comfortable things. A whole wardrobe. I'm getting to know her, so I'm hopeful that something I buy will strike her fancy."

Lucky bitch. "What's my budget?"

"There's no budget."

Of course not. In revenge, I pick out a ton of stuff. I just go down the racks and pick out one of everything. Well, not everything but most things.

He's following me and fingering a few items. His strong, tanned fingers look ridiculously sexy against the fragile satin bows. I squeeze my thighs together as I imagine those panties on my body and his fingers gliding all over them. *You suck,* I tell my body. *Stop lusting after an unfaithful jerk.*

"You wouldn't be willing to try a few things on, would you?" His eyebrow is raised again. I wonder if he practices these looks in the mirror. Each one seems perfectly crafted to make a girl want to drop her shorts right then and there.

"You're a dick, you know that, right?" I ask.

"Why's that?"

"Because you are flirting with me and buying lingerie for another woman. That's the definition of a dick. In fact, if you looked it up in the dictionary, your face would be there."

"They could be for my mom," he says mildly. Jesus, does nothing offend this guy?

"Then you've got a weird thing going on with your mom."

"Am I Oedipus instead of Batman today?"

I stare at him blankly. I have no idea who the fuck Oedipus is. I haven't ever heard of the guy's name before. Better that way, I think. Safer.

The sales associate is beaming at us. "So all of this?" Her arms are laden with tiny folded packages.

"All of it," Ian says immediately.

As she is ringing it up, I start feeling terrible. The prices are so high, and while I knew it when I walked in, the enormity of my spitefulness is sinking in. "Wait," I say. "I don't think she needs all this." I try to scoop away half of the loot.

He places his hand on mine and I'm frozen. "No. This is just the right amount."

Both the saleslady and I are gaping at him. I'm completely torn now. Part of me is raging mad that some chick is getting this stuff, and then I feel guilty for being petty and sad that I don't have anyone buying underwear for me.

"Box it up," he orders the clerk.

She does, folding each piece into its own separate tissue. Another associate brings a big, white box. Every piece goes into the gold-lined box, and it takes three of them to wrap up the box with a bow and stick it in a bag.

"Anything else?" She writes her name on a card and gives it to him. "Just give me a call. For anything at all."

"Thanks, but I'm not taking it. I want it delivered." He writes down the address. She starts to say it out loud, but he reaches out and taps her lips. They fall open and I think I see her tongue creep out to lick his finger, but it falls away before she can get to it. I don't blame her. I'd have wanted to lick the finger too. He's a menace. He should be locked up.

He taps the card he just wrote on and says, "These are all the details you need to know."

He leads me outside by the elbow and doesn't let go until we're in front of a nightclub whose metal gate is down and tagged with graffiti. He pulls out his wallet and hands me three crisp hundred-dollar bills.

I shove it back. "I can't take it," I say miserably. "I bought way too much stuff just to punish you."

He folds the hundred-dollar bills in half and then half again. I look longingly at them and then force my eyes up to his striking green ones. I kind of hate that he's so good-looking. I wish whoever was in charge of looks gave them out to reflect how a person was *inside*. There are so many good-looking people walking around who are absolute monsters. My stepbrother is Exhibit A and this guy is Exhibit B. Or vice versa. Either way, they are both prime examples of how karma never, ever works. What goes around never comes around. The next person who says "karma" near me will get a throat punch.

"That's a fierce look. I hope you aren't directing it toward me." He's still holding the folded bills between us.

"What were you doing here anyway?"

"I have a couple of businesses I was checking on."

"Is that what we're calling them now?"

"There's another word for *business* that's been approved in the *Oxford English Dictionary*? I thought the only new words allowed were *wassup* and *hashtag*, neither of which is a euphemism for *business*."

I start laughing. Those words coming out of that elegant mouth seem hilariously profane. He smiles at me and then places a finger on my forehead. It's like he's pressed a mute button because my laughter dies immediately and saliva starts pooling in my mouth. He drags his finger down between my eyes and over the ridge of my nose. Time's suspended now and I can't move.

"If I ask you to have a meal with me, are you going to say no?"

I nod my head. "Will you give me the job?"

"You don't want it." His hand drops away.

"I do." I pause and clarify. "Or at least I want the money."

"Money's easy."

"Only because you have it." I walk back toward my bike and climb on. Ian is right behind me. With one hand on the top tube of my frame, he keeps me from riding away.

"I haven't always," he admits. "Is that what your reservations are? You like a certain type of Joe?"

I give him a once-over. Today he does look more like a blue-collar city worker than a white-collar one, but there's still something about him that exudes wealth. His hair is so precisely cut and his plain cotton T-shirt fits as perfectly as if it were custom-tailored for him. "I can find any number of people to take me out to dinner"—though not really because I haven't had an offer in months—"but I'm desperate for a job."

"Are you?"

"Would I be working for Malcolm if I wasn't?"

"Good point." His finger rubs along the tube and the side of his hand almost brushes the inside of my thigh. I nearly fall over and have to grab him for balance. He grips my upper arm and steadies me. The heat of his palm burns through the lightweight fabric in a nanosecond. When I get home, there will probably be an imprint there. That *might* be wishful thinking. I force myself back on topic. "And what's your excuse? Why are you working with Malcolm?"

"Malcolm has certain connections that I thought would be useful."

"But it hasn't worked out."

"Not as well as I would have liked."

"Are you sure I can't help you?"

His fingers close around the frame and tip me toward him until I have no choice but to brace my hand against the hard wall of his chest. His hand leaves my arm and comes around me like a shackle.

"Let me be perfectly frank with you, Victoria. There are lots of things that I'd like you to do for me. Some of them involve you on your knees. Others require you bent over a table. All of them require me to be between your legs. But I don't pay for that."

"No, I wouldn't think you would," I say faintly. No one has ever spoken to me in such a graphic and explicit manner and I don't know how to respond—at least not verbally. My body is reacting by getting hot and tight.

He nods in confirmation that I've heard him. "I don't dip my pen in the company ink. Nothing good comes of that. So let me ask you again. Are you certain you wouldn't rather let me take you out to dinner and then home, where I would make you come so hard that you wouldn't be able to remember your own name let alone that you have money troubles?"

I'm finding it difficult to breathe normally and it's hard to remember exactly why I'm resisting him so hard. His hand has moved from my waist to my hip and his fingers are curling around my ass and pulling me as close as possible despite the bike frame between us. I can even feel his erection against my hip. "The money troubles will still be there, regardless of my memory," I manage to choke out.

His eyes narrow because he doesn't like my rejections. "You should know that when small prey runs away, it only whets the appetite of a predator. Someday, Victoria Corielli, I'm going to get you to say yes."

He pushes the bike frame upright and my body reluctantly follows.

"I'll be in touch," he says, and then turns and walks away. I stare after him like a dumbass for at least five minutes.

CHAPTER 6

When I get home that night, there's a package waiting for me in the super's apartment. It was too big for the mailbox slots in the first-floor lobby.

"If you can afford this, then I don't think you'll need that extension on your late rent payment. It's ten days past due," the super says as he points to the box on the table behind him. It's big and white and has a gold B embossed on the top of it. It looks expensive and exactly like the box that Ian had told the sales associate to deliver.

I stare at the box as if it contains deadly, hazardous materials because it does. If I open that box, something is going to happen that could wreck me. Slowly I back away. "Yeah, sorry about the late rent." I pull out a small wad of cash from the payment Malcolm had given me the other day and hand it off to the super. "Two months there."

He grunts and counts it out slowly, not moving from the doorway. The box is calling to me, luring me in, or at least holding me in place as if Ian is here with his warm finger pressed against my forehead.

"Any chance you have another place I could rent out? Somewhere with an elevator? Or a first-floor apartment?"

The super draws back. "Think I'd be here in this shithole if I had some other place to live?" When he's satisfied I've paid him correctly, the box is shoved into my arms. Before I can ask another question, the door slams shut. There's nothing to do but take the box upstairs with me.

The rest of the cash Malcolm paid me is in my bag. My thoughts flick back to the folded hundred-dollar bills that I stupidly turned down. When did my pride come before money? I should have grabbed those bills and ran.

"Did you pick up your box?" my mom calls from the bedroom. The apartment is filled with the smell of delicious baked pastry dough and my stomach growls appreciatively in response. "The super called."

"Yeah. It's from Malcolm," I lie. "A package he wants me to deliver." This second falsehood is told so she won't open the package. I dump it on the other side of the pullout sofa that I have called a bed for the three years we've lived here.

She comes out into the living room looking rail-thin under the velour sweatpants that I bought her, also from Malcolm's money. "I made some dinner tonight."

"You look great, Mom. I'm glad to see you're up."

"I went to church today. Louise picked me up."

"I'm so glad." I give her a hug, careful not to squeeze too tight. In the kitchen, I see her homemade potpie. "You must be feeling better. I prescribe church every night."

"Yes, it's good to get out."

The words are an unintentional dagger.

"Dear, I've been thinking that perhaps I won't go to treatment tomorrow."

I nearly drop the plate of potpie I'm about to place in the microwave. "What are you talking about?" I ask, pretending as if I don't understand.

She pushes my lax hands away and starts the reheat cycle on the microwave. The overhead fluorescent light illuminates everything in the tiny room and I can see how tissue-thin her skin is.

"I'm just tired of it." She sighs and looks out the window at the brick wall. "I'm tired of being sick all the time."

"I have some grass for you—" I start to offer, but she cuts me off.

"Don't you think I know what you're doing?"

That's such a loaded question. It's one of those trick questions moms ask to extract confessions of wrongdoing—like the time I was fifteen and had given my V card up to Jimmy Hostedder after the senior prom. I'd drunk liquor that night, smoked some weed, and had sex, all for the first time. When I came home the next morning, Mom was waiting up and the first thing she asked me was essentially that same question. I'd spilled out the sex thing and the drinking thing and the weed thing and when I was done vomiting my sins, she'd merely replied, "I was asking about why you didn't call me last night like you promised, but now that I know you've done all that, I think it's time for the pill."

Funny thing was that after I got on birth control, I had no desire to have sex with Jimmy or anyone else for a year. I'd felt so guilty about keeping Mom up all night.

"Working hard?" I ask weakly, trying to feel her out so I can confess to the sin she knows instead of the one she's fishing for.

"I know you're making ends meet by working for Malcolm, and I don't want that. You could get hurt."

"Malcolm won't hurt me," I protest. Yeah, he's got a temper, but he wouldn't lay a hand on me. Throw a fork in my direction? Mash my nose against some papers? Yes. Actually do me harm? No way.

"It's not Malcolm I'm worried about."

The microwave dings and Mom turns to pull the food out. She picks up a napkin and fork before leading me to the small table sitting next to the sofa. I follow with a large glass of milk.

"Eat," she orders. "And just listen. I'm the one who foolishly let my insurance lapse, but even if I hadn't, I don't want to go out like this, Victoria. These drugs they inject into me are designed to kill my bad cells, but they kill good cells too. I'm weak and sick five days out of seven. It's no way to live. I don't want to go through this again."

I want to put my fingers in my ears and pretend like I can't hear her. "You're going to beat this. A round of chemo. A stem cell transplant. It's all going to work out." The potpie that I love so much tastes like dust, really dirty, awful dust, and it's coating everything inside my mouth. I take a huge gulp of milk, but even that threatens to come right back up.

"There's a one-in-five chance of surviving more than three years. The odds go down dramatically with reemergence."

"Dr. Chen wouldn't have recommended all that treatment if he didn't think you would have a chance. You beat it the first time. No doubt in my mind you'll do it again." I give her a big smile.

She looks at me sadly. "All right, dear. We won't talk about it again."

I don't know what to say so I just squeeze her hand, afraid if I open my mouth, I'll start crying. "You just wait and see. You'll be the survivor that everyone looks to for inspiration." *You have to because you're all I have left.*

I give her a quick peck on the cheek and then pick up my nearly full plate. Dumping the contents of the pie into the trash, I pretend like the conversation never happened. Mom retreats into her room, and I make up a new playlist for tomorrow's ride.

I've got courier jobs for my real employer and then maybe an end of the day run for Malcolm. After I make my playlist and make sure my phone is charging, I pull out the sofa bed and prepare for the night. I kick the box to the side and the cardboard wall gives way, making it look crushed and kind of pathetic. Like how I feel right now. I'm not opening that box, though.

The lumpy mattress and the metal bars don't make for a good night's sleep, but the soothing sound of my mother's gentle snores? That's a lullaby no one can reproduce. Tomorrow I'm going to talk to the doctor and see if I can't get my mom some extra drugs either to stop her nausea or alleviate her pain. And if I can't get them from her doctor, then Malcolm will help me out. One in five are good odds. They are. I just need my mom to believe. I fall asleep gripping my blankets.

The next morning I get up extra early and check on Mom. She's not awake yet and chemo won't start until ten. I tiptoe out of the apartment, taking the big box with me. It's almost too big to strap to the back of my bike, but I manage. The stretchy cords, however, squeeze the box tightly, making it look almost like a weird bow.

I'm not even going to knock. I'm just leaving the box at the back door because it holds too much temptation, and I don't have the emotional wherewithal to deal with a man like Ian. He's too . . . too much of everything. Too tall. Too good-looking. Too confident. And too rich, apparently.

A small mechanical whoosh sounds and I see a camera protruding from the doorway, a camera that was formerly recessed. It looks almost alive and kind of freaks me out. I stick out my tongue.

He responds immediately. "That's pretty close to a yes, Victoria. You better run while you can."

This time I do. I get on my bike and pedal as fast as I humanly can. I'm scared now. Because I want to go back so much.

CHAPTER 7

Chemo is as terrible as we both anticipate. The IV drips always take so long. There are two televisions in here and Mom has her old laptop, but she's abandoned both at hour two, saying that the chemo is making her queasy and she wants to rest. I've sat here looking at the two apartments I've picked out. They're both in the same neighborhood we currently live in and close to the hospital. I can cover the rent so long as I continue my side deliveries, but since my on-paper salary isn't going to pass the application review, I need Malcolm's help even more.

Dr. Chen comes to check on us at the halfway point, four hours into the eight-hour-long drip.

"Everything looks good, Sophie." He gives her a pat on the shoulder. Mom barely opens her eyes, lethargy making her almost non-responsive. Dr. Chen frowns and gestures for me to step outside.

"Found a new place yet?"

"Not yet."

He shakes his head. "Don't forget her mental well-being. She can't stay cooped up in that apartment of yours."

As if the thought had ever left my mind.

The next four hours I spend in silence, playing solitaire and flipping through magazines to look at pretty clothes and shoes I'll never be able to afford. At the end of the day, I carry my mother up the five flights of stairs and place her in the lone bed. She rolls over immediately and faces the wall. I can't think of anything to say to comfort her. It's time to go down to Neil's anyway and take up the afternoon and evening shift.

I'm halfway done with my deliveries when my phone rings, the notes of "Killing in the Name" by Rage Against the Machine signaling a call from Malcolm. I've assigned ringtones to everyone in my phone. Neil's is "Price Tag" by Jessie J and Mom's is "Beautiful" by Christina Aguilera. My old friend from high school was Pink's "So What," but I haven't called or heard from Sarah in six months. My fault, though, because she kept asking me to go out with her and I kept telling her no. I couldn't afford a night out with the ten-dollar drinks and the twenty-five-dollar covers.

"You need to get your ass over to my apartment. Nine sharp," Malcolm barks into the phone.

"OK, that's fine. I've got . . ." I start to reel off my remaining delivery jobs but Malcolm interrupts.

"I don't give two shits about what you've got left. Just be here at nine or your side job will be given to someone who can do the fucking job as they're asked." He's shouting into the phone, so I hold it a few inches away. I can still hear him. In fact, I'm afraid if I hold it any closer, a rain of spit will drench my ear.

"Got it. Nine sharp." I hang up on him while he's still raining profanities down the cell line.

At eight fifty-five, I show up sweaty and tired at Malcolm's apartment building. There's a big, gray, expensive-looking car idling a few blocks up. I only notice because it's completely incongruous. Maybe Malcolm's supplier? Who knows? I should care, probably, but I don't want Malcolm any more pissed off than he already is.

"Lucy, I'm home," I yell into the intercom speaker. The buzz of the lock being disengaged sounds moments later. I take the elevator up and then knock on the door. Malcolm is there before I can drop my hand away, and as the door swings open I see *him*.

He's sitting there, his hand over the white box, which is all crushed and kicked-in. Ian doesn't belong here. It's not that he's wearing a suit or anything, although I expect his expertly distressed jeans cost as much as a bicycle and that his big leather boots—black this time— could float my rent for the month. It's just the way he holds himself. He's commanding and looks like he owns the place. Malcolm stands to the side, his hands dangling out of the tops of his jeans pockets, shifting from one foot to the other as if he's the visitor rather than Ian.

"Tiny," Ian drawls out. Apparently he and Malcolm have had a long talk if he's discarded my real name for my nickname. The way he says it, though, is so different than either my mom or Malcolm. With Mom it's loving and with Malcolm it's an insult. Out of Ian's mouth it sounds like a caress. "Thanks for joining us."

I decide that confronting this situation head-on makes the best sense. Tossing my helmet on the living room sofa, I drop into the chair opposite Ian. "Nice car out there."

"Thank you." He's wearing his amused look. "You put that together quick."

"Uh, it's not hard. Rich guy. Rich car. Neither belongs in this neighborhood."

His eyes slide almost imperceptibly toward Malcolm. "Not everyone made the connection."

I shut up then because even though I might not get along with Malcolm, he's still family, and I don't want anyone else insulting him. Other than me.

Ian cocks his head and we sit in extended silence, engaged in a weird battle for control. *I can sit here all night*, my stare conveys. But under the table, I'm pressing my legs together and my pussy is clenching as if in anticipation of something other than my own fingers being shoved inside me.

His smug smile says *I've been playing this game for a long time*, but his eyes are burning right through me. If I lean under the table, I suspect I'd see a bulge in his pants. It takes superhuman effort not to check it out.

Malcolm breaks the tension. "Ian has a proposition for you," he blurts out.

I bet he does. Even Ian's unflappable face breaks into a tiny smirk at the double entendre delivered by my brother. We continue staring at each other, and I continue getting more and more turned on. *Fuck.*

Ian decides to give in first. "I do. I need someone to work for me for a period of two, possibly three months."

"What's it entail?"

"I'll explain further only if you agree." He snaps his fingers, and Malcolm immediately produces two pages that look a lot like the contract I delivered, only with fewer words. "This is a non-disclosure agreement. It's very simple. I'll disclose some information to you, and in exchange you'll receive a weekly sum of money, along with other props necessary for you to carry out the work required of you—all of which you are free to keep after this project is completed. The only caveat is that you can never reveal anything I disclose to you. Very standard."

I finger the document but don't pull it closer. "How much?"

"How does $10,000 a week strike you?"

"What?" I push away from the table. "What kind of lunatic pays that kind of money for anything?"

"I'm guessing you don't know who I am, is that correct?" he asks. I shake my head. "I made $27 million a day last year and this year I'm on pace to make $37 million. A day." He emphasizes the time period. "This amount is so paltry that I doubt my accountant will even need to expense it."

The mention of an accountant eases my fear a bit because surely if he's got an accountant, everything he does can't be illegal, right? I slide into my chair because the sums he just spouted off are knee-shakingly high. No wonder Malcolm jumps when Ian snaps his fingers.

"Then it sounds like what you're proposing to pay me is too low," I say slowly, trying to decide whether I want to work for this man who I'm insanely attracted to and who has warned me at least once that he intends to hunt me down and . . . I have no idea what he'll do with me when he catches me, and I can't spend much time contemplating the scenarios because if I do, I'll end up being a puddle of goo on the floor.

Behind me Malcolm sounds like he is choking, but by the glint in Ian's eye, I can tell he's not offended at all.

"If the job you do is satisfactory, you'll get a bonus." And then he names a sum that makes Malcolm start coughing and me dizzy. A half-million-dollar bonus? I could *buy* an apartment when I was done working for him.

"What do I have to do?" I ask, but I don't know if I care right now. So long as I don't have to kill or torture or spread my legs, I'm pretty sure I'm on board, and maybe I'd even do those things.

"Sign the NDA." He slides the paper over to me.

"Do I have to sleep with anyone?"

"No."

"Not even you?" I peer at him between my eyelashes, ignoring Malcolm in the background. Amusement flits across Ian's face. He leans toward me so only I can hear.

"Only if you want to." He waits just a beat and then adds, "And you do."

Sniffing like it smells bad to disguise the heat that suffuses my entire body at his provocative words, I eye the papers with disdain. "What holds me to this?"

"If you disclose, I take back all the money, Malcolm fires you, and I ruin your life by ensuring you never get another job again." He says this calmly, as if he's reciting a grocery list. This time the zip down my spine is one of fear. "But I don't think you will disclose."

"How do you know that?" He's right, though. I wouldn't tell, even if the deal went south. I'm not a narc.

"Because you're loyal. Very loyal. You didn't want me to talk badly about your brother here, and you're engaged in business with unsavory characters in order to provide a better life for someone else in your family."

I wonder what Malcolm has told him. "But *you* aren't family."

He leans closer, so close I can smell his aftershave and beneath that his warm male smell. Happiness is not a warm puppy. It's the deeply masculine smell of someone who has got his big arms wrapped around you so you are wallowing in his scent. And right now, I'm tempted to climb over the table and into his lap—he smells just that good.

"For the money, you can pretend, can't you?" he asks.

When he draws back, the gleam in his eyes is one of satisfaction and pure masculine desire. How will I work for him for three months and not beg for a spot in his bed?

"I don't even know what that means. Am I going to do anything illegal?" I ask.

He taps the paper with his well-manicured finger. "Not until you sign."

I can turn away from him. I can beg Malcolm for help, but the vision of my mother turning away from me in her bed, of Dr. Chen asking me when our living conditions would change, of all those medical bills piled up in the corner . . . I could deliver packages for Malcolm for years and never get out from under that debt.

There's really no need for me to think even one more second about this. I scrawl my illegible signature across the straight black line next to Ian's finger. "Nice pen to go with your nice car," I say, handing the heavy rollerball back to him.

"Everything I have is nice," he says, and the innuendo makes my tongue feel two sizes too big for my mouth.

"How's your mother, Malcolm?" Ian asks, never once taking his eyes off mine.

"She's fine." Malcolm responds tightly. It's apparent to all of us that she really isn't fine.

"Still down in Atlantic City?"

He nods brusquely and I feel bad because Malcolm's mom has a gambling problem, which is partly the reason why he's into half of this shit.

"You should get her out of there. Atlantic City kills people." Ian's nonchalant attitude is suddenly grim. Apparently he does have more than one expression. This one looks scary. I prefer his smirk. Folding the contract in thirds, he stands. Business is over.

"I look forward to working with you . . ." he pauses and a fiendish gleam appears in his eyes. "Bunny."

"You really are the devil," I gasp as I catch his reference to our earlier encounter when he told me I was small prey.

"Ah, stroke my ego a little more. It's my second favorite nickname." This time he winks at me.

"What's your first?" I ask like a half-wit.

"God," he whispers in my ear, and walks out.

"What'd he say?"

"Bruce Wayne," I lie. The box is still lying there, and I guess there isn't anything to do but take it home.

Mom's asleep and snoring softly, her rhythm sounding perfectly healthy. I set the box on the table, make up my bed, and go into the bathroom to run through my nightly ritual of facial scrub and moisturizer. As I brush my teeth, I wander back into the living room and stare at the crumpled box.

Finally I climb onto the mattress and situate the box between my legs. Opening it means something. If I return it to him again, I think he'll back off. After flicking the light off, I set it on the floor and crawl under the covers. And lie there. And wonder. And wonder some more.

With a curse, I sit up quickly and turn the light back on. Ripping off the bow, I pull off the lid of the box, revealing the golden tissue inside. I push it away and see a riot of gorgeous, mouth-watering lace in every tropical shade in the beach crayon box—from aqua to coral to sand. But as I lift out the items reverently, I notice that there are only bottoms. Everything we bought, but just the bottoms.

There's an envelope and in it are the three hundred-dollar bills, still perfectly creased, and a small MP3 player. I grab my earbuds and listen.

His smooth voice plays out like a velvet chocolate spread—sinful and completely irresistible.

"I couldn't decide if I wanted to keep the tops or the bottoms. Did I want to imagine your breasts wearing the silk or satin, or your sinful secret part? I opted for the latter. You know where the rest of the sets are. Come and get them."

CHAPTER 8

I call the number he leaves for me at the end of the message even though it is very late. He answers on the first ring.

"I thought you didn't want to have sex with people you paid. Something about contaminated inkwells."

He laughs and the low sound vibrates throughout my body. "I've decided that I'm particularly skilled at compartmentalizing, so I'm going to make an exception."

"Do I want to know why?"

"Probably not. You're not ready for it. But it can be drilled down to the fact that I'm not interested in self-denial."

"You should look into it. I hear it's character building. Anyway, thanks for the awkwardly intimate gift."

"You're welcome. I prefer to think of it as generous and intimate rather than awkward. And my character was set at the age of fifteen. It's immutable now."

"Fifteen?" There's a story there.

"Yes." He offers me nothing more, and I'm not ready to push.

"Are you always so confident and knowing? It's not attractive."

"Then I guess you'll have no problem resisting me."

I stick out my tongue again since he can't see me being childish. "I'm not sleeping with you."

"Who says we'll be sleeping? I anticipate a lot of rigorous activity followed by a complete loss of consciousness."

"That's not sleeping?"

"No, that's fucking until you're nearly dead."

"Sounds terrible." It sounds amazing. I've never had someone talk to me so boldly. They certainly don't talk like that in the movies. It's more about showing soft lights and wide-opened mouths. Although, I wouldn't turn that down, either.

"Tell me about yourself," he invites, and in the background I hear the rustle of sheets as he gets more comfortable. There's not a doubt in my mind, he's nude. I wonder what he looks like in his bed, his golden skin contrasting against his white sheets. Does he touch himself? Malcolm always has a hand down his pants. When I asked him about it once, he said his balls itched. I figured that was a sign of some kind of STD and never asked again.

"What do you want to know?"

"Anything you'll share with me. I can see that you aren't much for social media. Your Facebook profile hasn't been updated since your mom was deemed cancer-free three years ago."

"I'm just not that social." I'm not sure why I'm talking to him. I have to get up in a few hours for work, but I can't put the phone down. Not while he still wants to hear me. "I'm Sophie Corielli's daughter, a bike courier." *I'm boring.* "Who are you, besides a rich man?"

He ignores my question and asks his own. "Is it just you and your mother, Tiny?"

I glance over at the wall separating the living room and my mom's room. "Yes, just the two of us. My father died when I was a baby. He was a deliveryman too. Trucks, though. Large-scale items. Made more money."

"My father passed of a heart attack when I was thirteen." *My character was set at the age of fifteen.*

"Then you understand."

"I do." His words are like a balm, a soothing cloth on my aching heart.

"It's not like I want to work for Malcolm." *Or turn you down.* "But my circumstances . . . I don't have better options."

"Your mother needs you. Is it dire? Malcolm seemed to think so."

My first instinct is to deny and pretend, like I have for the past four weeks, that everything will be fine. But he's so understanding, his voice almost caring, that I find myself telling him things I never intended.

"During the year that Mom was fighting cancer, I didn't have time for friends, not girls or boys, and when we came out victorious at the end, I found many of my friends had moved on. And by then, I just wanted to spend time with my mother more than anything. She'd become my best friend. We do everything together. Go to museums, the park. We love going to the Central Park Zoo. I can't imagine my life without her." I fall silent for a moment, my throat tight with emotion. "Yes, it's dire. That's a really good word for it."

"You'll be alone then? If she is gone?"

I nod, which he can't see, but he seems to sense the answer. "I know what that feels like. I want to help you, which is why—against my better judgment—I've agreed to let you do this project with me. I could offer you a thousand different positions working for me, but I sense that you wouldn't accept because your sense of fair play would be offended. Somehow you think that doing these things for Malcolm, you've earned it."

"Yes." My voice is nearly inaudible. "I guess I figure that no one gets hurt that way. That I'm not taking advantage of anyone. That my debt is paid. But hey, if you want to just give me a million, I guess I'd be OK with that."

"A personal jackpot? It's yours. I'll send a cashier's check over in the morning." He's dead serious.

"I wish I could accept it."

"But you won't because you think you can do this job for me, right? What if I said that you could deliver packages for me and earn the same money?"

"I'd know I was ripping you off."

"And you'd never sleep with me then, would you?"

"No, because it would feel like you were paying me for sex." I hurry and add, "Not that I'm going to ever have sex with you anyway."

"Of course." His voice is colored with mild amusement. "Good night, Tiny. I'll be thinking of you wearing the peach-colored panties with the flowers. You have very good taste."

After he hangs up, I pull the box onto my lap. I know I shouldn't but I can't resist. Inside I find a coral pair of panties. The lace is shaped in little rosettes with vines and leaves weaving them together. The band has side bows made out of some soft stretchy material. I'm surprised that the lace isn't itchy but rather conforms to the curves of my butt like it was custom-made. I don't know what to believe. Did he really buy all this stuff just to get me into bed? If he only knew. I'm way easier than that. Maybe that's how the rich do it, though. Like, they exchange presents as a courting ritual. If he expected one in return, then he was going to be sorely disappointed.

That night I sleep in the forbidden panties and dream that I am a rabbit being chased in Central Park by a big lion. I hide under a park bench and the lion transforms into Ian, only he's in his Batman garb and the rustling of his cape tells me it's windy. I hop backward and hunch down to make my small body less noticeable. As his big black cape is wafting in the wind, he leans forward to wave a carrot at me.

I creep out and grab the carrot with my paws. I'm nibbling when the net falls around me. I wake up, my little bunny heart pounding five thousand beats per minute. Taking a deep breath, I orient myself. Ian scares and attracts me at the same time, and by my accelerated heart-beat, it seems the best thing I can do is to stay away—or as away as I can now that I'm his indentured servant.

Despite the expert fit of the panties, I feel constricted, as if he's tightening his hold on me through my dreams. I can't escape him—and worse, I don't even want to.

CHAPTER 9

The next morning, I wake to the default ringtone on my phone and I know even before I answer it is Ian. "Bunny." He sounds pleased.

"I don't really like the name bunny. I had bad dreams about being a bunny last night."

"What was I doing?"

"Why do you think you were in my dream? I said I had a nightmare about being a bunny."

"I'm imprinted in your brain now. It's why you knew it was me before you even heard my voice."

"Huh." I don't know how he knows this, so I remain silent.

"So what was I doing?"

"You were wearing your Batman costume, holding a carrot." I'm not good at subterfuge.

"Did you come out and get your carrot?" The last word comes out slowly. There's some high-level player skill at work here. He's making the name of a vegetable sound like a sexy caress. I press my palm to my forehead like I'm a Victorian maiden. I'm not swooning, though; I'm trying to keep my emotions in check.

"I think you were going to kill me, but I woke up before that gruesome event occurred."

"If you suffered death at my hands, bunny, it would be in my bed and you'd still be breathing after you rode it out."

I cough at his explicit suggestion that he'd be giving me an orgasm. "So is the gift part of the extras that come with the job you want me to do?" It had bugged me last night.

"No," he says curtly. "What we do together is between us and completely separate from the job."

I'm not sure what to think of that. How do you keep those things separate? Maybe that's another rich-people thing. "I think you play in areas above my pay grade."

"We're all equals when it comes to the personal, Victoria."

I guess he means that we all get the same hurt if someone breaks our heart, no matter how fat the wallet is.

"So if I break your heart, you'll eat a carton of Ben and Jerry's to recover?"

"Maybe. What flavor?"

A reluctant laugh tumbles out. "I'm a fan of cookie dough, you?" I drop my hand from my forehead and slide back under the covers.

"I like vanilla bean. The original. There's a place over on Second and Twenty-Third that serves up homemade ice cream. I'll take you there." Everything he says is like a declarative. There's no asking. He only orders and directs. I suppose that's how you get into a position of earning $27 million a frigging day.

"Do you really earn $27 million a day? How is that even possible?"

"Stock valuation of a holding company increases exponentially, thus leaving you wealthier at the end of the year than you started in the beginning. Averaging out the increase results in a per-day amount. It makes the financial page journalists wet between their legs. Overall, it's meaningless unless you are cashing out a position."

"I understood only every other word of that sentence." I'm snuggled under my covers and the phone is pressed to my ear. Too bad I wasn't wearing my headphones. There's something awfully intimate about being in bed while talking on the phone. It's not exactly like he's right there whispering in my ear, but it almost feels like he is. "If you have so much money, then why me?"

"Why you for what? The job or the ice cream date?"

"Both."

"The job I can explain to you later. The other should be patently obvious, but since you seem obtuse about this unlike most everything else, I'll share. You turned down my money, returned my box of gifts, challenged me in my loft, and spurned my advances. I'm not sure you could have made yourself more irresistible."

"Because you like the chase," I conclude grimly. It's all because I turned him down. "I dated a guy like that once. He wanted me up until the point that he caught me and then dumped me three weeks later. He said I was too pushy." Did that sound bitter? I hope not.

There's a beat of silence and it makes me anxious. *I've turned him off already*, I think sourly, and then in the next moment I chastise myself for even caring. One thing Ian has said about me is right. I have a weak bunny heart.

"The chase," he says slowly, as if trying to parse out exactly the right words to make sure I don't hang up on him, "just whets the appetite. And if what you catch has no substance, then yes, the chase was the only worthwhile part of the whole game."

The mass in my stomach feels like hard stones. "At least you're honest," I say, faking some brightness so he doesn't hear my disappointment. I have no right to be upset. Colin once called me a stage five clinger because I'd been upset about him sleeping with other people. At the time I was angry with him for being a cheater, but maybe relationships aren't about fidelity but enjoying the experience. I don't think I can do that. I fall too quick, too fast, too easily.

He sighs at this. "When is your next outing with your mom?"

"In a few days. She has chemo on Monday, so we do something the weekend before." The thought of spending time with my dear mother outside while she's feeling healthy immediately lightens my spirits. Who cares what my new employer thinks of me? I've got no time for game-playing men.

"Specifically," he adds.

"Saturday probably." I wonder if he is finally going to tell me what this secret project is all about.

He hums. "All right, have a nice day." With that, the line goes dead. Tossing the phone aside, I actively fight the feeling of disappointment at the abrupt ending to the conversation. I recite all the positive things in my life. I'm in good health. My money situation looks better today than it did yesterday. My mom is still alive. She and I are going to the park. These are wonderful things, and I certainly don't have room or time for a half-baked relationship with someone who undoubtedly wants to screw me and leave me.

Renewed, I get up and fold the bed away.

CHAPTER 10

"Ten deliveries downtown and then come back," Sandra orders. With a nod of assent, I'm gone.

The deliveries downtown consist mostly of shuttling paper between law firms. Sometimes it's tubes of architectural or design plans, but mostly it's still just paper. All these firms and all their technology, but nothing can replace the signed blue signature on the bottom line.

Makes no sense to me, but as long as there are things to be delivered, I still have a job. It's about all I'm capable of doing. The thought makes the space between my shoulders pinch and all morning long when I'm usually able to just enjoy the activity of being outside and whipping in and out of traffic, my useless future rides me.

By mid-morning, I've nearly run into four cabs and one bus. I'm behind because I swerved into the curb and punctured my tire to avoid getting leveled by a bus. As I'm patching my tire, I lecture myself. If the last few years of dealing with my mother's cancer have taught me anything, it's that you can only deal with one day's worth of shit at a time. Otherwise you're paralyzed by the fear of tomorrow.

I don't hear from Ian for the rest of the week, and I wonder if all of his talk about helping out really was nothing more than niceties mouthed to a pathetic girl. I put him out of my mind the best I can.

Malcolm keeps me busy along with my regular job. I deliver drugs to three celebrities—two Hollywood actors and a Broadway star. The famous people are very uncomfortable. I stare at the ground and pretend not to recognize them. The rest of my deliveries are mundane. Rich housewives, a few business people based on the briefcases in the entry hall or suits that they're wearing when they answer the door. Some try to tip me—hoping, I guess, that the extra money will help keep my mouth shut. Don't they know that we're all in the same boat? I'm not going to tell anyone I'm delivering drugs to these people because I don't want to go to prison. I just tell them that discretion is part of the service. They nod and I leave, both of us feeling uncomfortable.

Most deliveries are to different addresses, although there are a couple that I've delivered a package to each week. I try not to think about what the drugs are doing to these people. Maybe they all have cancer and it's just weed I'm delivering. I'd like to think that were true, but I'm sure it's not.

When Saturday rolls around, I deliberately start humming in order to put myself in a good mood. I don't want to ruin the day.

"Have a good week, dear?" Mom asks as I putter around our small apartment getting ready.

Today I'm getting my mother out of the house and springing for a nice meal with the money I've made.

"It wasn't bad, but how can I not be happy on a day like today? The sun is shining. I'm spending the day with my best friend. And we're going to see cute animals." I give her a gentle pinch on the cheek and she grins back.

We hold hands on our way into the park, Mom swinging my arm like she did when I was a little girl. I realize in this moment that nothing I could ever do for Malcolm or Ian wouldn't be worth seeing the smile on my mom's face. We reach the zoo's open gates and join the other families going inside. Is there any place happier than the zoo? I think not. Glancing at my mom, I give her a huge smile and refuse to allow the worry to color our day together.

Leaning over, I give her a smooch against her forehead. "Love you, Mom."

"Love you too, sweet dear."

"I can see where you get your looks."

My head snaps up. It's Ian. Ian fucking Kerr is lounging against the iron post of the left zoo gate, looking for all the world like he owns the place. Hell, based on what he told me the other night, maybe he does. He's wearing his standard uniform of boots, jeans, and a big watch. Instead of a T-shirt, he's wearing a Henley with the top three buttons undone and the sleeves pushed up to showcase muscular forearms, sprinkled with dark-colored hair over heavy veins.

"Were we meeting someone?" My mom turns to me with a twinkle in her eye. "You should have told me you had a surprise for me. No wonder you're in such a good mood this morning."

Oh, shit. She thinks Ian is my boyfriend and that I'm bringing him to meet my mom.

"Mom," I protest. "I was in a good mood because you and I were going to the zoo!"

"Mrs. Corielli, I'm Ian Kerr. Friend of your daughter's." He picks up the hand that she offers and actually kisses it or presses his face to it. It's archaic but causes my mother to flutter like she's a tween at a One Direction concert. "Come on in, I've bought the tickets." He waves three tickets in front of my face. My mother heads toward the ticket attendant.

"Malcolm?" I mutter under my breath as I pass him. The side of his lips twitches but he says nothing. "Hope you paid through the nose for the information."

"If I did, it'd be worth every penny," he responds. Not waiting for my retort, he catches up to my mother, who was apparently trying to give me a moment with my new boyfriend. He tucks her hand into the crook of his arm, and I follow sullenly behind them as they stride toward the sea lion exhibit. My mother is asking him what his favorite animal is. His response is low-toned and I can't quite make it out, but it sounds like he says "bunnies."

Ian escorts my mother around the zoo for two hours, and I dawdle behind them, in part because I don't mind staring at Ian's fine ass, but mostly because I'm trying to gather my wits and figure out what his angle is.

Ian takes us to lunch at the Boathouse, a restaurant in the middle of the park. I don't want to go because it's far too expensive, but he insists and my mother looks elated. He begins flirting outrageously with my mother from the moment we are seated.

"Medical transcriptionist? You must have the best stories," he declares.

My mother coos. "Hair-raising tales, but unfortunately none that I can share. Confidentiality, you know."

"Your daughter must have all your best features. Bright, funny, gorgeous." He leans toward her and spreads the napkin on her lap. "Did she go to school here in the city?"

"Mostly, although there were a few years we lived in Queens." The Malcolm and Mitch Hedder years. "But Tiny is a born and bred Manhattanite. I don't think you could get her over the river now, even for all the money in Jersey."

"Tiny's such an interesting name for Victoria." He butters bread for her and then moves a water glass closer to her hand. Every action of his is focused on ensuring both she and I have everything we need even before we think of it.

"Didn't Tiny tell you how she got her nickname?" Mom shakes her head as if I've engaged in some outrageous behavior. "She can be so closemouthed about herself."

"Tell me about it," groans Ian. "I feel like I'm always doing the talking. She's more mysterious than the Sphinx."

He's so infuriating yet so smooth I can't help but be impressed. Watching the volley of words back and forth would be extremely entertaining if the topic wasn't me.

"Well, she was the tiniest baby. A thirty-three-week preemie. So small that I started calling her Tiny from the very beginning. It's almost more her name than Victoria."

"Victoria is a lovely name." Ian pats her hand, and she flushes with pleasure under his approving gaze. Incredible. I shake my head when he gives me a surreptitious wink.

The entire lunch continues in this vein, with Ian anticipating every want of my mother's, sliding me mischievous grins whenever my mother reveals something about me that he finds particularly interesting, and charming the pants off my mom, the waitstaff, and anyone within a ten-foot radius of our table.

"How will you be getting home, ladies?" he asks as we finish our dessert.

"Bus," I say.

"I suspected as much." He stands and pulls out my mother's chair. Holding out his elbow for her to take, he heads toward the door, stopping only to sign a slip of paper discreetly slid to him as he exits.

"Did you pay?"

"I did." He holds open the door and motions for both of us to exit. "Dining and dashing isn't considered good society anymore."

My mother smothers a giggle at this. "What my daughter means to say is thank you very much."

"Yes," I agree, chastised a bit. "Lunch was very nice. It was good to see you again, Ian, but we should be going."

My mother's energy is waning. I can see it in the slowness of her walk and the way her brow is slightly furrowed. I consider splurging on a taxi given that I have a little extra money because I didn't buy lunch.

"Please, allow me to see you home." He tucks my mother's hand in the crook of his right arm and then gathers my stiff, wooden frame with his left. "Perfect day. One gorgeous woman on each arm. Best Saturday ever."

I want to say something bitingly clever, although I don't know what it would be. My brain cells are shorting out because I can feel his warm hand gripping my waist through the thin T-shirt I'm wearing. Despite the cool temperatures under the canopy of leaves, I feel as if I'm in danger of overheating. Plus my right arm is awkwardly mashed against my side between his body and mine. It would be so much easier if I allowed myself to drop my arm behind his back and grip his shirt.

Never once in my twenty-five years do I remember walking in the park with my man and my mom. This is something I hadn't even fantasized about before because I never imagined it would feel so good, but there's a sense of rightness to this setup. A belonging that I've never felt before. Not only do I feel cared for, but the gentle concern Ian showed my mother all morning and throughout lunch made me feel like she was cared for too.

By the time we reach Fifth Avenue and East Seventy-Second Street, I notice my hand has crept behind Ian's back. It's resting on the top of the waistband of his jeans, the Henley he is wearing providing the only real barrier between his naked flesh and my questing hand.

I drop my hand immediately, but it brushes his ass. Ian leans down and murmurs against the top of my hair. "Feel free to touch me all you want, bunny."

Before I can retort that I'm not a small garden animal, Ian's expensive gray vehicle pulls up to the curb. "I can't allow you ladies to take public transportation. After all, I've invited myself to your morning excursion and your lunch. This is the least I can do."

"Such pretty manners." My mother pats him on the face and climbs into the back of the vehicle. He waves me in next so that I'm seated in the middle between him and my mom. "This is quite nice, Ian. Have you owned it long?"

"A few years. I have another sedan I'm testing out, but Tiny likes this one, don't you?"

He adopts my nickname like we're old friends.

"It's ostentatious," I say. I have no idea what other sedan he's talking about. I've only seen him in this big shiny gray monster.

"I'm sure she means it's lovely," Mom interjects. "How many do you own?"

Her delivery is airy, but it's no idle question. This time my mom's the interrogator and Ian's in the hot seat. He shows no resistance to her, though, and reels off a fleet of cars along with properties he owns, including a townhome recently purchased on the West Side plus real estate in London, Hong Kong, and Tokyo. I can't tell if he's bragging or trying to make my mother believe he'd be a good provider, and then I wonder why he even bothers. Is this part of the chase?

After a few more questions—such as where he went to church (he was agnostic) and where his family was from (native, ma'am)—Mom subsides and then ultimately falls asleep against my shoulder. Without the volley of words to distract me, I feel Ian's big body even more keenly. His arm has been thrown across the back of the bench seat and my mom's weight against my side presses me ever closer to him. His thigh feels like granite next to mine, and he smells delicious. I'm too agitated by his presence to talk. He somehow senses that and for once leaves me be.

When we arrive at my apartment building, he taps the underside of my chin and draws my face around. I notice for the first time his lashes are really long, almost girlishly so, and they give his dark-green eyes a seductive cover.

"Stay here," he instructs, swinging his large body out and coming around to open the passenger side door. With an ease that belies the difficulty of the maneuver, Ian leans in and scoops my mother out of the car as if she's a child. I follow. He cradles her to his chest tenderly, and my hard heart melts into a puddle of goo. Tears prick my eyes and I'm glad that I have to hurry ahead of him to unlock the outer door.

I hold it open while he turns sideways so as to avoid bumping my mother's head on the doorjamb. The run-down condition of my apartment building is embarrassingly evident. The linoleum of the entranceway is yellowed and cracking, with the corner peeling away from the floor. There is a smell of rot from garbage left out too long that permeates the lobby from the propped-open door leading to the alley in back.

Swinging my keys around my finger, I glance up toward the stairs and then sigh lightly. There's no way he's carrying Mom up five flights of stairs. Leaning over her, I smooth her hair away from her face and give her a soft kiss on the forehead, again struck by the role reversal. It's as if Ian and I are the parents and we're carrying our child home after a long day at the zoo. It's such a wistful thought my heart squeezes a little too tightly.

"Thanks for being so great with my mom, but I can take it from here," I say.

He looks at me skeptically and makes a minute adjustment to lift Mom higher in his arms. "Your mom is fairly light, but even feathers get heavy after a long period. Mind if we talk on the way up? You can thank me when we put your mom to bed."

Without waiting for a response, he starts walking up the stairs. "Fifth floor, right?"

My mouth is open and I'm gaping at his rapidly disappearing ass. Collecting myself, I race after him. "How did you know?"

"Your apartment number is 525. Not terribly hard."

"Malcolm again?"

"Malcolm," he acknowledges.

CHAPTER 11

The five flights of stairs go by quickly without having to carry either my mom or my bike. Stepping ahead to unlock the door, I let Ian in and show him my mother's room. He lays her down carefully and then exits the room. I remove her shoes, slacks, and sweater, leaving her in the light-knit shell she wore. She's all worn out, and my heart pounds heavily. Monday she'll spend hours hooked up to an IV as the poisonous chemicals enter her bloodstream trying to kill off the cancer. Her plaintive cry that she wasn't going to make it haunts me.

"Love you, Mom," I whisper. I feel myself teetering on the edge of an emotional breakdown. I'm not prepared to fence with Ian, and I spend an inordinate amount of time smoothing blankets and straightening things. Intently, I listen for the door to close and signal his departure, but there's nothing but silence.

Finally, I give up and head out into the small living room and kitchen area. Ian is sitting on the sofa, one leg thrown carelessly over the other, looking like an autocratic ruler in charge of everything he sees. It's a small and pitiful kingdom. We don't have much. A couple of bookcases full of used DVDs for me and books for my mom. There's a laptop that's about eight years old that my mom used for work, but it's done more time as a coaster in recent months than actual computing. I don't use it at all, given that writing is even more painful than reading.

We have a small wooden table and two nice chairs. The furniture isn't bad because it's part of a set Mom had bought before she got sick, but our impoverished situation is unmistakable.

I'm too tired to be embarrassed over this. We're doing the best that we can, and if I could get Ian to allow me to do this "job," I can make the whole situation better. It's painful, though, to have him looking at me and judging.

"Your mother's lovely," he says. His words are so unexpected that a laugh escapes me. "What?" he asks, one brow quirking upward in a query.

"I don't know." I rub my forehead. Ian rises and leads me over to sit beside him on the sofa. It's because I'm tired that I don't resist.

"Where's Malcolm's father?"

The question is unexpected. "Who knows? Far away from us. We haven't seen him in years, and that's a good thing." I avoid Ian's eyes. He's too perceptive. "I'd offer you something to drink, but I think we only have milk and orange juice. We're eating healthy."

"I ordered some food for us. I thought your mom might be hungry when she woke up." He's uninterested in a beverage.

"Ian—" I start to protest, but he raises his hand. I don't have much energy to fight him. It feels too good to sit and rest my head on the back of the sofa.

"No. I don't want to hear any objection. It's done." The finality in his voice shuts me down. I don't have the energy for a fight over food.

"Fine. Why don't you tell me what you wanted from Malcolm and how I can best deliver it?"

He makes a noncommittal humming noise and is saved by a knock on the door.

No one ever knocks on your door in the city unless it's a mad neighbor. I don't ever talk to my neighbors. I get up to answer, but Ian beats me to the door. As if he lives here. Outside is a burly blond guy who looks as if he belongs on a beach somewhere instead of standing outside my apartment carrying bags of food with an Asian symbol on them. This isn't ordinary Chinese takeout, I'm guessing.

"Tiny, meet Steve. Steve's in charge of me." Ian takes the food but doesn't back away, leaving me two inches of space to duck under his arm—which is holding the door open—reach forward, and shake Steve's giant hand. It's a brisk movement, and Steve's face is as impassive as the presidents' heads on Mount Rushmore. I can't tell if he hates me or if he's irritated that he's reduced to delivering food, but there's not a hint of "happy to meet you."

"Um, thanks for the food," I offer lamely.

He gives me a nod before he and Ian exchange silent words with their eyes. None of the conversation is decipherable. Maybe if I put on heels and stood up higher, I'd be able to intercept a word or two. But since I'm about eight inches shorter than the both of them, I figure I'll let them have their relative privacy—even though this is my apartment.

Unsure of whether to wake Mom up to eat or let her sleep, I pause and peek into her room. Her face looks so peaceful, I decide that sleep is better than anything. Behind me I hear the door close and the locks engage. Ian's body brushes past mine on the way to the living room. The scent of delicious peppers, ginger, and garlic trails behind him, and I follow like a puppy.

"Do you want orange juice, milk, or water? Your choices haven't magically changed since the food came," I say, detouring into the kitchen to grab plates, silverware, and napkins.

"Bring the plates," he orders.

On the table is an assortment of boxes Ian has unpacked from the sack. Next to him is a bottle of wine. I didn't see that delivered. "So Steve's in charge of you? How come I don't believe that?"

"He's in charge of where I can go. He gets very irritated when I'm in new places, and then I have to soothe him with expensive bottles of Scotch and free trips for his family to come visit him from Australia. It gets pricey. I try to keep him happy," Ian says. The food is all unpacked and my stomach growls in appreciation, which evokes a low laugh from Ian.

Ian's laugh, like the rest of him, is sexy and affects me in ways I wish it didn't. There are a lot of questions still unanswered, like why he was at the park and what he wants with Malcolm, but I decide that I'll tackle those subjects after a meal.

"Not sure what flavors you enjoy, so I ordered a variety." He sweeps a hand over the spread that could feed six instead of the two of us. The thought of leftover Thai food for days has me rubbing my hands together in gleeful anticipation.

I set down the plates and utensils and hurry back into the kitchen for glasses. Mom has some wonderful Waterford crystal glasses she received when she married Dad, and I pull those out impulsively.

"Part of me wants to complain about your high-handedness but the food is too good," I tell him while spooning a shrimp-and-vegetable concoction onto my plate. It smells so good I'd swear my taste buds are watering.

"Complain and eat at the same time. I don't care," he says easily.

"You seem very casual and laid-back, but I don't think you can be."

"Why's that?"

"Because . . ." I pause, wipe my mouth, and take a sip of the white wine he's poured me. So good. I try not to swallow the whole glass in one gulp. "You're very successful, and I don't think you would own properties all over the world if you were as completely laid-back and easygoing as you'd like people to believe. It's a sham."

He stares at me for a moment, and the look on his face is fierce. Some unfamiliar expression lurks behind his eyes, but it passes before I can decipher it and his normal, humorous, "life's my personal game" façade takes its place.

"I like how quick you are."

"That's a non-answer. Fine, you don't want to engage in normal conversation like a human being, then I'll eat." I reapply myself to the food.

"I don't like that you live here," he says over his noodle dish. He wields his utensils firmly and confidently, as he does everything else.

"Thanks, but this is all we can afford," I respond tartly. Being criticized about my financial decisions when I'm doing the absolute best I can makes me irritable.

"What about Malcolm?"

"We have a complicated relationship."

His gaze sharpens. "Tell me about it."

Oh, what the hell. It's not like it's a big, bad secret. I take another bite of my food. "His mom hates us because her husband, Malcolm's dad, had an affair with my mom. But she didn't know he was married!" I defend my mother. "So Malcolm's dad moved in with my mom, and they spent four years together, half of which Mitch Hedder apparently spent finding a new woman."

"Sounds like a real winner."

"My mom was lonely," I say defensively.

"No judgment from me," he says, holding up his hands. "Like I said earlier, your mother is lovely. Why don't we just eat? I didn't order all this food only to ruin the meal with nosy questions." His smile is a bit lopsided. "I'm intensely curious about you."

The statement embarrasses me, so I hide my face in my food. Despite our lunch, I'm actually so hungry I want to eat it all and not save any of it for tomorrow, but I force myself to stop. And it's like my cessation of eating signals an end to the meal. I'm a little sorry as we begin to wrap up the leftovers and then stick them in the refrigerator. The detritus of our meal is all gone but for the glasses of wine. Mine is low until Ian reaches over and empties out the bottle.

I can hardly believe I've helped him drink a whole bottle. Fatigue sets in and I stumble when I rise from the table. Ian is by my side, instantly leading me over to the sofa. He settles into the corner and draws me down right next to him and—maybe because I'm full of food and feeling sleepy from the long day and the wine—I lean into him, curling my legs up on the sofa cushion.

"We're a lot alike, you know," he says. His arm is around me, and his hand is threading through my hair. It's relaxing and arousing at the same time, which seems impossible, but it's Ian so I guess everything is possible. He could find gravity in space.

"How so?"

"Your mother's illness has turned you into the care provider." I make a sound to protest, but he shushes me. "It doesn't mean she loves you less or she isn't a wonderful mother; it means that you're taking on a responsibility sooner than you expected." He takes a large swallow of his wine, and I'm mesmerized by the muscles of his forearm, and how the light catches on the silver links of the band encasing his strong wrist. His arm flexes as he lifts and then lowers his glass. "But you're a lot braver than I think I would be in your situation. My mother was sick, and I didn't realize it. If I had taken better care of her . . ." his voice trails off and then picks back up. "She died, so I understand your grief."

I place my hand on his heart and my head finds a nesting place in the hollow of his shoulder. His heart beats soundly and regularly. It's strong and I feel in this place, within the circle of his arms, no harm could come to me.

"I'm sorry," I say. "When did she die?"

"Years ago," he says, and there's only acceptance in his voice and not the grief he spoke of earlier. "I'm a strong believer in what doesn't kill you makes you stronger."

"I hope so." The thought of my mother not beating her cancer and of the frightening aloneness I see in my future if she's not here isn't bearable. I shudder slightly at that bleak landscape. The emotions of the day overwhelm me and tears start running down my nose. I duck my head because I've never been one of those girls who look tragic and delicate while crying.

Vainly, I don't want Ian to see me like this, and I burrow my face against his chest. The cotton of his shirt smells like sun and heat. Against my hip, I feel an insistent pressure, which surprises me but makes me feel welcome. I'd like to stay in this position, curled up and hiding from it all, but he tips my head back and wipes away my tears.

"I want you to know that I'm not hard because you're crying, but because any normal man would have this reaction if you sat on his lap for more than a second."

This makes me burst into laughter, which is, I suppose, what he intended. He stands up, ensuring that I'm stable, and orders me to walk him to the door. At the doorway, he leans down and lightly brushes his lips against mine, leaving me wanting so much more.

"I want you, bunny, and I'll have you. This will be the last night you cry alone."

With those words, the door closes behind him. He's right about one thing: I cry into my pillow for a long time. I'm not certain about the exact source of my tears. It could be my mom, but it's more than that. The emotion is almost . . . relief.

That night I dream of Ian again. He's in his Batman costume and he flies into my bedroom, cape swirling behind him. This time I'm not a bunny. I'm me but I'm still quivering. With fear? Anticipation? I can't tell. His gloved hands are at his utility belt. "I want you," he says, and I spread my legs like a wanton.

The belt, the cape, the clothes all magically drop away, and then he's on top of me. His hands are palming my breasts and his mouth is leaving a heated, wet trail down the side of my neck. If this is fear, I want to be afraid all my life.

I hook my legs around his hips to draw his hardness down against me, but he's immovable. All I feel are light caresses from his hand and his tongue and his lips. The need for more pressure, for the hard thrust of his cock against me, builds until I wake up gasping for relief. But Ian is nowhere to be found. It's me and the sheets and the cool morning air. I roll over onto my stomach, close my eyes, and see if I can recapture the fantasy—but it's gone. I slide a hand between my legs and rub myself to a small release.

CHAPTER 12

On Sunday Mom and I putter around the house. She doesn't bring up Ian and I make inane chatter about how cute I thought the sea lions were. On Monday, we quietly prepare for the chemo trip. We'll need to be outside for the bus in about twenty minutes. The blender whirls, mixing up the banana, strawberries, and protein powder that will be Mom's breakfast. We've learned through trial and error that this is about the most that she can handle before her drip. Too much food and she's violently ill. Too little and she's weak and ill. Always ill, but Dr. Chen agreed that the protein powder and fruit in a drinkable form was our best option.

"I wish you wouldn't take the morning off to sit with me," my mom says as I hand her a hard plastic drink container full of her breakfast.

"I earn more today than any day of the week," I say, my sound muffled as I pull a long-sleeve shirt over my head.

"Because you're riding at night, and that's very dangerous."

"Even if you didn't have treatment, I'd still take this route." Kissing her lightly on the cheek, I ignore her further protestations and pack up my supplies. Because I'll be riding in the evening and it will get chilly, I make sure I have long biking pants and a windbreaker.

"Because of the money," she says with some disgust. The treatment, the illness, our circumstances, the whole situation is eroding our patience. I bite my tongue to prevent saying anything I'll regret.

"Ready?" I ask. Before she can say another word there's a knock on the door. We exchange puzzled looks, but I go to see who it is. It's Steve.

Pulling the door open but not unlocking the chain, I ask with suspicion, "How did you get up here?"

"Trade secret."

I can't tell if this is a joke because Steve's expression is no different than at our previous meeting, but the two words do reveal something about him that I wasn't aware of before: He has an accent. Then I remember Ian saying that it was expensive to fly Steve's family over from Australia.

"So are you here to pick up the leftovers?" I think forlornly of the mounds of leftover Thai food that I planned to gorge myself on later tonight after biking around the city for hours.

This time he shows a real emotion—confusion. "Leftovers? No. Hospital."

Ian. Sighing, I unhook the chain and open the door so Steve can come in. "We're almost ready."

There's no fighting this, I can tell. Steve would pick my mother up and carry her down to the car. "Hey Mom, look who's here."

She looks at me, puzzled, and then I remember she was asleep when Steve came to deliver the food. "Mom, this is Steve . . . um, I don't know your last name."

He looks like this is more painful than a root canal. He's standing in the middle of our living room, legs slightly spread, arms straight at his side like he's some soldier awaiting orders. Oh, holy crap. Ian said that Steve doesn't like it when he can't keep track of Ian. It hits me that Steve must be Ian's bodyguard.

And then I wonder why Ian needs a bodyguard. I give Steve a frown and he glares back at me.

"Thomas." He doesn't even move to shake my mom's hand, and my mom looks completely flustered.

I pick up my pack and then Mom's handbag and steer her toward the door. "Jerk," I mumble under my breath, but they both hear it. My mom gives me a reproving look but doesn't disagree. Steve grunts like a Neanderthal. Why does it not surprise me that Ian surrounds himself with guys like Steve? There's probably a whole bunch of grunting cyborgs back at the Bruce Wayne fuck pad ready to take Steve's place if he utters more than three words or, heavens to Betsy, cracks a frigging smile.

The car Steve is driving is not the gunmetal gray one that idled outside Malcolm's building, but a black one, and it's amazingly luxurious inside—even more so than Ian's other vehicle. The interior is covered with sumptuous tan leather. In the back, there are two bucket seats separated by a polished wood console where glass tumblers rest in the cup holders. One is full of orange juice.

After my mom climbs in, Steve bends down and—with a flick of a switch—her seat reclines and a footrest pops up. Mom releases an audible sigh of comfort as she settles into the butter-soft leather.

Once again I'm overwhelmed with Ian's thoughtfulness. It's touching yet disturbing at the same time. He wants something, and it must be more than a quick roll in the hay. Surely he doesn't need to be this . . . kind to get a fuck.

I'm sure the models who hang out in his neighborhood would pull up their skirts and ask for it on the brick-lined road if he seemed interested. Based on his body and looks alone, some would probably even be willing to pay for it. Add in his money and there's just no way that he doesn't have women—and some men—beating down his door. None of this makes any sense to me.

Mom rubs her hand along the creamy leather. "A recliner in the car. Have you ever seen such a thing, Tiny?" she asks in wonder.

"No, never."

"Steve," Mom calls up to the front. She has to raise her voice slightly because the distance between our rear seats and the driver's seat is sizable. "What kind of vehicle is this?"

"Maybach, ma'am," he answers.

"Your man, he's very nice." Mom picks up the orange juice and sips it. "Mmm. Even fresh squeezed."

Of course it is. The oranges are probably flown in from a special orangery kept in some remote island that is full of dirt specially formulated to create the best juice in all the world. I can't even be angry because Mom's eyes no longer look dull and disinterested. She fiddles with various buttons; one raises and lowers her footrest and another flips open a panel and offers up a phone.

"Look at this, Tiny!" she coos.

It is so amazing that we are almost reluctant to get out of the car. "Maybe you could drive around the city for a few hours," I joke when we arrive at the hospital. Steve ignores me and climbs out of the driver's seat to open the door for us. The Maybach is left illegally idling at the front while he silently assists us into the waiting room.

Inside, we head to the nurse's station to check in. Mom's chemo is done in a room with other cancer patients. It's fairly cold in the room, and I always ask for another blanket.

"Mrs. Corielli," the nurse calls out, "I have a big surprise for you today."

The staff at New York Protestant Hospital has always been great to us even though we're criminally behind on our payments. Perhaps they've fixed the broken footrest on the recliner she normally sits in, but we don't stop at the main treatment room. Instead, the nurse leads us down the hall to the very end. Inside is a hospital bed, a comfortable chair, and a big-screen television. It's a large enough room for four patients.

"What's this?" Mom looks askance at the room. It screams "expensive" and that's not a cost we can manage right now. Or ever.

"Your new room!" The nurse throws out her arms like she's a game show host displaying one of the grand prizes.

"Um, didn't realize Medicaid paid for private rooms now." We're on state aid, and I know it doesn't.

The nurse drops her arms and looks flustered for a moment. She walks over to the bed and picks up the chart hooked at the foot. "Sophie Corielli?"

Mom nods.

"No, no mistake." She pats the bed. "Why don't you climb up and we'll get started."

"Go on," I say. "I'll get everything squared away."

It's going to be a tiring day, so rather than argue, my mother nods and climbs into the bed. With the help of the nurse, we get the head and foot of the bed raised so she's comfortable. Once the drip is started, I follow the nurse out of the room. "What's this all going to cost?"

"I'm sorry," she smiles at me and pats my arm. "I'm in patient care. You'll have to call billing."

A young girl, likely in her teens, brushes by and enters the room. I hear her voice echo out in the hallway. "Mrs. Corielli?"

"Yes?"

"I'm Hallie Sitton, a volunteer. I was wondering if you might like to be read to today? I have *Emma*?"

"That'd be lovely, dear."

While Mom is occupied, I call billing with the number left me by the nurse. "Hi, um, this is Victoria Corielli, and my mother is a patient here at NYPH. She was moved into a private room today, which we never asked for or authorized. Can you explain this to me?"

"Sure, please hold," the bored voice says. A few moments later, the voice returns. "The bills are being covered by your new employer, Kerr Industries, under their family plan. The transfer was made today."

"Oh, OK," I mumble.

"Anything else?"

"No, thanks." I end the call and walk into the room.

"'Emma Woodhouse, handsome, clever, and rich, with a comfortable home and happy disposition, seemed to unite some of the best blessings of existence; and had lived nearly twenty-one years in the world with very little to distress or vex her.'" Hallie's voice is surprisingly soothing, and while I'd like to drop into a chair and give myself over to the story of the rich, spoiled, good-looking girl who tries to arrange everything in her life to suit her, I have my own Emma to deal with.

I'm starting to feel like I've already accepted that million-dollar payment, and for what? I haven't done anything. I'm unbalanced and the vertigo is making me sick.

"I have to make a phone call," I tell Mom. When she waves me away with a smile, a little kernel of resentment lodges in me at her apparent happiness. I can't read to her. I can't really support her. I feel so fucking useless. Stomping out of the room, I press CALL on the one number in my phone that I don't know by heart.

Ian answers on the first ring, and I unload. "I don't know what you think you're doing sending Steve, paying for a private room, and saying I'm your fricking employee!"

"Bunny, I've missed you too." There's a *creak*, as if he's leaned back in his chair and thrown his feet up on a desk.

"I'm not joking," I seethe.

"Hallie is the daughter of a friend, and she needs the volunteer work so she looks well-rounded on her college applications."

"Seriously?" Forgetting my anger for a moment, I peek into the room and see my mother is completely enthralled. Hallie's gesturing with her hands and using different voices to bring the story to life. "Is she some kind of theatre major?"

"Not that I know of. I believe she wants to be a doctor."

"Can't Hallie read to Mom in the common room?"

"Too disruptive," he says smoothly.

"How am I going to pay for this?" I say finally, because I can't deny Mom this pleasure, at least not today. Somehow I'll come up with the money for one day spent in a private room.

"I'll send you a complete accounting when it's all done."

"When do I start?" This is it, then. I'm going to do his secret job.

"I can send a car for you immediately and we can go over to the warehouse where I'll explain what I need from you."

His home. I think he's asking me for sex, but I'm not entirely sure. I have nothing to lose by just asking him outright. I know that I'd do a lot of things for my mom but I can't have sex with Ian for money. I wouldn't be able to look at myself in the morning. "I thought you didn't pay for sex."

I can almost feel the gust of wind through the phone when he sighs. With a touch of exasperation, he says, "I'm trying to do a good deed, and you're making it out to be something nefarious. Can't you accept a gift? That's all that it is."

"Let's just say you're making it easy to resist you right now."

"Again with the challenges. It's like you want me to chase you, bunny."

I hang up before the curse words spill out. I'm sure he's laughing somewhere in Manhattan.

When we exit the hospital, it is no surprise to me that Steve is sitting there in the emergency lane. He immediately jumps out of the car and hurries over to help my mom into the car. When the numbers of the cross streets get below eighty-six, I lean forward. "You're going the wrong way."

He meets my eyes in the rearview mirror and they tell me I can't be that stupid. I slide back into my seat. Ian's taking over my life. We stop outside a new condominium tower in Midtown that was completed last year. I remember hearing about it because it was one of the new developments that had views of Central Park. Steve lifts my mom out of the car and helps her into the elevator. There's no point in objecting now. I'll let my mom sleep before I take her home.

The lift stops on the fifteenth floor and we walk to the end of the hall. There are only six doors on this floor. The door to the end unit opens before we reach it—Ian's just inside the entrance. He's not wearing his usual uniform of boots and jeans. Today he's attired in another perfectly tailored suit. This time, it's a staid navy blue paired with a red-and-white checked shirt and a blue-and-white polka-dotted tie. His welcoming smile dies out as we march past him, a row of surly, unhappy soldiers. Well, Steve and I are surly and unhappy. Mom is out of it.

"Where to?" clips Steve. Even Ian only gets a few words. Steve is directed down the hall to the last door. Inside, I find a sizable room with a huge bed and a window overlooking Central Park. The view is incredible, but I'm too angry to appreciate it. I help my mother get into bed. She looks bewildered.

"Where are we, Tiny?" Her frail hand grips my arm, and I shoot Ian a furious look. He's wearing Steve's default expression now. Impassive, unyielding. I'm thinking that's his guilty look, the one where he knows he's gone too far but can't—or won't—acknowledge it.

"Shh, Mom, rest. We'll be back home soon." I cover her in a soft down comforter with teal and yellow embroidered accents. The whole room looks fresh and inviting but the glare from the windows is too much. After she's comfortable, I head toward the windows to pull the drapes, but I can't find a dang cord. I feel along the edges because I can see the shades hanging beneath the curtain valance. A whirring sound startles me and I jump back. The shades start to close, and I turn to find Ian pressing a remote control, which he lays carefully on the nightstand.

"Of course," I fume. "Of course there are fucking automatic blinds. Everyone has them."

"Language, Tiny," my mom says in a scolding tone.

I stomp out of the room and both Ian and Steve back away from me. Steve slaps Ian on the shoulder, says, "Good luck, mate," and leaves.

It's just the two of us now. I stand at the other side of the starkly modern living room furnished in whites and blacks with splashes of yellow. A long, low-slung sectional sofa is arranged in front of the windows. A large TV hangs to the right, and in the corner to the left is a large chair that looks like a giant, scooped-out egg. Upon closer inspection, the windows are actually French doors that lead onto a small balcony. The apartment is good-sized for the city, but it's cold and impersonal. I can't be bothered with what it looks like or how it feels because right now I am royally pissed off and Ian knows it.

"I don't know who you think you are, but you don't get to appear in my life and then dictate what I eat, where I live, and how I spend my time." I actually have my mom finger out and I'm waving it at him. I fist my hands and fantasize about popping him one in the arm.

He holds out his hands as if he can stem my barrage of complaints. "I'm trying to make things easier for you. That place you live in now, Christ—" He rubs the back of his neck, one hand on his hip pushing his jacket back and exposing his shirt-clad flat stomach.

"You're a jerk, Ian Kerr. A presumptuous, I-get-what-I-want-no-matter-what jerk." I stomp down the hall with my pack. I need to change and get ready to go. He's right behind me. Fine. He wants to watch me change, then fuck it. I drop my pack on the floor and kneel down, pulling out my shoes, athletic socks, and leggings. I pull off my jeans, acutely aware that Ian hasn't moved an inch and that his eyes are all over me. Well, he can look all he wants, but he's not ever getting in my pants. And I tell him that. "You might as well take a good look because this is the closest you'll ever be to seeing me naked."

CHAPTER 13

Leaning one shoulder against the wall, he sighs like I'm some tiresome child. "Bunny, what did I tell you about challenging me?"

"You can shove your hunter metaphors up your tight ass, Kerr." I hop around, pulling up the leg of my pants.

"I'm glad you've noticed. I had started to think I wasn't making an impact. My huge ego was being crushed. By the way, I like the rose panties you have on," he comments. "I particularly like how there are tiny bows right under the dimples in your back."

Is that a smirk in his tone? Is he fucking smirking at me because I wore some of the underwear he bought? Then fine. I don't need this stupid underwear either.

"You think you're so cute, but what happens when you're done with me? When I'm no longer interesting prey? When your little project is over? You must think my pussy is lined with fucking gold if I'm worth a million-dollar apartment overlooking Central Park." I hiss at him, pulling at the sides of the panties in an effort to jerk them off. Jesus, the lace must be made of titanium. People are constantly getting their underwear ripped off in movies.

"What are you doing?" he demands, and brushes my hands away. I fight him, wanting him to let me go, but he pushes me up against the wall and thrusts his big, heavy thigh between my legs, stepping downward so that the spandex of my bike pants is down around my ankles. I feel hobbled and, worse, I'm turned on. His steel-hard muscle is pressing right up against my clit and his hands are pressing me backward so that I'm imprisoned between his chest and the wall.

"What makes you think I'll be done with you?" he says as he moves my hands upward until they meet in an arch above my head and he can grip my wrists in one big fist. Free, his left hand slides down my arm, leaving a trail of goose bumps in its wake. His mouth is on my chin, my jaw, and then my neck. He's tasting me, pressing the flat of his tongue against my racing pulse. "Maybe I'll never be done with you and your solid gold pussy." At the last word, he closes his mouth over that pulse point and sucks hard. The only thing holding me up is his hand around my wrists. He pumps his thigh against me and an involuntary moan escapes my lips.

"I don't care," I manage to choke out. It's an obvious lie; my body cares a lot. "I'm not a toy. You don't get to put me in Barbie's expensive town home and play with me until you're bored. I'm a fucking real person, and my mom's a real person. And we don't need this shit right now. I say who I sleep with and whose bed I'm in—and right now, you aren't even in the same conversation."

"I am the entire fucking conversation." He sucks hard at the spot where my neck curves into my shoulder, and his hand is under my ass, moving me backward and forward along his thigh. His other hand has worked its way under my shirt and is palming my breast, a large thumb rubbing my nipple.

I realize my hands are free and that I've been holding them above my head while he rubs all over me. When I drop my hands to his shoulders I find I don't want to push him away. Instead, I use his shoulders as leverage to grind down on his thigh.

The nerve endings of my sex are hypersensitized and I swear I can feel every thread of his superfine wool pants. His leg moves, a tiny hitch, but it interrupts the rhythm and removes the pressure. "Don't you stop," I threaten him, all the heat turning from anger to throaty desire.

"Shh, bunny, I got you." He lifts me completely and spins me around. I have no option but to wrap my legs around him. A few quick steps and we're in another bedroom with one giant bed and nothing much else. He tumbles us onto the bed and then lowers himself over me. There's nothing in my field of vision but the hard planes of his face and the ruddy flush of desire on the high points of his cheekbones. He looks fierce and hungry.

Before I can capture another thought, his mouth is on mine and his hand is pushing aside the lace of my soaked panties. I'm moaning from both the feel of his thick tongue inside of my mouth and the sensation of one and then two of his fingers thrusting inside me. Sucking hard on his tongue, I lift my hips to grind against his hand.

His free hand spears my hair and tugs my head back as if he can't get his tongue deep enough inside me. He tastes of spearmint and earthiness, of true desire. My whole body is alive and it's straining toward him, toward completion. I brace my feet against the mattress, seeking more pressure. Breaking away from his mouth, I pant, "Harder. Fuck me harder with your fingers."

He shoves a third finger in and I cry out in surprise, but it ends in a deep groan as he begins thrusting relentlessly. "Oh, I'm going to fuck you hard. I'm going to shove my thick cock inside you, and you'll be feeling it for days after. Is that what you want?"

"God, yes," I cry.

"Your greedy pussy needs me, doesn't it?" he demands.

"Yes." It's the only answer I can give.

"Next time, it won't be my fingers inside you. Next time, you'll be riding my cock, squeezing your tight pussy around me, and coming all over me like you've never come before."

Instinctively I know that this man, for all his faults, can bring me to higher plateaus than I've ever visited. And I want to go there. Right now. I grab his wrist and squeeze my thighs around his hand so tight I can feel the bones in his wrist between my legs. "Make me come, Ian," I order. He's not the only one who can demand things.

He gives a hoarse, dark laugh and bends down to bite my nipple, right through my T-shirt and the cotton of my bra, and that's apparently all I need because the first tremors of my release start shaking my body. He sucks harder until I swear half my breast is in his mouth. The left breast is being squeezed and tormented while his other hand continues its relentless fucking of my pussy. He doesn't stop the sharp, hard movements of his hand even after my thighs fall open and I collapse, shuddering, on the coverlet. No. He continues to work me. He's covering me with his body, and his mouth is over mine again.

"You've another one in you," he growls against my lips.

"No," I say weakly, and try to push him away. "I'm done."

He's immovable. "You're done when I say so. Your pussy still wants me." His long fingers are still stroking my post-climactic nerve endings, more gently now but still firm. His thumb caresses my clit lightly, and I shudder with each pass. "You're so wet and hot and fucking beautiful right now, and I want you to come. *Now.*"

And somehow he's right. I come again as he commands. The white heat of my second orgasm overtakes me, and my body bows against the mattress. My toes curl as the power of my release draws all my attention inward, coiling my spring and then exploding outward.

He slips his fingers out of me but presses them flat and tight against my sex to soothe the ache left there. In my ear, he whispers how beautiful I look and how sweet I'd sounded during the height of my pleasure, and how he can't wait to taste me—all the while, I'm trying to gather myself.

"I'm still mad at you," I mumble as I lie like a beached starfish.

He chuckles and leans down to pull off my panties and leggings that are still attached to one leg.

"What're you doing?"

"Cleaning you up, bunny. Stay here."

"I'm only staying because I want to," I call after his disappearing back. "Not because you tell me to."

"That works."

I hear the sound of a faucet running. Moments later, he returns with a washcloth in one hand and a towel in the other. He ignores the massive hard-on that is tenting his wool pants as he tenderly cleans me down with one and then dries me with the other.

"You confuse me," I whisper as he ministers to me, but I can't deny how good it feels to be taken care of instead of the other way around.

"I'm pretty simple." He tosses the towel and rag aside and then begins to pull up my bike leggings.

"Yeah right, and the Eiffel Tower was built in a day. Hey, what about my underwear?" I protest, finally sitting up and taking over for him.

"They're damp. You sure you want them?" He dangles them from one finger, and when I move to grab them, he closes his fist around the pink lace and tucks them into his pocket.

"Fine," I huff. "Be a pervert. Keep them." Pulling up my pants, I notice the time on his wristwatch—a large black leather-banded one this time. "Shit, I'm going to be late."

Running out the door, I scoop up my shoes and socks. I've got to catch a cab across town to my apartment and get my bike.

"Whoa, your bike's right here." Ian takes me by the shoulders and points to the bike mounted right by the door. I missed it when I came in. Its presence and the mount itself give rise to so many questions that I don't know what to say.

Pulling it down, I check the air in the tires and am happy to see they are both fully inflated. I pull out my headphones from my pack and settle the helmet over my hair. I'm a mess and likely stink of sex, but the city will air me out.

"You're not a toy to me," Ian says.

Buckling my helmet and then pulling on my gloves, I give him a quick once-over. His suit is ruined. He never even removed his coat when he finger-fucked me, and I'm guessing the fragile wool wasn't meant to be worn during any intense physical encounters. There are creases in the arms and shoulders where I clutched him, and was that a . . . stain on his thigh? I duck my head to hide my embarrassment. "You owe me a lot of explanations."

"I'll be here when you're done. Come back and we'll talk."

I give him an absent nod, but it's not a sufficient response for him. He strides over and tips my head back. "I'm having this suit bronzed, you know."

My cheeks heat up because I know he's referring to the mark in the wool made from my arousal. He leans down and gives me a hard kiss. "Come back here tonight." It's a demand and not a question.

Sighing, I give in. "Only because my mother is here."

He strides to the door and holds it open as I wheel the bike out into the hall. "If it makes it easier for you to return, then yes, by all means use that excuse."

CHAPTER 14

I'm still late—should definitely not have given in to Ian—and my supervisor isn't happy.

"Two deliveries on the West Side," Sandra orders. I pick up my radio control unit and shove my phone in my backpack. "By the way, Neil is going through some hormonal crisis. If you're late again or miss another day, he's going to fire you."

My heart thuds heavily but I manage to give her a nod of acknowledgment. "Thanks."

I work extra hard that night to make sure my deliveries go without a hitch. I wonder where Ian's company is. I don't remember delivering anything to a Kerr office.

My phone stays mostly silent, which is rare because I usually field at least one phone call from my mother during my early evening runs. She doesn't like that I do them because she's convinced someone is going to hurt me. I tell her that there's more traffic in midday Manhattan and, therefore, a greater likelihood of getting hit by a bus or taxi in the sunlit hours than at night. She's my mom, though, and part of her job is to worry over me. At least I know someone out there's thinking of me.

As my shift winds down and I deliver my last set of documents to a law firm in Times Square, the ringtone for Malcolm thrums in my ear.

It plays for three measures before I'm able to maneuver out of enough traffic to answer. "Yo, big bro," I yell into the phone.

"Thanks for the eardrum-breaking hello, Tiny."

"No problem. Got a job for me?"

"Three packages for a.m. delivery."

"I'm on my way."

"Where are you now?"

"Midtown. Be at your place in thirty." I press the release button on my headphones and head over. I'm a sweaty mess by the time I get to Malcolm's. It's a good thing he has an elevator because I don't feel like carrying my bike up eleven flights of stairs.

Music is pumping outside of his apartment, and I wonder what the neighbors think of his rowdiness at nearly ten at night. It takes three hard poundings on the door and a kick before it opens. Stale smoke wafts out, smelling like someone's been doing bong hits all night long. Malcolm himself abstains from all liquor or addictive drugs. He told me early on, the only way to stay alive in the game was to never partake of the product.

Good for him, I guess.

"God, it reeks in here." But I shoulder my way inside and find a spot next to the entertainment center for my bike. "A.M. deliveries, huh? So people are taking hits of Molly in the morning? It's like the name of a morning show."

Malcolm takes my arm and drags me away, even as I'm pointing at two girls and a guy who look like overdone hot dogs on an outdoor grill—puffy and burnt around the edges. "Any of you bud heads touch my wheels, I'll come after you with a crowbar."

Malcolm glares at me. "Don't try to be funny. It's not your thing."

"The other day some dude opened the package right in front of me. I'm trying not to know!" I protest, following him down the hall into a bedroom he's made into an office, complete with a big wooden desk that he likely picked up off the side of a street, and two leather chairs. I think in another life Malcolm would have liked to have been . . . well,

Ian. A wealthy investment guy who had a big office overlooking the Hudson River and lots of lackeys. Malcolm would totally get off on being driven around the city by Steve.

I slump into one of the leather chairs as Malcolm picks up three packages and throws them on my lap.

"First thing," he says.

Ordinarily I would jump up and leave, but this time I linger, running my finger along the edges of one of the envelopes. I need answers, and Malcolm might be a person who can provide them.

"How do you know Ian Kerr?" I finally ask.

The question takes him by surprise, and he looks over his shoulder as if expecting someone to swoop down and crush him. "Why?"

"He's holding my mom hostage."

"What are you talking about?" His voice is full of disbelief, as if I'm a silly child making up some silly story.

"I ran into him during a delivery the other day and—"

Malcolm interrupts me. "Wait." He closes the door and then sits in the leather chair next to mine. "All right, go on."

"He showed up when Mom and I were leaving for the zoo yesterday. Apparently someone even told him our apartment number."

Malcolm isn't ashamed of this at all but simply motions for me continue.

"This morning he sent a car over to bring us to NYPH. When Mom's chemo was done, the car was there again. Only this time it doesn't take us home. Instead, we went to that new Century development over on Eighth and—"

"—Midtown Mini Mansions, yeah, I know," he interrupts.

I roll my eyes. Malcolm knows everything. Always. "Do you want me to finish the story?"

"Whatever." He motions for me to continue.

"Mom isn't feeling well, and it's not like I can pick her up and carry her off, so I put her to bed and then—"

"What's it look like?"

"What's what look like?"

"The view? The apartment?"

"Malcolm!" I snap my fingers in front of his face. "Are you even listening to me? He has my mother. Now tell me what he wants from me."

He sticks his knuckle in his ear. "I'm right next to you. Do you have to shout?"

"Yes!" I give a little scream and kick him in the leg. "Because you aren't listening to me."

Malcolm shoves me back and I feel like we are adolescents again, living in a tiny two-bedroom apartment in Queens, not too far from his current place, arguing about who gets to play the next game of Sonic. It was usually Malcolm because he's always been bigger and stronger and meaner than me.

"Hasn't he told you?"

"No. If he had, would I be here, talking to you?"

He shrugs. "I don't know. He contacted me asking me if I knew someone who could handle a delicate situation. I sent him a couple of people, and they didn't fit whatever idea he had about who he wanted. You were kind of a last-ditch effort."

"How much are you getting paid?"

He looks down at his shoes, but not before I see the flash of greed in his eyes.

"How much?" I ask again.

"One hundred," he mumbles.

"He's paying you a hundred thousand dollars to find someone to fulfill his little job? There must be more." Folding my arms, I glare at him. "Malcolm James Hedder, you tell me the truth."

He slouches down in his chair until his head is resting on the back. Blowing a big stream of air out, he gives up the rest of it. "And I have to make sure you never tell."

"We both know I won't." It still doesn't all make sense. Why Malcolm? His specialty is small packages, as far as I know. Not people. "Your mom's in that much trouble?"

Malcolm exhales heavily and shakes his head. "When is she not? Don't you think we'd be better off without our moms sometimes?"

"Bite your tongue," I cry. "I love my mom."

"So that's a yes."

"It's not." She's not a burden to me at all. "Besides, she's going to get better."

"I don't know if it's good for you to keep lying to yourself about that or not."

Furious at the direction of the conversation, I spring from my chair, but Malcolm's there before I'm able to wrench the door open. His hand presses the door closed again, and he murmurs into the top of my hair. "I'm sorry, Tiny. I need the money. I knew you'd be the right person for the job because you needed it too."

"He's got us by the short and curlies, then?" I rest my forehead against the door, feeling drained and not a little frustrated. "You need the money to pay for some bad gambling debt that your mom racked up, and I need it to move to an apartment with an elevator."

"Yeah, tell me the rest of it." Malcolm leans against the door, and it's clear that I'm not getting out until I give more detail. So I tell him everything. The zoo. Lunch at the Boathouse. The private room at NYPH. Everything except where Ian finger-fucked me twice. I leave that part out.

"I don't know much about him," Malcolm admits. "I've never done any work for him in the past. His kind only come to me for one or two things and whatever his vices, currently I don't have the goods to meet his demands."

"Until now."

"Right." His face shows something darker than greed this time. I don't really want to know either. Ian's game with me is confusing because he can't just want me. He must need something from me, but I've offered to do his job. Maybe he doesn't trust me. Tonight I'll try to convince him that no matter what it is that he wants done, I'll never tell.

As we walk out, the three in the living room are engaged in some heavy petting. Malcolm's eyes grow hooded. Time to go.

After I put on my helmet, he chucks me under the chin. "Be as safe as you can."

I head across the river toward Midtown, each revolution of the pedals getting heavier and heavier as I get closer to the Central Towers. Guilt bears down and so does insidious want. Would it be so terrible to stay in that posh apartment, I wonder. Until my mom gets better? It's not like I'm so full of morality. After all, I'm nothing more than a drug mule for my second job. Can't I suppress my pride to allow my mom to sleep on a bed with a view of Central Park and ride an elevator every day?

But at what cost? What does Ian want from me? The vague details provided by Malcolm don't give me much peace of mind. And the man himself? He's been infuriatingly closemouthed.

CHAPTER 15

When I get up to the apartment complex, it's late. I'm wondering if he's gone by now, but the door at the end of the hall swings inward as soon as the elevator doors slide open. Ian stands framed in the doorway, fists at his sides and a muscle jumping at the left side of his clenched jaw. His anger confuses me.

"Why are you upset?" I push past him.

He follows closely and kicks the door shut. "Your mom said you'd get home at ten and it's half past midnight."

He grabs my bike and we struggle a bit before I decide I'll likely end up on my ass if I don't let go. Giving in, I release the metal frame and watch as he lifts the bike onto the wall mount.

"What business is it of yours? You kidnapped my mother, but you aren't the boss—" I pause because he is kind of my boss now. Trying for a more restrained tone, I ask, "How is she anyway?"

"She's asleep. She was worried, by the way. She doesn't like that you work for Malcolm." His voice sounds labored, as if speaking in a normal tone is a chore for him. Even that gives me a petty sense of satisfaction. "We called."

"I ran out of battery around ten. Sounds like you had a real cozy chat." In the kitchen, I hunt around for food inside the refrigerator, which is packed with fruits and vegetables but none of the awesome Thai we had the other night. "Where are the leftovers?"

"Leftovers?" He clearly has no idea what those are.

My stomach growls and I realize I haven't eaten in hours. "You know, from the Thai food you had delivered?"

He looks befuddled. "Why do you want old Thai food? This is a full-service building. There's a chef on call twenty-four seven. What do you want?" He holds out his phone. I finally notice he is out of his rumpled suit and is now attired in jeans, no shoes, and a blue T-shirt that's so worn it's nearly white.

Food, Tiny. My stomach rumbles again. "Um, a grilled cheese sandwich and tomato soup."

Eyebrows raised, he calls in the order. What a place. I walk over to look out into the dark park. Without the sun, the dense foliage looks eerie.

"How did you explain all of this?" I signal toward the living room. Mom had to have questions about the private room, the volunteer, and now this amazing apartment overlooking Central Park.

"I told her you were doing me a favor," he says, joining me at the windows. "That this place has been unoccupied for several months, and I've been holding it off sale as a favor until the building is over half occupied."

"So sell it."

"I will. In fact, the broker came over and met your mother today. She promised to help keep it clean and that you and she would vacate the premises when it came time to move. Sophie understood that it was easier to sell if it looked like people were living here instead of a sterile, staged place that couldn't get off the market for some hidden reason."

"Oh." That sounded really reasonable. "I guess I won't get used to being here. How long do we have?" I try not to sound completely deflated by this news. I'd spent the entire day justifying how it was OK to accept this generosity, only to find we will be pushed out soon. I cast a longing glance behind me at the marble counters and the white, shiny glass appliances. This place is so nice that stainless steel is too down-market.

"Long enough for you to find your own place. With the money I'm paying you and the money you're likely getting from Malcolm, you should be able to find something better and safer than where you were living."

The doorbell rings, and Ian strides over to retrieve my food. Less than fifteen minutes. That's some amazing service.

"What's this about insurance?" I ask, taking a huge bite of the grilled cheese. It's delicious and I gobble down half the sandwich in no time.

"Jesus, Tiny, why is everything a battle?" He runs a hand through hair that already looks like it lost a pillow fight.

"Jesus, Ian, why does everything have to be your way?"

"My way is best." He leans forward and grabs a bite of the other half of my sandwich. I bat his hand away and he retreats, sucking some extra cheese off his thumb. My lower body stirs at that simple sight.

"Arrogant much?"

He just smiles and taps the side of my plate. I finish eating in silence. Leaning back in the chair, I stretch and then pat my belly. "God, I'm going to sleep so good tonight," I say absently.

Ian makes a sound—something between a grunt and a cough. "I hope so."

"By myself." I look at him reprovingly. "I want you to explain to me why I'm an employee of Kerr Industries. Is this for real? I thought the project was an off-the-books sort of thing."

Instead of answering my question, Ian asks, "How many boyfriends have you had?"

The non-sequitur is so bizarre that my answer tumbles out before I can stop it. "A few."

"And did you have such an immediate visceral attraction that you couldn't stop thinking about them? That thoughts of them interrupted meetings and business deals and evenings out with other people?"

The thought of what *other people* constitutes burns the back of my throat like an acid wash, but I've no right to be jealous that Ian has had other women. "So you're saying that the sight of me in my spandex bike shorts made you instantly attracted?"

"Maybe. Maybe it's instant attraction followed by finding out other things that make you more intriguing." He is leaning toward me now, both elbows on the table, fingers clasped together.

"Because I'm this challenge?" I roll my eyes and force out a laugh because earnest Ian is too much of a threat to my self-control. It's easier when I'm mad at him, when I'm counting all the imperious means he employs in an effort to control me. "That's such a lame pickup line."

"Do you know how many people tell me 'no' right now? Maybe five. None of them are sleeping with me. I won't give you a sob story about how hard it is to meet women because obviously that is not a problem. The challenge is finding the right one who is more interested in things outside of what I can provide."

"Really? Because you play so hard to get with your funds. Christ. The only reason I'm here is for the money." I gesture toward the apartment.

"If I believed that for an instant, you wouldn't be here," he retorts.

"I think your cock is deluding you. My hard limits aren't very hard when it comes to money."

"Fine," he says impatiently. He flexes his fingers as if imagining how good my neck would feel being squeezed between them. "What else will you do for money? Will you come over here and suck my cock?"

"How much?" I say recklessly. His green eyes are glittering with anger. Or maybe with desire? I don't really know, and I'm a little afraid to find out.

"How much do you charge?" He flings back.

It's like we're playing verbal chicken, neither one of us wanting to swerve off our stupid road regardless of the impending injury.

We stare at each other, the air around us so charged I'm surprised the whole place doesn't explode. I start to rise from my chair and he shifts backward, his powerful thighs falling open. Are we really doing this? I hold my breath and sink down onto my knees between his legs. Our eyes are locked together, and though I can't read his clearly, he must see the disbelief in mine.

As I place my hands on his knees and then slide them slowly up his jean-clad legs, I admit that while I want him, this act will ruin whatever chance we have for something tender and meaningful. There's a line here I'm breaching because if he pays me for sex, I'll never feel like his equal. I'm not sure my actions are even sexual anymore.

This is a battle for control, and I'm not going to call a halt to it. If he lets it continue as if I'm some paid whore, we'll be done. We might have great sex a couple of times, but it won't ever be more than that. Certainly not the fulfillment of this great attraction he speaks of. Maybe I'm dumb for even thinking that his lines are anything more than rehearsed come-ons designed to get me to drop my panties and jump into bed with him.

And now that I'm on my knees and my hands are on his thighs, creeping ever closer to his zipper, I'm wondering why I've even started this challenge. There is no winning here. There is no tenderness. No sweetness, only crass commercialism. But I can't seem to stop from hurting both of us. Tears splash down my face onto the backs of my hands and slide off onto his jeans.

With a muffled curse, he reaches down and drags me into his lap. Burying his head in the crook of my neck, he tucks me close with one hand affixed to my waist and the other forked into my hair, his entire palm cupping the back of my head.

"No more," he breathes. "I give."

I wrap both arms around his shoulders, reveling in the solid muscle mass beneath my hands. I wipe my tears against his shirt as unobtrusively as I can, but we both know why he stopped.

He's a beast, I guess, but he wants to be my beast. I don't make the mistake of thinking I've tamed him, though. We sit there like that—him holding me tight on his lap—for what seems like a long time before he presses his lips briefly onto my neck. Deciding he's done baiting me for the night, he picks me up and carries me into the bedroom. Maybe he can sense my flagging energy. It's way past my bedtime.

"I can walk, you know."

"So can I." He jiggles me a little in his arms, as if to say I weigh nothing, which isn't true. "Isn't it great how physically capable we both are?"

He tosses me on the bed and starts pulling off his shirt.

I'm tired, but I haven't lost all sense yet. "Wait a second." I hold up a hand.

He pauses, and then gives a little shrug and finishes taking off his shirt. In the lamplight, the planes of his chest look golden, almost amber in color. It's like looking at an ancient stone statue come to life, and it takes a lot of effort to not reach out and stroke my hands across the light mat of fur on his chest and follow the treasure trail down into the very worn jeans. When his hands move to start unfastening his jeans, I'm awakened from my sensual stupor. "What are you doing?"

"Getting ready for bed," he says implacably.

"Here?" I say dumbly.

"Yes." And he proceeds to shuck his jeans. Underneath he's wearing slate-gray, silky boxer briefs that hug his very manly form. He's half-aroused and the shape behind the fabric looks enormous. My vagina clenches in either excitement or trepidation. Both, probably. "I usually sleep in the buff, but because it's been a long day for both of us, I'll keep my shorts on tonight."

"You can't sleep with me," I squeak. "I'm not ready for that."

"We're sleeping, bunny. Nothing else," he says and heads for the bathroom.

"But . . ." I trail off. "Is this because of what happened earlier?"

"No." He comes out of the bathroom with a toothbrush in his mouth. Speaking around a mouthful of foam and water, he says, "I was always planning on sleeping with you tonight." He disappears, and I hear him spit and then the faucet running. "Actually, I planned to pick up where we left off, but it's too late now. We both have to get up in the morning."

The door closes and I hear the flushing of a toilet and more running water. Then he's done with his nightly bedtime routine, which I guess consists of brushing his teeth and peeing. Men. Totally unfair.

Pulling back the covers, he pats my ass again. "Don't look so disappointed, bunny. I plan to fuck you until you pass out tomorrow night."

I flounce out of bed like an outraged maiden and hide in the bathroom. I can tell there is no moving him, and right now I'm so tired that I give in. On the marble counter are all my bottles of personal care products, from my facial soap to my toner to my moisturizer. My outrage meter is so overworked that I can only sigh at this sight. I run through my nightly routine, which is far more extensive than Ian's, and strip out of my confining spandex. It's too late for a shower, so I grab a washcloth to clean my underarms and between my legs. Realizing I don't have my pajamas—an old, oversize Giants T-shirt that I filched from Malcolm's house—I wrap a towel around my body and confront Ian. "Where are my clothes?"

"There's a walk-in attached to the bathroom. Should be in there." He leans up on one arm, the blankets falling aside to reveal his perfect chest. "Or you can wear this."

He tosses me the blue T-shirt he had on earlier. Reflexively I catch it and hold it to my nose, breathing deeply of Ian Kerr. God, he smells so good. Over his shirt, our eyes meet. His have taken on a feral glow. "Wear the shirt, Tiny," he commands. And this time my reaction is a purely sexual one.

I imagine him ordering me to do all sorts of things in this bedroom and me liking it very much. I back away into the bathroom and lean against the door, breathing heavily. It's like he can touch me with his words. Against my better judgment, I slip the T-shirt over my head.

He says nothing when I climb into bed next to him. I notice he sleeps on the right side of the bed, closest to the door. When my back hits the mattress, I release a moan of pleasure.

"How long has it been?"

"Months."

He grunts. "Who was he?"

"Who was who?"

"The guy you were sleeping with months ago." He sounds like he's speaking through gritted teeth. When I look at him, it's too dark to tell if his eyes are even open.

"What are you talking about?"

"What's this 'months' you are referring to?"

"That's how long it's been since I've slept on anything but the pullout." I shake my head. "How long has it been for you?"

"I sleep in a real bed every night, bunny," he says with obvious amusement.

"Ha ha. Fine." I turn over on my side and thump my pillow. "It's probably yesterday. FYI, I'm an only child. I don't like to share."

"Back at you," he says. "I'm not fond of the idea of you sleeping with anyone else ever again."

I don't fall asleep immediately because having a man in bed with me is just strange. I hardly ever slept with Colin, my one serious boyfriend, and the few random hookups since him didn't warrant a sleepover. Sleeping with someone can be more intimate than fucking him.

"Ever again?"

"Ever again." He confirms in a husky voice, knowing immediately what I'm talking about.

"Ever again seems like a long time, or is that a rich person's term for like six months?"

He chuckles. "You define the length of time that makes you feel comfortable, bunny."

"I can't decide if 'bunny' is a term of endearment or an insult."

"Endearment."

"Seems kind of insulting sometimes. I need to pick out a nickname for you."

"I thought I was Bruce Wayne."

Ian rolls me to my side and begins to rub my back, his hand underneath my shirt, lightly stroking my shoulder blades, tracing my spine, and then sweeping back up again. It feels good and would be non-sexual if not for the hard-on the size of the Empire State Building pressed against my ass.

"That's not insulting in any way."

"You're right. I like being compared to a superhero."

"But you call me 'bunny.' That's not kick-ass or super in any way."

"You looked like a scared bunny the day I saw you outside the wig shop. You wanted to come with me but were afraid, and you hopped on your bike and rode away." He sounds so smug, but I'm tired. The feel of his hand as it rubs away the pains of my long bike ride is too good to mount a protest against. "I appreciate the Bruce Wayne imagery, and I have to tell you I've always wanted the Batmobile."

"You can't buy that with all your money?"

"Unfortunately, no. Technology hasn't advanced that far yet."

"So if I ever come into a lot of money, the perfect gift for the man who has everything is a Batmobile?"

"Don't forget the butler. I want Alfred too. Steve is no Alfred."

"I'm telling Steve that the next time I see him." I can barely force the words out as I get drowsier with each pass of his hand.

"You do that. And tell him I want him to start dressing like a butler and referring to me as 'sir.'"

"Do you think he'll change his behavior?"

"Yeah, I think he'll become more of a prick."

"If you don't like him, why do you employ him?"

"Who says I don't like him?" Ian pulls me snug against his body. I feel his hard chest around my back and the massive boner wedged even tighter against my ass. He throws one arm around my waist. A heavy calf slides over my legs, and I'm pinned down like a butterfly on a mat. And it feels great. "I fucking love Steve, but he's got two emotional settings: stoic and a little less stoic." His quiet laugh ruffles my hair.

As I'm falling asleep against the cave of his body, I whisper, "I don't get you."

"I'm going to tell you a little bedtime story, bunny. Once upon a time I was in Japan and I discovered this plastics company. I knew after the first tour of that company that I had to have it. They were manufacturing plastics using clean energy and in a safer way than I'd ever come across. I begged, cajoled, and finally bought my way in. It's one of the best decisions I've ever made and one that I arrived at in a day." He pulls me even tighter to him, if that's possible. "This is how I'm wired. By the way, I haven't been with another woman since I saw you on the street."

And then I'm dead to the world. His words run around my head as I sleep, but I can't process their meaning even though I know he's telling me something really important.

CHAPTER 16

When I wake up, I am hot and aroused. There are two fingers between my legs rubbing the lace of my panties in circles, and at my back there is a furnace of male flesh.

"I thought we weren't having sex until tonight," I say, sounding a bit like Marilyn Monroe—all breathy sexuality. His chest rumbles behind me as he chuckles.

"We're not." But his fingers are playing out a different story. As they circle and press, I push back against the thick length snugged against my butt.

"It feels like sex." It feels hard and long, actually, and despite the fight we had the night before and my lack of surety about what Ian really wants from me, it's difficult to concentrate on anything other than the languorous feelings he's generating with such simple movements.

"No, this feels like sex." On the last word, he presses the tips of his fingers inside me, the fabric of the panties restricting him to shallow thrusts. Whimpering, I open my legs hoping for deeper penetration. I mean, he's here. Why not use him?

He pulls my left leg back over his hip, shoves the fabric aside, and slowly pushes his middle two fingers all the way inside me until I can feel the palm of his hand rest against my clit. His palm stays there almost motionless, the heel against my sensitive extrusion, while his fingers scissor and stroke inside me until he finds that soft little sponge of flesh that makes me gasp out loud.

"Right there, hmm?" It's not a question that requires an answer—at least not a verbal one. My body is telling him he's stroking me in exactly the right way. My hips thrust toward his hand, and when he dips his head to nip at my ear, my arm reaches up hook his head closer to mine. His comfort doesn't enter my mind. Am I pulling too hard on his hair? Are the nails of my right hand that's moved down to press on the back of his hand digging too tightly into his skin? I don't care.

I'm swimming in a tide pool of sensation that I want to wallow in forever.

"Not yet," he whispers as he rolls me over onto my stomach. His fingers pull out of me, and I let out a sound of protest that is muffled by the pillows. Even if I were louder, I don't think he would cease. He pulls down my sodden panties and shoves a pillow under my hips. Then his mouth is where his fingers used to be. His broad shoulders have spread my thighs apart and his tongue is spearing inside of me. I'm grateful for the pillow at my mouth because I can hear myself moaning.

"Right there. Oh god. Faster, please." But my pleas are ignored. He has his own rhythm. His tongue is savaging my clit while two of his fingers are thrusting into me, curling and seeking until they hit that same spot he'd discovered earlier. Once found, he relentlessly fucks me with his fingers, all the while sucking and tonguing and licking me. Tension coils within me, curling my toes and causing my fingers to dig into the mattress.

From between my legs I can hear his groans of satisfaction—as if he's getting as much out of eating me out as I am by being the recipient of his gifted tongue.

But every time I think I'll climax, he brings me down again, slowing the pace and moving his fingers in an unhurried fashion, in stark contrast to the frantic thrusts seconds before.

"You're killing me," I gasp out.

"I hope not." There's so much smug amusement in those words that if

I wasn't ass-up and facedown with his head between my legs, I'd have to punch him. But he knows that I'm too delirious with desire to call him out.

"Stop teasing me," I beg. Thinking he needs more encouragement, I spell out explicitly what I want. "I need your big, hot cock inside me. Fucking me hard and fast."

His fingers tighten and he groans, but instead of rising up and thrusting inside me, he slaps me on the ass. It's almost a little too hard to be affectionate, but because I'm so hot for him, all I do is raise my butt in the air higher in a "Please, sir, can I have another?" move. This causes him to speed up the thrust of his fingers, and soon I'm too lost inside my own head to care that it's not his cock inside of me, not when his magical tongue is back between my legs.

Desperate and needy, I gyrate against the pillow and alternately pant out commands and pleas. "Don't stop. Please, don't you ever stop."

And he doesn't. He's relentless in his assault. It's as if he doesn't even need to breathe down there. His mouth is attached to me and his tongue is like a lash against my clit. Inside me, I can feel the drag of his calloused fingers against the swollen tissues of my inner walls. With each glide in and out, he rubs against the front flesh, causing my whole body to tighten. And then it's faster, until the combined force of the suction of his mouth and the push of his fingers causes a cacophony of sound and light to explode in my head, and I'm lost on delicious waves of feeling.

He does rise up behind me, but doesn't move his fingers. He's cupping me as if he's trying to keep tendrils of my orgasm inside me for as long as possible.

"I want to fuck you bad, Tiny." His husky voice raises goose bumps all over my body. "But I'm going to need at least eight hours of uninterrupted time." The goose bumps turn to shivers.

Ian holds me, running his fingers over my back and down my arms and over the tops of my thighs, trying to soothe my shattered nerves. After a few moments of comfort, he rises from the bed with a slap on my ass. "Too bad we both have to work today."

I roll over and watch him stretch next to the bed. His erection bobs right in front of me. The hard length of him is flushed an angry red.

"What about you?" Suddenly I want a taste. Scrambling up on my knees, I lean over the edge of the bed and grab his arm. "You can't go out like that. Heart attacks will happen. Think of the elderly."

He looks down at me with amusement but then presents his back to me. "Climb aboard, then, and you can take care of me in the shower."

If pressed later about the decor of the bathroom, I'd have to say it was full of steam and tile. Ian spends most of the time kissing me while I stroke him with both hands. While his large hands cup my face, he caresses me with his mouth and tongue, showing me that I hadn't really been kissed before.

It's not enough for me to hold him between my hands—his flesh pulsing against my palms. I want him in my mouth. I want to know the flavor and the smell, the girth and the length. I want to know it all.

This time he doesn't stop me as I slide downward. The tile is warm from some underground heater, and the steam rises from the hot water that sluices around us. He drops a thick towel onto the tile and I slip it under my knees. Droplets drip down his hard abdomen and cling to the hair that surrounds his thick, heavy erection. The head arrows toward me and follows my tongue as I lick delicately at the top and the sides.

Ian's hands come down to push my hair aside, and when I glance upward through my lashes, his eyes are heavy lidded and he's breathing heavily. Finally, I take him into my mouth. He's very thick and my lips are stretched to their fullest. One of his hands drops away from my hair to stroke my jaw and chin. Then he cups my face, holding me under my chin as he begins to shuttle in and out in short, shallow lengths.

"I can feel myself in your mouth," he says above me. "I can feel my cock through your cheek. Your lips are stretched and you can barely take it, isn't that right?"

I would've nodded but for the steady hand under my chin.

"If I touched you right now, how soaked would you be?" he asks. "Is all the moisture from the shower or are you so fucking wet right now that it is *dripping down your thighs?*"

The last few words are growled, and I can't keep a moan from slipping out. Above my mouth, his taut abdomen flexes as he pants and grapples for control. I grip his thighs for balance, my nails digging into his flesh.

"You look like a fucking goddess right now," he continues. "Hotter than the desert sun in August. I want to come down your throat. Will you swallow it all?"

I nod, flicking my tongue against the bottom of his cock. He presses slowly to the back wall of my mouth. I gag and then swallow it down, feeling the cockhead swell in my throat.

"Open up for me," he says, moving his fingers down to rub my neck as a little more of him eases down my tight throat. He hisses, "Jesus Christ, bunny. That's so fucking good. So good."

He withdraws, flexing his hips, and then slowly glides back in. This time it's easier. I'm prepared for the fullness and hungry for his taste. This time he slides so far in that the coarse hair of his pubis tickles my nose. His hands are on either side of my face, tipping my hair back. I can feel my hot arousal trickling down my leg, a thicker, more viscous fluid than the water. I'm consuming him, eating his essence, taking him inside me in a way I had never envisioned possible.

With his hands around my face and neck and his rigid length down my throat, I'm entirely his. His cock drags along the soft tissues of my throat. I feel the ridges against my tongue and his firm grip against my chin. My entire world is his cock and fingers and the smell and taste of him.

I drop my hand to my clit and start to rub furiously, unconcerned by balance or resistance. Ian has me in his hands. He's thrusting now, not as deeply, and his movements lack his regular precise control.

"I'm going to come now," he grits out. I think he tries to push me away, but I lean forward and open my mouth as wide as possible. I want to drink him down. A shout sounds and then he comes, the thick, ropey jets of semen coating the inside of my mouth. There's so much of it that it leaks onto his hand and spills out onto my face, and it is hard to tell where the soap stops and the evidence of his climax begins. I lick as much of it as I can before the water washes it away.

Ian lifts me into his arms and kisses me, uncaring that he's tasting himself. His slick tongue is devastating. "I want to be inside you. Soon. I have to have you, Tiny."

"Yes, Ian, yes," I moan between kisses.

His fingers slip inside me again, pumping me to the release that had been building the entire time I had sucked him down. It takes only a minute for him to rub me to an orgasm.

"God, bunny." His eyes darken and his breath quickens, and for a moment I think he'll impale me right there in the shower. But for that brief moment when I was on my knees before him, Ian's self-control governs him more strictly than the never-smiling guards outside Buckingham Palace. Instead, he lowers me to the ground, kissing me gently. With his hot gaze on my every move, I quickly shower and step out. As soon as I am out of the enclosure, he blasts the cold water but his eyes never waver from me. I swear the steam rises from the heat of his gaze.

I have to turn away before I'm burnt. He gives me a wry smile and finishes his shower.

"You can leave your bike with the doorman. They'll store it," he tells me as he's dressing. I try not to dwell on the fact that he has a couple of suits in the walk-in closet next to my jeans and spandex. I'm too chicken to ask him what it means—mostly because I don't know what I want the answer to be.

"They won't think it's weird?"

"They are paid too much to say anything but that you look beautiful and that biking is good exercise."

Ian moves too fast for me. I understood his bedtime story last night. He likes making quick decisions, believes in them. But I'm not a manufacturing company.

"Do you still own the plastics company?" I ask him.

"So you did hear that?" His eyes flick from the mirror to me and then back to the mirror. His collar is flipped up, and he's wrapping the large end of his tie around the little one in expert, practiced movements. I don't have the first clue how to tie a man's neckwear, so his morning rituals are fascinating. In about thirty seconds, his tie is knotted and his collar is back into position. "Yes, I still own it. It's a very profitable company. Maybe you've heard of it." And he names a company that I thought made shampoo.

"Wait, they're a plastics company?"

"They were when I bought it. Now they are a much larger business with many diverse interests. Cuff me?" In his hand he holds out two mother-of-pearl cufflinks. They're almost feminine in their appearance, but against his masculine hand, they look exotic and are a perfect match for his oyster-pink tie.

"Did you pick this tie out?" I flick my index finger against it.

He looks down. "No, personal shopper."

"She has good taste," I say sourly—but like all my other feelings involving Ian, I'm confused about this too. The thought of another woman dressing him somehow bothers me, as if she's got intimate knowledge of him that I don't have, or maybe even a longer, more personal relationship with him.

He taps my nose and says, "It's a him, but I like your jealousy. Gives me hope."

As he sits on the end of the bed to put his shoes on, I slip on new panties, spandex bike shorts, a sports bra, and a T-shirt.

"While I'd love to stay here all day with you, I have meetings to run."

"People to ruin?" I joke.

He pauses in the midst of pulling his laces tight. "People to ruin."

He gives me a quick kiss on the forehead, which is fast becoming his go-to region. I'll put a sticker there that says "Ian's landing spot."

And then he's gone in a whirl of custom-made superfine wool and hand-stitched shoes.

Mom is still sleeping when I let myself out. I make my three deliveries for Malcolm as he requested, but my thoughts are still in the shower. I'm wet all day and not just from sweat.

Around noon my mom calls, diverting my thoughts away from Ian. "Hey sexy momma, what's cooking?" I say brightly.

"This place is so beautiful, dear. I swear I can see all the way across the park," she exclaims.

"That Ian boy is so nice." Leave it to my mom to call him a boy. *Shit.* I don't even know how old he is or what his middle name is, yet I'm living in an apartment that he's paying for and my clothes are sharing the same closet as some of his clothes. I wonder what goes on at the fuck pad down in the Meatpacking District—the one with the cameras that look like live creatures.

"Yeah, don't get too comfortable," I warn.

"Did you know that there is a concierge for the apartments? As if we were staying in a swanky hotel!" She continues on, gushing about it as if my warning never happened. Each compliment increases my concern over taking her out of there and back to the walk-up. It's my own pride that makes me want to leave.

"It's a nice place," I say begrudgingly.

"I can't believe he's having trouble moving this place. I wonder if there's been a crime in the building." Mom speculates on all the ways that the apartment building may have lost value. "It's also very cold except for my room, and the bed in your room is far too big. It makes the room look crowded. He should hire a stager."

"I'll mention it to him the next time I see him." When she hangs up, I stare at the phone for a moment. There's no way I can move out now. Part of me feels elated, but that's the dumb, foolish part of me. The part of me that's going to not understand when he loses interest. The part of me that will be crying into the pillow for weeks after he's moved on.

CHAPTER 17

I'm in the midst of patching a tire when "Room at the Top" by Tom Petty starts to play.

"Hello?" I answer tentatively, wiping the residual tar off my fingers. Thank god for Bluetooth headphones.

"Bunny." Ian's low baritone slides down my ear and right into my belly.

"Is this call for work or pleasure?"

"Do you spend the entire time brooding on that bike? You should quit and do something else that occupies your quick mind."

"I don't have time to brood. I'm too busy trying to avoid the taxicabs who treat bikes as the enemy." In truth, I daydream. I dream about my mother being cancer free. About having a family. About reading to my own kids. They would be whip-smart and go to Harvard or Princeton, and I'd beam proudly in the crowd when they graduated. They'd be scientists or lawyers or writers. They wouldn't be me. They wouldn't be locked into a job that doesn't require reading or writing skills. I say none of this to Ian.

"Thanks for reassuring me," he says dryly. "Unfortunately, I can't be there to watch over you this week. I have to go to Seattle and look over a possible venture. Wearable military tech. What do you think?"

"Would Tony Stark buy it?"

He chuckles. "Should that be my investment measuring stick from now on?"

"I think so. You aren't as successful as he is. I haven't seen you in anything but those old cloth suits. So twenty-first century."

"I've already admitted that my sense of fashion is pretty poor and I pay someone to shop for me."

"Like the lingerie?"

"That is some of the best money I've spent." His voice is husky and the weak and vulnerable part of me responds with a swifter heartbeat and a throb between my legs.

In the background, I hear rustling and a pleasant voice indicating that a flight is about to take off. "I need to go, Tiny. I should be back on Friday. I trust you'll still be at Central Towers when I return?"

"Probably. I can't move my mom right now."

"Don't sound so glum. I have a task for you. Friday night you'll need to get yourself to the Red Door Spa on Fifth Avenue at seven p.m. Can you make it?"

"Sure, but why?"

"I'll need you to get properly armored at the Red Door at seven, and I'll pick you up there at ten. The Aquarium is," he pauses, searching for a word, "a shark tank. I want you to be properly armored."

"OK. Is this for the project?"

"Yes. I was going to explain it to you this evening, but obviously that's not possible, and it's not something I want to do over the phone." He says something indistinguishable to another person and then returns. "Where are you going next?"

"I have deliveries in Midtown and then on the East Side. I'm at Tenth and Fifty-Second Street. I'll be going crosstown because I have a delivery over on Designers' Way. Probably dropping off fabric samples."

"Have you considered not doing your messenger job?"

"No," I say shortly. "Does it embarrass you?"

"It worries me."

That shuts me up. Only my mother worries about me, and the idea that this bothers Ian touches me in a deep way. I blink rapidly to stave off any physical reaction to his concern. Why am I so hormonal lately? "I'm safe."

"You told me earlier you spend each moment thinking about how to best avoid an accident. That doesn't sound like a safe job to me. Do you know that there is an actual New York City government study on bicycle fatalities? Between 1996 and 2005, 225 bicyclists died in crashes."

I don't have anything to say because my thoughts are caught on the idea that he's concerned enough to look up statistics about bicycle safety. In fact, I'm certain that if I spoke, I'd start crying—so I remain silent. I don't even point out that those numbers are from ten years ago.

Ian sighs then and says, "I'll pick you up at ten on Friday."

"Good-bye," I manage to croak out, but he's already gone.

The week crawls by without Ian here to hassle me. He does call, though, more than I expected, and the pleasure I feel just listening to him tell me about his day is worrisome. Each day I wait for the call as if I'm a drug addict and he's my heroin.

♦ ♦ ♦

When I arrive at the Red Door on Friday, I'm flushed and sweaty from the day of work and I'm wearing at least an inch of city grime all over my body. Steve is leaning against the Bentley, his arms folded and aviators covering his eyes. He looks like a bodyguard rather than a chauffeur.

"Hey Steve," I say, wondering if Ian is in the car.

"Hello, sheila," he says in return. "Can you pop off your wheel?" he nods his head toward my bike. "We need to stick it in the trunk."

"Right." I bend over to disengage the quick-release mechanism and hold up the front tire. Steve takes it from my hand and then picks up the frame and easily carries both to the now open trunk.

He closes it with a thud and then, with a little wave good-bye, climbs into the driver's seat and jets off.

Inside the building, soft music plays and a woman so slender she makes reeds look fat totters over to me on six-inch heels. "Ms. Corielli?" she inquires. For a moment I don't know who she's addressing, and I look over my shoulder to see if there is another lady who walked in behind me. But no, she's addressing me. I nod and try shaking her hand, but she backs away a little unnerved. Who shakes hands with the receptionist? No one, but I've never been in one of these swank spas before. The closest I've ever been to a spa is one of the nail salons that populate every city block.

She gives me a wan smile and leads me up a circular staircase and into a fairly large room. There is a garment bag with "Barney's" lettered discreetly on the left side hanging on the back of the door and a shopping bag in the corner. A robe and slippers are laid out on a massage table and to the left is a hair station. Apparently everything is done in this one room. No mingling with the masses for me.

"Please remove all of your clothing and jewelry and press this when you are ready." She hands me an iPad with a big red button that says ATTENDANT.

Over the next two hours, I'm rubbed down and then done up. Inside the garment bag is a top that could be called a sweatshirt. It has a ribbed bottom and cuffs but, except for the front panel, the entire shirt is made of a heavy, deep-red lace in a beautifully modern floral pattern. The neckline is wide, giving it a tendency to slip off my shoulder. As I root around in the bag, I am unsurprised to find that there is no bra—only a pair of sheer red panties with tiny bows all over them. I slip on the delicate panties and then pull on the silk shorts that I also find inside the bag. They are black with tiny pinstripes mimicking a man's suit pants. I'm relieved that they aren't booty shorts and actually manage to keep all the private parts of my body fully covered, even if I bend over.

The shoes are black with lace fretwork running around the sides and up the middle. A delicate strap encircles my ankle. There are bangles for my wrists and a pair of red stone earrings. I wait to put those on.

"That's a gorgeous outfit," my stylist, Robin, comments as she winds my hair around a hot curling iron. After my massage, a team of people trooped in. Robin is the hair stylist and Mark is the makeup artist. Robin and Mark take turns holding my chin and nodding to each other about how my eyebrows need help and my hair color has no depth. Limp as a noodle from the rubdown, I endure the inspection without comment.

"First hair," Robin declares, and Mark leaves to round up more tools and the eyebrow artist. They actually have someone designated only for eyebrows. I try not raising mine when I hear that.

"Thanks."

"Your legs are so toned. Pilates?" she asks.

"Cycling," I say and then hurriedly add, "cycling class." Bike couriers can't afford three-thousand-dollar outfits to go to a nightclub. Whoever shopped for Ian had failed to remove the price tags.

"Going somewhere tonight?"

"The Aquarium."

"Ohhh," she breathes out in awe. "Private party?"

"Don't think so."

She nods at me in understanding, although I don't know what we're agreeing to. "They always say it's closed to private parties, like at 1 Oak, but it's all who you know, isn't it?"

"Yes, probably." She's likely wanting to know who it is that I know, but I'm not drawing connecting lines for anyone.

We chat a little more about the city's best nightclubs, although it's really just Robin talking about all the hot places she's heard of or went to and me nodding along.

After she's made my hair look voluminous with big waves spilling down my back, Mark comes in with a team of people. One is focused on my feet and another on my hands. The eyebrow artist advances toward me with a tool of shiny implements strapped to her waist. I close my eyes and tip my head back because there's nothing else I can do.

Once they're done, I see that I look like an entirely different person. My cheekbones look more pronounced and my lips look fat and juicy. They also feel like they're tingling. "It's all in the shading," Mark says, whisking a brush one more time down my face.

"What if I sweat?" I ask, raising the tips of my fingers to a cheek that looks luminous even under the harsh lights. I didn't realize that makeup could actually make a person look this good.

"Don't," he says shortly. "There's blotting paper, a little foundation, blush, and gloss in your purse. Think of yourself as Cinderella. You'll turn into a pumpkin if you stay out so long that you're sweating."

"I think it was the mice that turned into the pumpkin, not Cinderella," I say. My eyes look huge and mysterious. I'm going to have to take a selfie because there's no way I'll ever look this good again.

"Cinderella got herself home before she started sweating, otherwise she would have been a pumpkin—a big, orange, sweaty, lonely pumpkin," Mark declares.

I'm shooed off. Downstairs, the receptionist gives me a slight nod of approval, which I take to be just as effusive as clapping.

"Thanks, everyone," I say and the team of specialists beams at me like I'm the best school project they've ever put together.

CHAPTER 18

Steve is waiting for me outside in the gray car. When I crawl in, I notice that Ian is sitting right behind the driver's seat. The light illuminates the interior for a few seconds after Steve closes the door. He rounds the front and then leans against the hood. I wait, a little breathlessly, to see Ian's reaction.

"So I guess we're staying in tonight," he finally says when the light flickers out.

"What?" I ask, confused.

"You're far too beautiful to be out in public." He slides a finger around the boatneck opening of my sweatshirt, and we both watch as his finger pulls the fabric down so that the ball of my left shoulder is exposed. "Clearly I need to give better instructions about what's appropriate attire. No bra, Tiny?"

His finger is circling my skin in some pattern known only to him. But that small contact is making me throb in a dozen other places. I slide closer to him, close enough to feel the fine wool of his trousers brush against my bare leg. I want to slip off my sandal and run my bare foot up the entire length of his leg. "No," I croak out. "You'd see it in the back." I turn slightly so he can see that the back of my shirt is just open lacework.

His hands sweep aside my hair to reveal my braless back. "How do your breasts feel without their restraint?" he asks, sliding two hands down my shoulder blades and then around to rest underneath my breasts. With a quick tug, I tumble backward so that I am leaning against his chest. I squirm a bit, wishing that there wasn't his suit coat, shirt, and undershirt separating us. His mouth finds the tender skin where my neck and shoulder meet and he sucks, causing me to cry out in desire.

"God, Ian," I moan.

"Your breasts," he says again, "tell me how they feel." His hands move downward and then sweep underneath my shirt. My breasts strain toward him, my nipples ache for his touch, but he doesn't move and he won't until I give him what he wants.

"They feel heavy. They ache," I say.

He bites softly in the same spot. "Good girl." I'm rewarded when he cups my breasts, one in each hand. He holds them loosely, almost as if weighing them to see if they are, indeed, heavier. "What do they ache for?"

"Your hands." I place my own hands over his and press them harder against my chest. "Your fingers."

"My mouth?" He sucks lightly on my neck. There'll be a mark there, but I don't care at this moment.

"Your mouth," I agree breathlessly. His fingers begin to pinch my nipples all the while he's palming the sensitive flesh. His mouth leaves my neck to place kisses and bites all along the back of my shoulders. My panties are getting damp, and I'm squeezing my thighs together, both to increase friction and assuage the ache that's growing.

I don't understand how he can affect me this way—make me so hot just by touching my chest or running his mouth along my shoulders—but I'm so turned on that I think I could come, given enough time and maybe just a little touch of his fingers between my legs. I can feel the rigid length of his erection press against my butt.

A car door slams shut and the lights flicker on again, just for a moment. "Ready, boss?"

Ian drops his head against my shoulder, and I almost cry out in frustration. "Ready," he replies. He places a soft kiss against my neck and then pulls his hands out from underneath my shirt.

"What exactly are we doing tonight?" I slump against the seat.

"Baiting the hook."

At the mention of being the bait, I draw away from him.

"Tiny." He grabs my hand. "No matter what happens tonight, it's only part of the job. The rest of this between us is separate. Whatever you think is happening between us is entirely real. Don't forget that."

I don't understand how he can separate business from pleasure. One minute he's telling me he can't wait to be inside me and the next he's saying I'm bait for something. But this is how I'm to earn my keep. I just need to remember that. It'd be a lot easier if he kept his hands to himself.

He hands me *The Observer*, one of the local city gossip papers. On *Page Six*, there is a picture of Richard Howe, son of mayoral candidate Edward Howe, his arm wrapped around his wife, whose name I can't recall.

"Our project involves Edward Howe?" I gasp.

"No, his son, Richard. Richard is a forty-seven-year-old going on eighteen. He's rumored to be in the throes of a serious midlife crisis and is spending his family money faster than the Treasury Department can print it."

I run a finger along the edge of the paper. Edward Howe was in his late sixties and came from old money. He was the type of guy whose family rubbed shoulders with the Rockefellers and Astors. While his name wasn't on landmarks around the city, his ancestors' buddies were. The city's residents weren't sure if they loved him because he was an institution or hated him because he was so wealthy.

Unlike most politicians, he seemed to have no skeletons in his closet, and despite his posh Fifth Avenue address, he lived austerely and without unseemly extravagance. The fact that he was wealthy meant that he would be shielded from graft and corruption—or so the thinking went. He has only one wife and campaigns on the promise that he'll be a solid, if unexciting choice. Whether he'd be the next mayor is hard to say. His campaign is running smoothly so far.

"You said that I wouldn't have to sleep with anyone," I accuse. My voice is reaching perilously high levels. "You want me to have sex with him and take pictures or something? Because I'm not going to do that."

"Calm down. No. Nothing like that."

"What is it, then? What do you want me to do that will cost you so much money?"

Shaking the paper, Ian taps his finger on Howe's face.

"Howe is no innocent. About fifteen years ago, he was an up-and-coming trader, but he had expensive tastes and decided that company funds would be used to finance his adventures. A friend of mine helped him out, and that friend ultimately got blamed for Howe's embezzlement.

"I don't know how many people Richard Howe has managed to ruin in the intervening fifteen years, but I've decided that he's a blight on this earth that needs to be stamped out. The Howe household is built on sticks. And one little gust will topple it over."

"You've decided?"

"Yes." His voice is implacable and as unemotional as if he's asked whether I want cream and sugar in my coffee. "There are rumors abounding that Howe has developed a taste for young women. That alone is neither surprising nor scandalous. But he's married."

"Can't you buy the intel you need from one of his conquests?"

He gives me a grim smile. "Tried that. The three 'conquests' my people have had contact with are scared. They won't talk and no amount of money is moving them. My guess is Richard is threatening something bad will happen to their family members. My best course of action is to hire someone to get me the information that I want."

"Why not date someone and use them?"

He gives a small, humorless chuckle. "And you call me ruthless."

I flush. Bad idea, but his idea isn't much better. I have no experience in the upper echelon of Manhattan society. "So I'm supposed to lure this guy in with my supposed charms and he'll give me stuff you can use to ruin him? I think your plan is seriously flawed. I'm not chopped liver, so won't cause a guy to throw up, but I'm also not beautiful enough to make him go crazy and put himself in jeopardy."

"You underestimate your appeal," he replies. Reaching out, he takes one of my hands in his. "Besides, Richard is a man of little imagination. He likes what others find appealing."

"He's that type of guy?"

"You have no idea," he responds wryly.

But I will, I think to myself.

"I don't know," I say. "It's not what I expected—that I'd help you make a scandal or ruin someone. What happens to me when it's over? Will I be hounded? I don't have any desire to appear next to him in a photograph."

"You won't. You'll only need to supply me with the pictures he sends. There does not have to be any information about you. I'll have someone else leak them."

"Why do you think there'll be pictures?"

"I don't. But there'll be something or these girls wouldn't be afraid."

I turn toward the window because I can't think with Ian staring at me so intently. "I can't do it. I'm not very good at texting."

"All the better. He'll know you can't write and will be forced to send you images."

"I swear you have an answer for everything." I start to rub my forehead and then remember the admonition of the Red Door people against touching my face.

"Do you have some moral objection? You do work for Malcolm."

Right, so a drug mule has no conscience, but it isn't the same thing. The people who are taking the drugs are participating in their own ruin.

"And what? We want bad things to be said about him on *Page Six*?"

"On *Page Six* and page one and all the pages in between," he says softly.

"And you expect that while I'm carrying on with this Howe dude I'm going to sleep with you?"

"Not expect. Hope."

"You're crazy." I push his hands away, feeling incredibly cold.

"I don't expect or want you to sleep with Howe. I only want you to talk to him, be friendly. He'll be interested because I'm interested. The idea that he could lure someone away from me will be too much to resist. A few pictures and we're done. I don't anticipate it taking him longer than a few encounters before he tries to express himself in some embarrassing fashion."

"Why don't you just ruin him financially? Can't you do that?" I fist my hands in my lap, wishing to be anywhere but here.

"I could," he responds. His head is turned out the window and in profile he looks less stern and more thoughtful. "Not yet, though."

Ian turns toward me and in his eyes I see both pain and determination.

My character was set at the age of fifteen.

Without conscious thought, I reach over to squeeze his hand. His grip is firm in response but implacable. Ian has been alone for a long time, and even though I don't entirely agree or understand his plans, I realize I'd do just about anything for him. That's an uncomfortable feeling.

CHAPTER 19

Steve drops us off in an alley in Hell's Kitchen, and the recessed door of a four-story brick building opens before we can reach it. Barely any light spills out, and once inside, I can see why. The door opens onto a shadowy landing with steps going both up and down.

"Mr. Kerr, I'm Priya Kulkarni. Mr. Kaga's assistant. He asked me to show you to the private viewing lounge first." She extends a hand toward the second floor.

"Lead the way," Ian responds, giving me a little push so that I head up the stairs in front of him. As Priya walks ahead of us, the stair treads begin to illuminate. I peek behind me and see that the entryway is again shrouded in darkness.

"These lights are so cool," I comment, allowing my mind to be distracted from the Howe deal.

"Mr. Kaga believes in the conservation of our natural resources. While the club itself does not run on solar power reserves, the offices and private areas do," she explains.

Behind me, I hear Ian snort. "Mr. Kaga is a cheap, opportunistic bastard."

"I heard that," a male voice from above us booms out. Whatever Mr. Kaga is, he has a voice well suited for the stage. It's loud but nicely modulated. When we reach the top, I see that he could easily be a star on the stage. His black hair and razor-sharp cheekbones could be seen from the last row of the upper deck of the Shubert Theatre. Even in the dim light, I can make out his effortless gorgeousness. I wonder if all of Ian's acquaintances are good-looking. It's not like Steve is hard on the eyes, either.

Priya gives him a short bow and disappears down the hallway, little lights flashing to illuminate her path as she goes.

"Tadashubi Kaga, at your service. All of my friends call me Kaga." He lifts my hand and simultaneously pulls me forward and presses his warm lips to the back of it. I nearly faint. I've never had anyone kiss my hand before. What is it with these guys and their old-school hand kissing? It should be banned! As I stumble backwards, two hands brace my fall—one tries to pull me back as the other tries to pull me forward. Kaga releases me with a smirk and I fall against the hard chest of Ian.

"Not yours, Kaga." His arm bands around my waist and he lifts me against him. The delicate knit and lace of my top gathers under my breasts as he half-carries me onto the landing and past Kaga , whose smirk has widened to a full-on grin.

"I thought I was the one of our little troupe who had a problem with sharing." Kaga follows us down the hall. I'm grateful the darkness hides that my cheeks are currently the color of my shirt—and not because of any excess makeup. If Ian and I were alone, I would share what I thought of his display of possessiveness. He doesn't deserve to feel territorial, not after what he's asked me to do.

Ian pulls me back so I can feel his hardness flush against my back. There's no give to any inch of his body. From his sternum to his thighs he's just marble. Into my ear, just slightly above a whisper, he says, "Just because I haven't stuck my cock in you doesn't mean that I'm not thinking of you at every moment, wanting you more than the world needs oxygen." The hand that had shackled my wrist drifts to the bottom of my shorts, and for a moment, I hold my breath thinking he's going to spin me around and kiss me until I pass out.

A cough interrupts us and my eyes shoot upward to see Kaga staring above my head, his face serious. A communication passes between him and Ian. Kaga nods and then winks at me. The silent message is clearly coded by testosterone as I can't figure it out, but perhaps it was his acknowledgment of Ian's totally fake claim over me. Unfortunately, the point of protest for me has passed. I've already exhibited my weakness when it comes to Ian.

"Victoria Corielli, meet Tadashubi Kaga, scion of the Kaga empire," Ian introduces us. "Tad's an old friend."

For the first time, I notice there are no obvious doors in the hallway. The floors are made of some kind of dark, striped wood and the walls are covered in gray squares with rounded edges. Every four feet or so there is a linear break from floor to ceiling, and it's only after Kaga pushes on one that I realize a few of them are doors. He gestures for us to enter.

Inside is a spacious room that overlooks a two-level nightclub. Longer than it is wide, the room reminds me of a stadium box where I once delivered caviar during a Giants game. A tech company ran out when hosting some Russian oligarchs. Sandra told me later that the caviar was worth nearly twenty grand. I only delivered five small containers of it. From the ease of both Kaga and Ian, I suspect that they wouldn't be surprised at all by the price of four-thousand-dollar cans of caviar. Life for some people is simply unreal.

The front of the lounge is all glass, from floor to ceiling, although there are heavy blue velvet drapes hanging on either side. In front of the glass panel are two stair-stepped platforms with cushions strewn across the padded surfaces. Up one level are club chairs and small tables. Where we are standing there are a few bar stools and a good-sized metal cart with glasses and bottles of liquor. There's no music inside the room, but the vibrations of club music can be felt under our feet.

"What can I get you to drink?" Kaga asks, positioning himself by the beverage cart. Ian turns to me with a raised eyebrow.

"Singapore Sling?" I'm not sure if I should be asking Kaga to mix me a drink, but since he asked, I'm not going to be shy. I figure I'm going to need a few drinks before the night is over.

He presses a button near the cart and says, "Singapore Sling and the new reserve."

"Right away, Mr. Kaga," a voice on the other side responds with alacrity.

"Uncorking a new barrel?" Ian asks with genuine eagerness in his voice.

"Eighteen years old with a little spice and cherries along with vanilla. I think you'll like it."

"Kaga's family owns the largest beverage company in the world and makes some of the best single malt whiskeys on the market," Ian explains, settling into one of the velvet-covered club chairs on the second level. He draws me down on top of his lap and wraps his arm around me, his hand finding a resting place at the top of my left thigh. I squirm, a bit uncomfortable at this intimacy in front of a stranger, but his hand clamps down to still my movements.

"We are but a blip on the map compared to the holdings of Kerr Industries," Kaga says dryly.

"Don't let him kid you, Tiny." Ian stretches out his legs. A knock on the door brings our drinks, which Kaga carries over to the table. He settles into a chair next to Ian and hands out the drinks. "His money is older than the United States and probably enough to buy a few territories."

The Singapore Sling tastes refreshing with only a hint of sweetness, a perfect combination.

"Usually guys are all about showing who's got the biggest of everything, but the two of you are arguing about how the other guy's bank account is fatter. This is the weirdest kind of dick posturing I've ever seen." I shake my head and take another sip. Kaga and Ian both pause and then roar with laughter.

"Where did he find you?" Kaga asks, wiping from his eyes the tears his gut laugh produced.

I look at Ian for guidance as I say, "Mutual acquaintance."

"No secrets from Tad," Ian says. "Tiny is Malcolm Hedder's stepsister."

This revelation causes Kaga to look at me with speculation. "So you aren't together? This is all for show?" He leans toward me to grab my hand, but Ian blocks him.

"Yes, for show," I say.

"Not for show. We're together," Ian replies at the same time.

"We're together," he repeats, giving me a hard look and a firm squeeze on the thigh.

I'm not one for arguing in public or doing much of anything in public, so I press my lips together even though I'm dying to give Ian a piece of my mind.

I settle for, "It's complicated."

From the owner's lounge, I can see the entire dance floor. Kaga presses a button and the plate glass turns into a viewing screen showing eight different security feeds. He selects one feed and zooms so that it overlays the other video. The security camera is focused on a well-kept man in his forties. I recognize him instantly as Richard Howe, my target. Forcefully, I push away from Ian and after a bit of a struggle he lets me go.

"Is this the source of your complication?" Kaga asks. I nod but my eyes are glued to Howe. He's leaning over the second-floor balcony, holding a small tumbler in his hand. There's a beautiful brunette standing very close to him. As we watch, she flips her hair across her shoulder a few times in a flirtatious gesture. They keep talking, and after a moment we see them exchange phone numbers.

Howe takes a picture of the woman and then they pose together for his camera.

"What does he tell his wife?" I ask, genuinely curious.

"Some say that she knows and doesn't care. Others believe she has no idea. This is a rather different crowd than Cecilia Montgomery Howe would associate with."

"Too old?"

"Too poor," Kaga answers dryly. Ian has been silent as I observe Howe, wanting—I suppose—for me to draw my own conclusions. How does Ian do it? If I saw him flirting with another woman, even knowing it was a charade, I'd be jealous and hurt. How can he keep everything so separate?

"You want me to go over there tonight and get his phone number?" I ask Ian.

For a long moment he doesn't respond, and then in a tone so low I can barely hear him, he replies, "No. I don't want that."

In one swift motion, he rises and hurls the whiskey glass at the side wall. "Sorry," he mutters, and then walks out. I'm frozen by the display of violence and more confused than ever. Kaga catches my arm when I turn to chase after him.

"Give him a minute."

Nodding, I allow Kaga to lead me to a chair.

"Richard Howe is a charming, likeable man," Kaga says. "And he wields those traits like a weapon. People do things for him that they wouldn't ever do for another. And behind him, he leaves a trail of ruined lives, broken hearts, and . . . orphaned boys."

Orphaned boys.

My character was set at the age of fifteen.

I look toward the rear of the room where Ian exited. This Howe thing was personal to him. It wasn't just about some "friend." Someone close to Ian got hurt by Howe. And now he is struggling between his feelings for me and his desire for revenge.

"Some say that the elder Howe's candidacy rests on Richard keeping his nose clean for the three months until the primary voting is closed. His primary voters want to see an intact family because that's part of Howe's platform. In the general election, it won't matter as much."

"I don't see how a cheating scandal is going to make a big difference."

"It might not to a lot of people, but it would matter to Richard Howe's father. Ian wants to separate Richard from everyone else."

I frown. "I'm supposed to attract Howe? I'm too old."

"You're with Ian. That's enough."

"What do you mean?"

Kaga crosses his arms and stares out the viewing glass. "Richard is intensely jealous of Ian. Believes that Ian is standing in his place in the sun. Whatever Ian has, Richard wants," he explains. "Ian needs only to show you some attention and Richard will be right over to see if he can peel you away."

"I don't get how Richard could possibly lure someone away from Ian," I grumble.

At this, Kaga shouts out a laugh and drops his arms to his side. "Loyal. I like that. Or deluded." Sobering, he replies, "Ian wasn't always this well situated and Richard comes from an old Dutch family whose roots can be traced back to the Knickerbockers. For some, that's worth more than all the money in the world."

"But can't Ian just ruin him financially? He said that Howe was spending money faster than the Treasury can print it."

"If Ian ruins Richard financially, all the Howes suffer. Papa Howe believes the mayoral position will right the sinking ship. They've poured millions into the campaign and convinced all their wealthy society friends to contribute as well. If Papa Howe doesn't win, the Howes will have to leave the city. They'll be disgraced, and it would be easy for Ian to tip that ship over and have it sink like the Titanic."

"But?" There's more to this; something Ian doesn't want to share but Kaga feels compelled to reveal.

He smiles in approval. "But when a ship goes down, a lot of innocents are harmed, and Ian feels strongly that only Howe should suffer. Publicizing his indiscretions will humiliate Cecilia, but she'll divorce him. Once Howe is isolated, Ian can bring all the influence he has to crush Howe. But not until all those bystanders are safe from harm.

"In New York society, you can exist if you have either status or money. Lose one and you can still belong. If Howe is ruined financially, it would affect his entire family. They are teetering on the brink of financial insolvency. But if Richard Howe becomes a liability, his family will cut ties with him and he'll be left without status or money."

Not yet, Ian had said on the car ride over. He isn't prepared to take out the bystanders. I could respect that in a weird way.

"Why me? Why not the other women that Malcolm sent?"

"They were too hard. Ian would never have dated them. He's always had much quieter tastes. Richard would have known right away something was up. But you?" Kaga looks me over. "You're exactly what Ian's always wanted."

I flush profusely at this.

"Ian needs you, and I can tell that asking you to do this for him has been an enormous struggle."

He needs me.

This thing with Howe isn't a job; it's a gift. Ian has bought me clothes, upgraded my apartment, and provided for my mother. Not because of any job but because he genuinely cared. And I can do this for him even if he doesn't want me to.

Straightening my shoulders, I turn to Kaga. "So what do I do?"

With admiration in his eyes, Kaga replies, "Go over to the VIP lounge and have a drink. Richard will inevitably approach as soon as Ian leaves you alone for a moment. Play it by ear from there."

"How do I act?"

"Be yourself."

◆ ◆ ◆

Ian is standing by the back door of the club where we first entered.

"He talked you into it?"

I nod.

"Don't look at me like that," he warns.

"Like what?"

Turning away, he curses. "I've tried to keep the two of you separate in my head. At first, I turned you down because I wanted to sleep with you. Then I convinced myself that I could sleep with you and have you ensnare Howe. Compartmentalize, I told myself." He shoves an agitated hand through his hair. "Now my Tiny boxes are scattered in every corner of my head. I think of you nonstop. When I get up in the morning, I wonder if you'll like the smell of the soap I used. When lunch rolls around, I wonder if you've eaten enough. By mid-afternoon, I'm so hungry for your body I have to go to the bathroom and stroke myself until I'm spent—only to find that I'm hard thirty minutes later when I think of your pink pussy convulsing under my tongue. But I wanted to delay making love to you until I was completely sure you were with me—mind, body and soul—because yes, Tiny, you are mine. And this isn't for show."

He pushes away from the door and climbs up the stairs. I haven't moved. I can't. His words have rendered me motionless. With each step, he's coming closer to me, until he's so close I feel the heat of his body. His eyes search mine, and in them I see not only lust but tenderness.

His mouth fastens over mine, punctuating his words or perhaps sealing them inside me. Does he know that he makes my heart sing? That the tender look in his eyes completely slays me? His right hand digs into my hair as he uses his left to lift me against him. The hard length of his erection is impossible to miss. I wish I could see him in his office stroking himself. That would be so amazing that I'd probably come from just the show.

His tongue rubs slowly along the side of mine, inviting me to play. Whatever lipstick I once wore is being sucked and licked and bitten off. His kiss is ravenous, and I feel like he's trying to devour me. Worse, I want him to. I open my mouth as wide as possible to swallow down all the sweetness and passion he's serving me.

Beneath my questing hands, his body feels like iron. I want to rip off his clothes and impale myself on him right here on the landing. With a last reserve of sense, I pull away from him and rest my head in the hollow of his throat. I hear his rasping breath above me, and underneath my cheek his chest heaves up and down as he tries to gather his own self-control. I allow him to soothe my trembling body with his big hands when I realize the long, sweeping caresses are just as much for his sake as they are for mine.

"Jesus, Tiny," he groans, dropping his forehead. After a minute he clears his throat and tips my chin up so I can see him. His eyes glitter in the darkness, lit from within. "I'll find someone else to do the job. Clear the table so there's just you and me."

Someone else? He'd have to feign interest in *her*, bring *her* out to nightclubs and events. The idea of someone else doing this . . . project with Ian makes me violently jealous. Like, I'd punch her if I saw her with him. "No," I say forcefully. "You hired me." I straighten up and push him away. "I'm your girl."

I am halfway down the second set of stairs when what I said sinks in.

"About time you realized that."

I bite my lip to keep from laughing because I don't want him to know he has yet again gotten the last word.

CHAPTER 20

The Aquarium is so named because it's full of water, blue walls, and blue light. There is so much glass and mirror used on the walls and even the floor of the second level that it seems like you are in a fishbowl. The entire place is painted blue, from the floors in deep midnight to a varying gradient on the walls. Even the lights are tinted blue, giving an under-the-sea feel to the space. The main floor has a circular bar centered around a real aquarium with . . . are those sharks in there?

Once I see the second floor, I understand why Ian picked out shorts for me to wear. Above us the floor is made of alternating tiles of clear and blue glass, about four feet square, and by looking upward you can see straight up the skirts of some of the female club-goers.

Around the sides of the room on the second level are people sitting in glassed-in plunge pools lit from underneath, like square mini hot tubs. Most of the pools are filled with women who appear to have stripped down to their underwear, although there are a few males in them too. There are butts and boobs pressed against the glass—and in at least one, there's a couple simulating a sex act. At least I think it's a simulation. I nearly break my neck staring as I pass. It's an exhibitionist's dream, and I'm very glad I'm wearing shorts as I walk up the stairs past a formidable bouncer clad in a navy-blue T-shirt with the word "Aquarium" stenciled in white across his massive chest.

The VIP area is a small balcony on the second floor that overlooks the first level dance floor and has a bird's-eye view of the hot tubs. As far as I can tell, access to the upper deck is communicated through a series of nods and hand slaps because Ian simply lifts his chin to the bouncer, who moves aside to allow us access.

Up here, I can see that there are bleachers set up next to the pools and people are lounging in bathrobes or on towels. There are a couple of well-known actors and athletes who I recognize. The other beautiful people must be moneyed or famous or—I think as a thin but bosomy woman walks by—arm candy like me.

"This is the weirdest place," I tell Ian.

"New Yorkers get bored easily," he replies. "You constantly have to come up with something new and seemingly innovative, and these days, the more risqué the better. It's frowned upon to wear swimsuit attire here because that's not considered edgy enough."

"So I'm wearing the pearl-clutching version of a club-goer's outfit?" I ask wryly.

"Given that your legs are hot enough to warrant a visit from the FDNY Ladder 21, I don't think 'pearl clutcher' is apropos." He drops his hand from my back and I feel it brush my ass as he reaches down to stroke my thigh, but his movements are interrupted when Richard steps into our sightline. Ian's fingers fall away.

Richard has the look of an Ivy League banker. His hair is expertly cut and lies in a *Dead Poet's Society* swoop to the left. I can easily superimpose a regimented striped tie and blue blazer with gold emblem on the pocket. Tonight he's attired in a well-cut suit, although the shoulders look almost too big for him, and I notice that the fabric is shiny, as if it has endured one too many trips to the dry cleaners'.

"Ian Kerr, you old dog. You keep ducking my dad's phone calls. It's like you don't want to donate."

It's hard to tell if Richard is serious or kidding. Neither Kaga nor Ian gave me any clue as to whether Richard supports his father or is rebelling somehow, but at his age, the north side of his forties, he should be too old for that shit.

"I've given up on donating to politics. Figure it makes more sense to burn it in the fireplace."

The words exchanged are sharp, but the two smile and slap each other on the back as if they are best buds.

"Who's this delectably dressed young lady?" Richard's attention turns to me, and I'm surprised that his gaze is warm and friendly rather than predatory. I think I was expecting something totally different. But Kaga did warn me that Richard is charming.

"Victoria Corielli, meet Richard Howe. His family is practically one of the original four hundred."

I hold out my hand, but Richard doesn't shake it. Instead, he pulls it toward his lips as Kaga had. Before he makes contact, Ian slides his large palm over the top of my fingers.

"So it's that way?" Richard says, one eyebrow quirking up.

"Kissing's too fancy for me," I interject, not wanting Ian to get into a pissing match when I'm supposed to be luring Richard with my non-existent wiles. "Nice to meet you, Richard."

"You are lovely but I wouldn't expect anything different from a companion of Ian's." It sounds like a veiled insult, as if I'm just one of many interchangeable women that Ian Kerr has had dinner with. Maybe he's right. He offers his hand and I take it. He has a firm, cool shake, and if he lingers overlong, it's not so noticeable that it makes me uncomfortable.

Under the bar lights, his hair looks shiny.

"Go for a swim?" I guess.

His smile is impish. "Yes, the pools are irresistible. I heard management over at 1 Oak is upset because some of its exclusive clientele can't seem to tear themselves away from the attractions here."

"I've never been there," I admit, but I'm curious. These are bars and clubs that I might have heard about in passing but have never had any interest in visiting, primarily because they would be too expensive and I doubted I could get in.

"It's an old-school establishment. Still entertaining." He leans close and in a low voice says, "I'll take you sometime."

I can't help but glance at Ian, whose narrowed gaze is focused with laser-like precision on Richard. Ian really dislikes this guy, and he's suddenly making no attempt to hide it. Discreetly, I step backward onto the tip of his shoe and press down, not too hard but enough to get his attention.

He shakes his head as if he's woken from a trance. "You look thirsty, Tiny," he says, and walks off before I can respond.

We both watch as Ian saunters away.

"You and Kerr?" he asks with a raised eyebrow.

I shrug in what I hope is a coy manner. "We're friends."

"He seems off tonight. Did you guys have a bad dinner?"

"No, I think he's tired. He just got back from a business trip."

"Oh, what about?"

"I'm not sure. I didn't pay much attention." I know instinctively that Ian would not like for me to share any personal information with Richard, no matter how innocent. "How did you get in here, or shouldn't I ask? All Ian had to do was nod at the bouncer."

"Turnover at these places is frequent, mostly because of the constant employee fraternization. The staff at these places cycles in and out. Go to enough clubs and you'll get to know the people who work the door. Once you've made your contacts, you have no problem getting past the guardians at the gate." He ducks his head and snorts. "There. I've now admitted I'm practically a barfly."

"No, not at all. Just social," I reassure him. His self-deprecation may be an act, but it's a good one. "Do you know much about the owner?" I'm curious if he knows the connection between Ian and Kaga.

He shakes his head. "I think it's owned by some Japanese conglomerate. They are taking over the city, you know, buying up our landmarks."

Not wanting to hear Richard launch into a dangerous and possibly racist rant about ownership of big-city properties, I attempt to redirect the conversation. "What is it that you do?" Men like to talk about themselves.

"Investments, like your friend Kerr." He gives me a strange, wry smile. "Only not as good, according to my old man. How about you? You work with your father?"

"No, I . . ." I hesitate, looking for the right words. "I was never very good in school."

"Don't work for a relative," he advises. "You'll never make them happy. Take me, for example. Haven't had an investment turn my way in a long time." He sounds almost wistful rather than bitter, and his obvious desire to please his father tugs at my heartstrings. My mother is my best friend, and the worst thing she's ever said to me was "I'm disappointed."

"I bet your dad is prouder than you think. Sometimes it's hard for them to express it," I console him.

"When I was like six or seven, my nanny would take me to the Central Park playground across from our condo complex. We live right on Fifth Avenue, a block from Embassy Row." He is bragging a tiny bit, but that's an impressive address. "Every time we went—which was like three times a week—there were two brothers. One was my age and the other was older. The older kid could do everything. He could catch the ball on the first try. Could swing across the monkey bars without stopping. Could leap over the fence with a single bound. A veritable mini-Superman. His mom or nanny, I don't really know which, would always say to the younger kid that he should be more like his older brother. The barrage of criticism was nonstop."

"Poor kid," I murmur.

"Comparisons don't motivate people," he says, and this time the bitterness has erased any wistfulness. "My dad hasn't learned that yet. Ian Kerr, once an outcast from city society, is now held up to every son and heir as the model. He left town impoverished and came back less than twenty years later with his *Fortune 500* cover and his pockets so full of money that he can barely walk."

We both stare at Ian, lounging at the bar and chatting with a Giants linebacker with the ease of someone who is familiar in this setting.

"I'm sorry," I say lamely, not knowing quite what the right response is. Richard is right, though—comparisons suck. And if all he gets at home are questions about why he doesn't measure up, then bitter is a normal emotion.

"Not your fault." He turns his bright white smile on me. "I don't usually run my mouth like that. You're exceptionally easy to talk to."

I duck my head. "Thanks."

"I need a smoke." He runs a hand through his thick hair. "Come with me?"

I toss a glance over at Ian. He isn't looking this way, but I sense he's fully aware of what I'm doing. "Sure, why not?"

I totter down the stairs on the unfamiliar heels. It's easier walking up on stilettos than down. Richard leads me through a mass of bodies to a side door manned by another beefy security guy.

"Need a smoke, man." Richard holds up a pack of cigarettes and the bouncer steps aside, holding the door open. There are others milling around in a small, bricked-in space with tall ashtrays.

"No thanks," I say when he offers a cigarette.

"We're the leper colony." Richard lights up and takes a deep drag. It's easy to see how young women could be charmed by him and engage in a flirtation despite his marital status. Then again, his left hand is bare of any jewelry, so perhaps he pursues women who simply don't know he's married. Many young New Yorkers couldn't name all the upcoming mayoral candidates, let alone their sons. "I should take up the electronic ones, but I find it offensive that everything is digital now—even our bad habits. From porn to cigarettes." He shakes his head and takes another deep drag. "On social media much?"

"Not really."

"I shouldn't be, but I can't quit it." The lit end of the cigarette creates a delicate lace-like pattern as Richard waves his hand up and down in front of my body. "But of all the people who should be taking pictures of themselves and posting them, it's you."

"I'm not a fan. Too busy."

"So if you don't work for your dad like me, what do you do?"

Be yourself.

"I'm a bike courier. I work for Neil's Delivery Service."

Richard coughs and strikes a fist against his chest a couple of times. His lack of breath is from surprise, not from the smoke. He can't believe that Ian would be with someone like me. I see it in his eyes. Though whether it's because I work such a menial job or because I'm not smart enough, I'm not certain.

"How'd you get into that?"

"Ex-boyfriend. Kept the job. Lost the boyfriend."

"And you delivered something to Ian?" he guesses.

"That's right. And one thing led to another and here I am."

"I'm sorry," he says when he regains his equilibrium.

"Why's that?"

"Because he's using you."

I freeze, wondering if somehow Richard knows exactly what Ian is up to. "For sex?" I answer glibly. "We're friends."

"Ian Kerr doesn't have friends who are delivery girls." The look on Richard's face is of pity, albeit genuine pity. "I hope to hell I'm wrong, but I think he's going to break your heart."

Richard takes my lax hand and holds it up to the light, examining the calluses along the base of my fingers that I've developed holding the handlebars of my bike. "You're such a hard worker," he says, rubbing the hardened pads. I jerk my hand away and hide it in the pocket of my shorts. It's a compliment, but it doesn't sound like one. Rather, he sounds like he's about to list all my shortcomings. "He doesn't insult you, does he? Make you feel small because you don't have as much money? I'm sure he doesn't comment about how you don't know the difference between leveraged buyouts and portfolio hedging."

"No," I answer. The money disparity has been huge between the two of us, but I hadn't considered our intellectual differences. I didn't— no, *couldn't*—read the financial pages. I knew nothing of how to run a business. When Ian jetted off to another state to look at "wearable tech," I'd made a comic book joke. Richard is invoking doubts I hadn't even realized I should be worrying about. The outdoor air is suddenly chilly.

"Don't feel bad. I'm not too good at that myself. It's why Ian looks down on me. Anyone who's not as successful as he is doesn't warrant more than a second glance. He's notorious for being even worse with women. No one's good enough for him. Not socialites or hedge fund managers. They've all got some kind of flaw." Richard takes another draw on his cancer stick, the ashes almost to his fingers. "I've seen way too many tears wiped away after he's tossed these poor girls aside. Guy's a menace. Should keep his pants zipped."

Each word Richard unfurls is like a punch in the solar plexus because they strike directly at my insecurity. I'm worried that I'm not good enough for Ian. That he's too rich for me. Too smart for me. Too every- thing. Hearing it from Richard's mouth batters me like a physical club.

Hadn't Ian said that he'd pursued me because I was a challenge? That's all I was. A convenient fuck and a big-ass source of amusement.

"We're friends," I repeat numbly.

"I'm not telling you this stuff to be mean. I'm right there with you in the undesirable pool. We rejects gotta stick together." Richard tosses the butt on the ground and grinds his foot on it. "What's your phone number?"

I give it to him without hesitation, and he inputs it into his phone and sends me a text—which I can't read. Richard leans close to me, the tobacco smell heavy on his breath. "Like finds like, Victoria. I've a lot of practice in mending broken hearts."

"I'm still whole," I say, and wonder if I can remain that way.

"Don't let him ruin it, ruin you," he whispers. His mouth is only inches away from my ear. "Come dance with me."

I don't want to. Richard isn't so charming anymore. His words have gouged me, and I'd like to go to the bathroom and lick my wounds. But Ian's absence must mean that I'm supposed to use this time to reel Richard in.

"All right." I place my hand in his upturned one.

"I'm a terrible dancer," Richard confesses as he leads me back inside. "I always need to stand next to someone so I don't look foolish."

I go with him because there isn't anyone to stop me. He takes me by the hand and leads me down to the dance floor. The press of the crowd pushes us closer together, and Richard places his hands on my waist.

"I don't want to lose you out here."

I put my hands on his shoulders so I don't look like an unwilling mannequin. Richard has lied, of course. He's a great dancer. His hips move easily to the rhythm and his hands drift lower, fingers splaying to reach more intimate parts of my body. I back away, but there's little room on the packed dance floor.

Under my palms, his body feels alien to me and I don't want to touch him, but in the small space that the crowd has allotted for us, I can't do anything about it. When he slides a thigh between my legs, the intimacy is simply too much and I feel claustrophobic. This isn't what I want. I don't want to have to touch him, dance with him, or kiss him. *God, will I have to kiss him?*

Before I can break away, there's a commotion behind me and then a familiar hand wraps around my waist and pulls me firmly against a hard body.

"I'm sorry, Rich, but Victoria has to leave." Ian doesn't wait for a response from me or Richard. Instead, he literally lifts me off my feet and carries me to the edge of the dance floor, the crowd parting before him with ease. About five steps beyond the dance floor, Ian sets me down and I totter, momentarily disoriented and unused to the heels. His hand, still latched to my side, braces me.

"Don't you think Victoria should be the one to decide when she leaves?" Richard has followed us, but Ian doesn't even turn to look at him. He buries his nose into my hair, and I feel the whisper of a kiss against my head.

"She's got an urgent task to take care of," he says flatly.

"At midnight?" Richard's voice is full of skepticism.

"Yes, at midnight." The hand at the small of my back presses me forward as Ian gently propels me toward the rear of the club, past the centrally located bar and the huge circular aquarium. Beyond the dancers, the partiers, and the watchers and out into the night.

"I don't get you," I mutter, shivering a little.

"What's there to get? I don't like other men touching you." His words are clipped. When we're at the street, the big gray car is idling, waiting like a giant gray panther to whisk us away. He opens the door and almost shoves me inside. Over the top of the roof I hear him say something to Steve, something like "long way around the park."

As Ian settles next to me, he presses a button and the privacy screen rises. I stare at it until Steve's head is completely cut off and we're entombed in silence in the back. There isn't even music and almost no street sounds inside this luxurious car.

"Are you really that compartmentalized?"

"Your change of subjects is dizzying." He reaches for me. "And you are much too far away."

"It's that you told me you wanted me and then you turned it off when Richard showed up. I can't keep up with that."

"You're wrong." His hand comes up to the base of my throat, his fingers curling around to press on the pulse of my heart. No doubt he can feel it beating rapidly.

"Stop it." I push his hand away. "What are you doing? You ignore me for twenty minutes and then pull me off the dance floor to grope me in the car?"

He lets out a loud snort and then turns to look out the window. The lights of the street and stores flash by as Steve maneuvers us around the north side of the park. In a gruff, low tone, almost as if he doesn't want to say it, Ian admits, "I always want you. Watching you with Howe was a miserable experience I don't want to repeat. I hadn't realized I'd feel this way."

"I'm confused too," I mutter.

Then he lifts me onto his body in one swift move and covers my yelp with his mouth. His tongue is inside my mouth before I am even settled against the hard column of his erection. His tongue is bold, and his lips move over mine with specific intent. This is no soft, romantic kiss; this is a claiming. He's growling and his one hand is tangled in my hair, holding me imprisoned against his mouth. The other hand is kneading my butt cheek through the silk.

I can't help but kiss him back, playing with his tongue until we are a tangle of tongues and mouths and wetness. I have no oxygen, but I don't need it. Ian is breathing for me. His tongue is everywhere inside my mouth. There is no place inside that recess he doesn't explore, and all the while he holds me tight against him.

Then he breaks away almost as suddenly as the kiss started and rasps out, "I want you, Tiny Corielli. I've wanted you since the minute I saw you and that desire has turned into a need I've not been able to shake. I tried to ignore what I was feeling, push it aside, but it kept returning. I'm not going to fight it anymore."

He swoops down before I can formulate a response. When his hands are all over me and his tongue is literally having sex with my mouth, I cannot remember why I'm mad, why I'm supposed to protest. He's so goddamned sexy. The effortless command he has over everything around him, as if he can snap his fingers and everything and everyone will fall in line, is as sexy as it is infuriating.

I want to be repelled because a sane, smart woman would be. But no, every autocratic action actually turns me on because with Ian, I don't have to think if I don't want to. I recognize that I could let him take care of me. That he would willingly make all my decisions for me—what to wear, what to eat, where to go.

And yet . . . if I do that . . . if I allow him that much control over me, then where will I be after my vacation with Ian is over? Back in a tiny one-bedroom walk-up eating ramen noodles and wearing polyester.

"You think too much," Ian says, smoothing his hands down my arms and then following the path with his wet mouth, leaving a pattern of nips and soothing kisses down my upper arms. His tongue finds the tender skin of the crook of my elbow and the soft spot on my wrist, causing me to whimper and grind against him.

"I have to," I gasp. "There's no one else to do it for me."

"Let me think for you then."

I weaken because the idea is so tempting. Not having to think, letting Ian take control? Would it really hurt that much to allow it for one night or even a few days?

"I can almost hear the cogs in your brain churning," he murmurs. His mouth has latched itself to the exposed skin of my throat. It's so much harder to remember why I was resisting when his mouth is moving up and down the column of my neck. His hands are holding my arms tight to my side. I'd like to blame my capitulation on alcohol, but I only had one drink tonight.

"I don't want you to think that if I let you have your way with me this one time, I'm giving in forever." I drape my arms over his shoulders and twine my fingers in the bottom of his hair.

"That thought hadn't even occurred to me, bunny. You like to fight me and I like the challenge." He licks behind my ear, causing me to shudder and squeeze him. "Like that, do you?" He repeats his action and I squirm even closer to him.

Dropping my head on his shoulder, I whisper a plea. "Don't hurt me, Ian."

His arms tighten around me and I feel the hard warmth of his body through the heavy lace and the thin silk of my shorts. "It's me who should be afraid." And then he plunders my mouth and I don't even notice that he didn't give me his answer. Or maybe he did and I don't want to accept it.

His tongue traces my collarbone and licks at the hollow of my throat. He shifts me slightly to undo the button on my shorts and release the zipper. Before I can form a response, his hand is down my shorts and pressing hotly against me. He presses his erection against my thigh and thrusts in a lewd manner. I know exactly what he wants.

"What about my doubts?" I ask, but inwardly I'm thrilled that he's finally, finally ready. His mouth crashes down on mine, devouring me and leaving me with little doubt as to his intentions.

His lips are wet from my saliva and his fingers are tight against me. "I'm going to fuck those doubts right out of you."

CHAPTER 21

"Can you do that?"

"Absolutely." His statement of arrogance is followed by his fingers piercing me. Two long digits push inside my wet channel, eliciting an audible moan.

"Oh hell, Ian. That feels so good."

I can see his smug gleam at my lack of resistance, at how my body is responsive to his very presence—not to mention his talented touch.

"Your panties are soaked. Have you been wet long?" he asks.

It's rhetorical because he's more interested in pushing up my shirt to bare my tummy and then higher to expose my breasts. My nipples are distended and aching. The light rub of the fabric only served to heighten my arousal.

"Ian, I want . . ." My demands trail off as he mouths the sensitive upper curve of my left breast.

"What, bunny, tell me," he commands. His fingers stroke me, curling toward my pubic bone and then dragging along the tissues all the way out. He repeats this gesture in an infinitely slow loop. He is burning me up. My thighs hug his hips tight, and I pull on his tie so that his mouth is against mine. I surge against his fingers, needing the release from the tension his fingers are stoking.

"I want you inside me," I tell him. I want his mouth on me, his cock inside me. I want him surrounding me so that all I can see, hear, and feel is Ian Kerr. He angles his head so that he can kiss me deeper. His tongue is again everywhere inside my mouth, pressing against the roof, licking along the sides of my cheek and the sensitive skin under my tongue.

The heavy erection in his pants is evidence of how greatly I'm affecting him, and I glory in that power. My thoughts of inequality are lying on the floor where I'd like our clothes to be. *We're both equal in this*, I think.

"Where is it that you want my cock?" he growls.

"Everywhere," I say, and my lips curve up into a tiny smile of satisfaction.

His teeth flash white in the dark interior of the car, and he pumps his hips obscenely between my legs. "Enjoy turning me on?"

"Yes," I admit, and my smile becomes a little bigger. I tunnel my hands under his suit coat and revel in the flex of his back muscles. He feels like a powerful machine beneath my palms—and that I can rev that engine and make it run hot? Hell, yeah, I enjoy that.

"You turn me on by breathing." Each word is punctuated by a hard thrust of his hand. My grin dies quickly as he begins to fuck me more thoroughly with his fingers. The palm of his hand slaps against my clit with each drive. "Let's see what else you enjoy."

My thighs lock around his wrist and I cling to him with both sets of limbs, my arms wrapped around his shoulders so I can either pull him toward me or press against him. My overriding instinct is to get closer. Blood is pounding in my ears, a rhythm directed by his hand. He's the conductor or the musician and I'm the helpless instrument in the orchestra.

"Tell me," he commands, but I've lost the thread of our conversation.

"Make me come," I half plead, half demand on his next stroke.

"Be specific." His fingers signal that he really, really wants to hear the words.

"I want you inside me. I want you to use me hard and long. I want you to drive every thought from my mind that is you. Me. Us." His body tenses above me, and his breathing becomes ragged. My words are turning him on so much that he's nearly panting, and that gives me the encouragement I need to continue. "I want your hard cock filling me, making me come endlessly." I choke out the last words because his fingers are drilling me now, hard and fast, rubbing that spongy spot on the front wall of my channel. He is relentless, and I'm nearly mindless with the pleasure he is generating.

"I'm going to fuck you so hard tonight that you will be left with only one thought. One concept: You belong to me."

"And you? Who—ahhhh," I cry out as he bites into the meat of my shoulder. The sensation rocks me, and I start to come. The waves of the release start small and then I'm overcome, dragged beneath the ocean of ecstasy. Through my half-closed eyes I see fierce desire painted all over Ian's face, in the ruddy flush on his cheekbones, in the half-lidded eyes, and in the slick wet of his mouth.

"I belong to you," he answers my unfinished question. "I'm yours."

He pulls his fingers out of me and sticks them both in his mouth, sucking hard and then licking his palm. I nearly come again.

"Oh god, Ian," I tug at his clothes, wanting no barrier between us, but before I can rip off his suit coat, the car comes to a halt.

Steve's voice sounds through the rear speaker system. "We're here."

Ian pulls down my shirt with a heavy sigh and sits up. With a rueful smile, he does up the zipper to my shorts. I'm still lost in a post-orgasmic state and want nothing more than to drag Ian back against me.

"Tell him to drive around some more," I say, pressing kisses along the sides of his mouth, over the bridge of his nose and across his eyes. I straddle him and rub my still throbbing pussy against his thick erection. "I need to take care of you."

Pushing away, I start to slide down his legs with the intent of taking that hot and heavy cock out of his trousers and swallowing down as much of his flesh as I possibly can.

He stops me and opens the door. "Inside." It's a guttural command.

He helps me out onto the pavement and I see we're not at Central Towers but his four-story converted warehouse in the Meatpacking District where I delivered the contract. His suit is rumpled and clearly abused, but Steve says nothing as Ian bids him a brusque goodnight. I falter on my heels as Ian pushes me in front of him. In one swift movement, I'm in his arms and he's striding to the door.

We aren't two steps inside the door when he drops me against the wall and we attack each other. My top and shorts are off, leaving me only in my sodden panties and stilettos. I pull at his suit coat, uncaring if I'm ripping some five-thousand-dollar suit to pieces. Ian clearly doesn't care either, as he shrugs the coat off and lets it fall to the floor. His tongue is in my mouth before the fabric hits the ground. Somewhere along the way, he toes off his shoes and socks but doesn't let go of me for an instant.

I suck on his tongue hungrily, feeling the ache renew itself between my legs. His hands are at the waistband of my panties, pushing them downward as I struggle with his buttons.

"You wear too many damn clothes," I cry, wrenching my mouth from his. In frustration, I pull the shirt apart and a few of the buttons fly off, making tiny pings as they hit the cement floor. With some effort and help from Ian, we unfasten the rest.

Then there's nothing but flesh against flesh. I climb up his body like a pole dancer and wrap my legs around his waist. He turns and the cool stone wall is smooth against my back. I dig my nails into his shoulders to gain leverage. The hard length of his erection rubs against my bare pussy and nearly sets me off again.

His mouth is ravaging me and I open my own wider to receive every bit of his kiss. We kiss each other thoroughly, tongues delving into every recess, teeth nipping and biting at each other. He wrenches his mouth away and leaves a wet trail along my jaw and down the column of my neck.

Behind my ear he finds a spot that makes me sob and convulse, so he sets to it, alternately sucking and biting until I'm mindlessly grinding against him. My hands clutch his head.

"Now, I want you now," I cry. But instead of acceding to my demands, he cradles my ass in his palms and lifts me off his cock.

"Not again!" I punch him in the back, furious that he's going to leave me wanting, that he's going to pull away once again.

Gruffly, he nips at my shoulder. "Damned if I'm going to have my first time with you up against the door. I can wait a minute." He climbs the stairs, still holding me. "And so can you."

I don't feel like waiting. I want him too much, so I reach between us and palm his erection. It jumps in my hand and swells. "You don't feel like you want to wait."

"You're going to kill me." He angles his head toward mine, and I take up the invitation to kiss him again. I'm ravenous and he's the only thing that will satisfy me.

Wrapping my arms around his head and hooking my ankles around his back, I continue to kiss him as he walks me up the stairs, across the long, open living space, and up another flight. His effortless strength is making me breathless—that and how his bobbing cock rubs against me with nearly every step. It's a tantalizing tease, a light brush, but it's enough to make me wetter than a fire hydrant on the fourth of July.

He walks down a hallway overlooking the main floor until we arrive at the second doorway. He doesn't bother to turn on the lights as we enter, but instead throws me on the huge bed. I get a glimpse of pale-colored walls before my entire vision is filled with Ian.

My mouth waters when I see his bare body illuminated by the night sky that can be seen through the two skylights in the ceiling.

"You're so beautiful," I say reverently as he stands fully nude, his magnificent cock arrowing directly upward.

"That's my line." He pulls the thick length so that it's perpendicular to his body and begins to stroke it. My mouth waters in response and I get onto my knees to reach for him. He has other ideas. He pushes me backward until I'm lying on my back crossways on the bed. His eyes burn into me as he stands like a conqueror ready to avail himself of the spoils of war. But he doesn't fall on me with hurried roughness. Oh no. He decides to take his time.

One hand wraps around an ankle and he carefully unbuckles the shoe before tossing it aside. The position of my leg in the air exposes my core and he takes a moment to stare at my center with undisguised lust. "Yes, you're the beautiful one," he says and reaches out a long arm to swipe two fingers up the outside of my pussy.

I jerk toward him, wanting a deeper, firmer, stronger touch, but he draws back. Resting my now bare foot on his shoulder, he kisses up my ankle. Whatever rush he was in before has passed. The time has allowed him to gather his vaunted self-control. I have none. Nor do I want to have any. Why would I want control here?

His deft fingers unbuckle the other shoe. He lifts my foot to his mouth and runs his tongue along the top, stopping to suck on the ball of my ankle and then the tender Achilles tendon. I cry out, not realizing I even had an erogenous zone there. He chuckles and repeats the action on my other ankle. Is it possible to come from having your ankle sucked?

He trails kisses up my legs, behind my knees, and then pulls me to the edge of the bed and kneels between my thighs. With my legs dangling over his shoulders, he places both hands under my ass and lifts me to his mouth like I'm a buffet of sexual delight. He begins tonguing me languorously. Over and over, he places the broad flat of his tongue against my pussy and licks from front to back. Anxiously, I try to get him to penetrate me with his tongue or fingers or anything. I need him inside me.

"Please, Ian, don't torture me. It's been so long." I tug at his silky hair and he raises his head, his face wet from my arousal. For a heart-stopping moment, I think he'll refuse me but this plea—perhaps the confession that I've been without for a period of time—moves him.

"I could eat you all night and be a happy man." With a firm squeeze of my inner thigh, Ian reaches over to the nightstand and pulls out a condom. With one hand on his sheathed cock and the other grasping my left hip, he rubs the thick head against me. He enters me slowly, giving me time to adjust to his generous girth.

He groans as my walls open to accept him. "I've dreamt of being inside you. Fantasized about it. Jerked off to it. But nothing feels as goddamned good as reality." When he is completely seated so far inside me I feel like I'm overflowing, I can't help but release a sigh of pleasure. I rock against him because my need is too strong to allow him to remain still. I want him to pound me hard and fast until we are one sweaty—and replete—mess of bliss.

"Stop," Ian grunts. "Stop moving or this will be over far too soon." He reaches between us and I feel his knuckles against my tender flesh as he squeezes the base of his cock. I try not to move but it's so hard.

He retreats, sliding back until he's nearly left me, and then drills me hard against the bed.

"Oh god, yes, fuck me," I cry out.

My eyeballs roll back into my head as his balls slap my body as he plunges inside me. My back is almost entirely off the bed as he uses both hands to pull me against him. His feet are braced wide apart, and the force of his propulsion would have driven me across to the other side of the bed if it weren't for his hands clamped hard around my hips. I drum the heels of my feet against his back, trying to urge him closer. He lifts one knee onto the bed and braces an elbow by my arm, still pistoning his hips against me in a relentless rhythm. My blood is roaring in my ears, and I can't hear a thing but the harshness of our breaths and the slick sound of our sexes battering against one another.

I've never felt so full.

Need. Want. Desire. Passion.

They are all one.

It is flesh against flesh.

He is steel with an iron resolve, a man who is intent on delivering one thing: pleasure.

The rapturous feeling of my climax hits almost unexpectedly, and as I convulse around him I feel his body tremble beneath my hands as he follows me down into the well of ecstasy. Our mutual pleasure shakes the bed and the very foundation of my life. I bite my tongue to keep the words of love and devotion from spilling out of me.

Collapsing against me, his chest heaving with his exertion, his next words echo in my heart. "I'll never have enough of you."

CHAPTER 22

He kisses me gently, and his wicked hands provide comfort instead of stimulation as he cradles me tenderly against him. One hand slides slowly over my back to palm my butt, but the touch isn't provocative. It's sweet and pulls at me with as much emotion as the vigorous bed play we'd shared.

When my shudders die off, my brain starts working again and all my questions resurface. I can't go on without knowing more about everything. Pulling away from his seductive mouth, I sweep a finger across his dark brows and trace down the side of his face and along his strong jaw. I avoid his gaze even though I feel the weight of it, preferring to watch my finger as it marks a path along Ian's skin.

"What's going on in that head of yours?" His voice is lower than usual and the rough, gravely sound makes me clench my legs together. In response, he squeezes my bottom.

"I'm trying to sort everything out." It's a vague but truthful answer. He leans forward to place a light kiss on my nose before rolling off the bed.

"Hold that thought," he says. His ass muscles clench as he walks toward an adjoining bathroom, and I prop my head up so I can fully enjoy the show. He returns only moments later and slides into bed, pulling me into his arms. "What is it that you need sorted? Us? The project?"

"All of it," I say. His arm is tucked under my neck, and I rest my head on one well-defined pectoral muscle. He tugs me closer so that I'm pressed up against his side with nowhere for my limbs to go but on top of his.

"It's pretty simple." I feel him shrug lightly beneath me. "You're becoming very important to me. Maybe even vital."

The words he utters are ones that I haven't ever heard spoken to me. My high school boyfriend told me he loved me, but no one other than my mother has ever viewed me as important or vital because I've never been that person. I get by fine, but I feel forgettable most of the time, so it confuses me that this wealthy, attractive man wants me more than one of the tens of thousands of smarter, prettier women that exist in the city. I'm not going to give voice to these insecurities, though, because I didn't realize that they even existed before Ian.

Before he came along, I dated. I had sex. But his words make me realize that I'd been missing something. *Important and vital.* It kind of makes me want to cry. "Why aren't you with a model? Or a celebrity or some rich socialite?"

"Rather than you?"

I'll need to keep my mouth shut to do a better job of hiding my crazy. I bury my face into his chest to hide the burn of embarrassment, but it's a question I'm dying to know the answer to.

"You're quite beautiful, Tiny. And it's not your looks. Anyone can buy those. They can buy a firm body or decent nose. Reshape their lips, install bigger breasts. But your spirit is what sets you apart. Your devotion to your mother. Your willingness to sacrifice for another. Your quick mind and," he pauses and slips a hand between my thighs, lightly teasing my pussy, "I fucking love your body."

The light touch causes a hitch in my breath and it's a moment before I can continue. "But you seem to be enjoying the bachelor life, right? I mean, look at this place." I wave a hand around. "You're rich and handsome and could be enjoying a different girl every night."

"Bunny." He *tsks*. "I'd appreciate a little respect. I am not and never have been interested in meaningless sex. And plenty of rich men have wives."

Wives? That's a word that makes my heart stutter. "So you're like a serial monogamist?"

"Do you think I'm unable to form a commitment?"

"It's that you don't have to commit, right? You can enjoy all the lovely fruit from the tree because if you tire of it, there's always more orchards to explore."

He laughs at my stupid analogy. "What about me? Why would you be interested in me rather than some nice young man who has no vendettas and doesn't require you to engage in subterfuge? I know it's not about the money for you. Should I be afraid of a wandering eye? I am several years older than you."

"Really?"

"Didn't Google me?"

It's an offhand remark, and I know he doesn't mean anything by it, but the casual question strikes at the core of my insecurities. I don't Google because I'm not comfortable reading. I'm not smart. Or at least, not book smart, and I never will be. Someone like Ian who trades in millions of dollars a day must be super smart. Ultimately, that's what I can't wrap my head around. Why would someone like Ian be with a dummy like me? "I don't use the computer much," I say dully.

Ian abruptly sits up and pulls me onto his lap so that we are facing each other, my knees on either side of his hips. His hardening cock is between us, looking ready to go again, but he ignores it. Framing my face with his two hands, he looks straight into my eyes. "You're a bright woman. I admire how fast your brain works. It doesn't matter to me in the slightest that you have problems reading or writing. That's not the measure of who you are. Can you even doubt how amazing I find you? You have a real handicap, but you don't let it slow you down, and it doesn't beat you down either."

I press my lips together because any minute now I'm going to start crying. A bit of wetness forms at the outsides of my eyes and Ian thumbs it away. "I can see my future in your eyes, Tiny."

His hands palm my ass and he pulls me flush against his burgeoning cock. "And I want to be inside you for at least fifty percent of that time."

"Already?"

"I've waited a long time for you. Weeks. I'm going to have to fuck you for a good twenty-four hours straight before my cock is appeased." He curves one side of his mouth up in a roguish grin.

"Since you put it so elegantly . . ." I tease, high on the words he's said. I lift my hips so that I can rub against him properly, which has the added benefit of scraping my nipples against his coarse chest hair.

"Wait a second, don't you have anything that you want to say to me?" He quirks an eyebrow up.

I hum a few bars of the 1970s song made popular by David Cassidy that my mom loved to sing. *I think I love you.* Ian looks at me, and then when the lyrics come to him, he throws his head backward and lets out a belly-shaking laugh.

"One of these days you'll feel comfortable saying it out loud, but I'll definitely be changing your ringtone tomorrow."

With that, he tumbles me onto the bed and proceeds to work me over . . . thoroughly. His mouth is heated and demanding, asking for surrender and giving me back power in the same breath.

"Lie back," I order. I want to be in charge this time.

Ian obliges me and places his hands behind his head, looking like an indolent god. His naked form *is* beautiful. It's not just the hardness of his abdomen or the obvious muscles in his chest and arms. It's the contrasts that make him stand out.

He has physical strength but a tender touch. The dark brown of his hair is set off by lightly tanned skin and a white, even smile. His neck is strong yet elegant. His thighs look powerful, yet they've cradled me. And his cock? His cock is the biggest contrast of all.

So smooth and soft, yet so firm, with interesting ridges and veins. Leaning over, I lick him from root to tip with the flat of my tongue.

He releases a strangled laugh. "I didn't wear you out, did I?"

"I'm just getting started." I grin. I reapply myself, taking his broad head into my mouth and working my tongue against him. Right under his head is a sweet spot, super sensitive, and I tease it until he flinches against me.

There's something wonderful about having him surround me like this, of breathing in his scent and feeling him swell in my mouth. His control isn't as easily held onto, as evidenced by the way his fingers grab the rumpled sheets and his thighs quiver from his effort to keep from coming.

He wants to rip me off him and plunge inside me but is willing to wait . . . for now. Crouching on my knees between his legs, I cup his sac in one hand and grasp the base of his cock with the other. With my mouth, I set a quick pace of swallowing and sucking and gripping him in long, unbroken movements along his length.

"Fuck," he pants. "Fuck, yeah."

His breath is harsh above me, a nearly wracking sound as he heaves for air. Beneath me, his body tenses and I prepare for him to shoot down my throat. I'm aching for the taste of him and the feel of his release as he comes.

But before he reaches climax, his hands clamp around my upper arms and he throws me off. I land on my belly next to him, and he's on me before my next breath. His hand finds my clit and rolls the small, sensitive flesh between his fingers. Breath searing my neck, he says, "I'm coming in your hot pussy tonight. All night."

I shudder at his raw words. He pushes my hips up and attacks me with his mouth. His rough, shadowed beard abrades my tender skin as he uses his entire face to make love to me. I arch into him, wanting more pressure. He is making me throb everywhere. In my neck, along my wrists, in the base of my feet.

He dips his fingers just inside, as a goddamned tease. I push back harder, but he fends off my movements with a firm grip around my hips. I'm at his mercy now and his pace. He hardens his tongue as he drags it up and down my sodden opening.

"Take me then," I gasp. "Right now. Fuck me hard."

He growls and I can feel the reverberations against my clit—and even *that* makes me shudder. I'm a hair's breadth away. The tear of the condom package echoes loudly in the room where the only sounds are our labored breaths.

With one smooth motion, he seats himself to the hilt. Both his hands are on my hips as he powers himself in and out of me. I brace my palms against the headboard as the force of his strokes pushes me forward on the mattress.

"Am I deep enough yet?" he murmurs into my ear. "Can you feel me all the way through your body?"

I nod my head, too aroused to even answer. The sensitive flesh of my core is swollen and tingling from earlier orgasms. The feelings evoked by every withdrawal and advancement of his cock is magnified.

"You're extra tight right now," he whispers, dropping his head to bite along my neck and shoulder. Tremors rock me, and I feel close to collapse.

Sensing my imminent climax, he pulls me upright so we're both kneeling. He places one hand on my neck like a collar and the other he drops to my mound. Unbalanced, I reach behind us and hook an arm around his neck.

"That's right," he croons. "Feel us, Tiny."

He drags my free hand to my sex. He covers me with his big hand, pressing our palms against my clit and arranging our fingers on either side of my opening. His fingers extend farther than mine, but I can feel his wet shaft arrowing in and out in rhythmic motions. "Feel how beautiful this is. How fucking hot this is. I think about this constantly. My cock inside you, covered in your juice. Wet with your arousal. I fantasize about your tight, hot pussy squeezing me until I can't breathe."

"I want you to come with me." He exerts more pressure against my clit until I'm delirious. Turning my head, I can see the thick veins of his neck prominently displayed. His eyes are heavy lidded but directed at me, and his lips are parted as he's caught up in our joining. The sight of him is breathtaking. Need, want, and pleasure are written in large, obvious letters on his skin.

It's that sight that sends me over. My body freezes up as the climax overtakes me, spiraling out. I can feel my own come flood our fingers. In a daze, I hear him groan and then the movements behind me, beneath my lax fingers, quicken. His hand moves away from my throat to grab my breast, and I'm imprisoned in his embrace as he works his cock against me with a ferocity I've not felt before. His hips surge against me in uncoordinated thrusts, and he takes a quick indrawn breath as his arousal peaks.

"My god, Tiny," he says, tumbling me down on the sheets. "I'm becoming addicted to you."

"Good, because I don't know if I can live without you either," I confess, trembling from the aftershocks.

"You won't have to."

CHAPTER 23

Morning comes too quickly for me. I don't think Ian allowed me more than an hour's rest last night, and I feel sore all over. But each twinge of pain when I stretch puts a smile on my face because I recall the sinfully delicious ways that I worked out muscles I didn't realize I had. I feel desirable and possessed.

"I hope you're OK with your mom knowing that I fucked you like crazy last night." Ian hands me a plate of perfectly poached eggs, wheat toast, and steak. It looks like a dinner but I guess I worked up an appetite because I fall on the meat like a ravenous beast. He actually made all of it, including the steak, which surprised me. I figured he was solely an order out and delivery sort of guy.

"Why's that?" I ask, running a possessive gaze over his shirtless frame. He's only wearing skintight boxer-briefs, which serve to emphasize the size of his package. *Mine*, I think. *All mine.*

"Because you have a smug but very hot look in your eyes. I think anyone would recognize what it means." His voice has dropped, and by now I know that means he's thinking about doing dirty things to me and with me. Predictably my body responds with clenching and moistening. I'll never get out of here at this rate. Dropping my gaze to my plate, I clear my throat and cast around for a safer topic.

"How'd you meet Malcolm?" I finally ask.

"Do you know what your brother does?" he asks.

"He's a drug dealer. I mean, I'm not sure, but I'm delivering a lot of small packages for him, and they aren't all full of legal papers."

"That's not the only thing he does. I went to him because he's got a certain reputation for dealing with a lot of very attractive women who'll do just about anything for money and are fairly discreet."

"Are you saying he's a . . . pimp?" My mouth falls open.

Ian presses his lips together for a moment. "You could say that."

This news rocks me, and I drop my fork onto the plate.

"So you needed a prostitute? You thought I was a prostitute?" My voice is getting unnaturally high.

"No. I knew you weren't right away." He repositions his chair so that he is sitting closer to me. "The women in the business have a certain look in their eyes that you don't have. Plus, you tried hard to piss me off and no working girl is that bad at customer service." He shakes his head and chuckles at the memory.

"You thought I was naive and could be taken advantage of?"

He shakes his head again. "Why are you always thinking the worst about both of us?"

Good point. I drop my eyes to my plate. "Just checking."

He folds his arms behind his head and leans back against the chair. "At first, I wanted to fuck you because you're so adorable. The attraction we had on the street," he pauses. "That's not normal, Tiny."

He plays with strands of my hair as he talks. "I didn't want you involved in the Howe project, but your need for money was obvious. When I discovered the situation with your mother, I caved. I knew you wouldn't accept straight-out cash from me and, frankly, you would be the perfect person for Howe to pursue."

Taking a sip of his coffee, he pauses for a minute and then continues in a darker, grimmer tone. "I just didn't realize that I'd want to smite him for even breathing the same air as you."

Stirring the egg yolks with the tip of my fork, I recall the meeting when Malcolm gave me the contract to deliver to Ian. "Malcolm once said that I'd need to service a train of guys to pay off my debt . . ." I trail off at the memory. "I guess he wasn't kidding."

Beside me, Ian stiffens. "What debt? And I'll kill him if he thinks he's going to sell you."

A pain, an unwelcome one, starts throbbing at my temple. "I had to borrow money from him after my mom got sick the first time. She thought she'd be able to continue to work even during her chemo treatments, but she couldn't. We ended up getting evicted. To live in the apartment we are in now, I needed first and last month's rent, which I didn't have because I'd spent it all paying rent on the apartment we'd gotten kicked out of. Then I needed more money because my mom is too weak to keep walking up five flights of stairs. Malcolm paid off my back rent, provided me the first and last month for the apartment, and promised to do the same when I found a new place so long as I worked it off."

Ian is seething. "He's going to be peeing from his asshole when I'm done with him."

"No." I lay a hand on his arm. "This is Malcolm's way." I pick up my fork again. Malcolm has his own problems. Big ones.

Ian's face is still rock hard, and I can tell he's having difficulty reining himself in. I ask him another pressing question. "So why the hard play in front of Richard? That didn't seem like part of the plan."

The topic of the project shakes Ian loose from his fantasy of beating Malcolm bloody.

"I didn't realize how angry and jealous it would make me to see you being held by another man, and when he dropped his hands to your ass and thrust his leg between yours I wanted to rip his fucking head off and then spin around the room holding it up like a warning sign." He drew a hand over his face. "Kaga has always been one possessive motherfucker. He doesn't like sharing anything. Not a room, not a cab, nothing. He's got this thing for the younger sister of a friend of his. We all see it but the friend. And he doesn't like any male to be within about five feet of her even though he won't make his own feelings known. I used to harass him all the time. And now, look at me . . ." He spreads his hands wide, inviting an inspection.

"Now what?"

"Just hearing his name come out of your mouth makes me want to end his time here on Earth." He glares at me. "Eat your breakfast. Rich's a work project and we're not on the clock."

CHAPTER 24

We part ways soon after, as I have to get to work. Ian explains he has a home office that he's going to work in today, and I leave him to review financial analyst reports or whatever it is that venture capitalists do.

Around noon my phone dings. It's a text message from an unknown number. I hit the speech recognition button and the little phone spits out a garbled message.

Victoria it was so nice to meet you last night sorry we didn't get to finish our dad like to take you to the high top Brooklyn next weekend give me a ring.

Dictation software sucks. I figure out that Howe is telling me that he is sorry we didn't get to finish our dance. I forward the message to Ian.

When I'm finished with that task, the phone rings. This time it's my mother.

"Victoria," she chides.

Oh no, the full name. I'm in trouble. I brace myself. "Yes?"

"You didn't come home last night, and if it weren't for Ian calling me, I would have been so worried."

I smack my forehead. Ian has overtaken my mind. "Sorry. I don't know what I was thinking."

"I think I know what you were thinking," my mom murmurs, humor palpable in her voice.

"Mom!"

"Don't sound shocked, dear. How do you think you came to be?"

I mumble something like "virginal conception," which elicits a full-throated laugh.

"I hope you're practicing safe sex."

"God, Mom, yes." My womb might be baby safe, but my heart is hanging out there.

"Good." Her voice softens. "I'm so glad, Tiny, that you've found someone. It's been so long for you."

"I've had you," I answer.

"You need more in your life. I love you," she concludes. "Stay safe."

"Love you too, Mom."

A beep sounds, and by the image, I see it's Ian calling. "It's Ian," I tell her. "Can I call you back?"

"No need. I'll see you tonight."

I flip over to Ian's call. I've never been such a popular girl.

"Did you respond to Howe's text?" he asks abruptly.

"Um, no. I don't text. Besides, I didn't know what to say."

"He invited you to a nightclub in Brooklyn. 'Victoria it was so nice to meet you last night. Sorry we didn't get to finish our dance. I'd like to take you to Hightop in Brooklyn next weekend. Give me a call.'"

I hear something crack. "I hope you aren't ruining anything of value."

He expels a heavy breath. "I rarely miscalculate, but I've really fucked things up. Don't text him back."

"I won't."

"Bunny." He pauses. "I'm sorry I've dragged you into this mess. I don't want you dealing with him."

"But I want to help you," I protest. "And if I don't help you, then I can't stay in the apartment or anything. It wouldn't feel right."

"Jesus, after last night, you still can't accept a goddamned gift?" He snarls.

"Especially after last night," I reply firmly. "I've got to get going."

Acid churns in my belly. If Ian doesn't let me do this project for him, then all these things aren't right. I can't accept them, but shit, does he have me by the ovaries, because I am loathe to move my mother from the apartment. She's been in such a great mood lately and hasn't once brought up quitting treatment.

The new location, the new freedom, the access to a car has made a huge difference. When I get to the Central Towers, it is around six in the evening and I'm starving and unhappy, having spent the whole afternoon brooding over my situation.

"Miss Victoria." The doorman greets me with a nod of his head and tip of his cap. "May I take your bicycle? We can store it downstairs."

I'm grateful that Ian had mentioned this, otherwise I would have reacted weirdly. The doorman's name is Jeremiah, and he promises to take good care of it. I reluctantly let it go. That bike is almost part of me.

As I exit the elevator onto the fifteenth floor I see a woman wheeling a rack of clothing down the hall. Her hair is black and stick-straight, the kind that you pay a couple hundred dollars for in upscale salons, but I'm guessing hers is all-natural. If not for the fact that she's toting a metal closet behind her, I'd think she lived here. Dressed in high heels and a black dress that accentuates her model-slender build, she looks like she stepped out of one of the apartments.

"Nice stuff," I say to make friendly conversation in case she is one of my temporary neighbors.

"Whoever lives in 1525 is one lucky bitch. You making a delivery there too?" It's a natural assumption from my bike uniform, helmet, and pack. Shifting awkwardly, I nod. My living arrangements are too complicated to spell out to this stranger. "Guy bought about fifty grand worth of clothes like it was a tall coffee at Starbucks. No change of expression. Not even when I told him one dress was five grand. He looks at the woman to his left and is all 'Will she like it?' If she nodded yes, it was a sale."

Did she say 1525? My eyes zero in on the end of the hall. I'm transfixed by this rack-toting woman and her tales of selling clothes door-to-door.

She eases out of her nude sky-high heels with red soles and dangles the back straps on one of her fingers. Leaning down, she rubs her feet.

"But a good day for you?" I ask.

"Yes, a great day—but fuck me, I'd like to be the recipient of all that," she waves toward the apartment door, "instead of earning a commission."

"I hear you." But inside I'm a churning mess because I suspect that I am the recipient of "all that." If I were still working the project, then clothes would be part of the gig. Now? I don't even know what to make of it other than I'm quickly losing my appetite.

The elevator door dings and she boards, flexing her feet into the tiled floor and not appearing to care at all that her feet are going to get grimy. She notices that I'm staring rudely at her feet and winks at me. "I can wash my feet off when I get home. Make sure you get a good tip. He can afford it."

I find my mom and Ian sitting in the living room enjoying a glass of wine.

"Tiny," my mom cries as I enter the room. I set my bike helmet on the kitchen island and survey the scene. Ian is sitting on the sofa, one ankle propped up on his opposite knee. He's turning the pages of a bound scrapbook that looks suspiciously like the ones my mother made before she was ill. She's in a chair at a right angle to the sofa, her recently held wineglass sitting on a rolling tray beside her. Clothing is draped across the rest of the living room furniture. There's a splash of orange and red along with several black pieces of cloth. There are about eight shoeboxes on the dining room table, and a number of felt drawstring bags.

And all of this largesse actually angers me. Oh, I know I should be thrilled, and I wish I could go into the living room and sit down beside Ian and drink wine with the two of them. There's something that bothers me about the two of them being so cozy and making plans. And my mom. I feel betrayed either by her or for her.

Knowing that this is irrational, I try to hide my pique by burying my head in the refrigerator. I see a plate of pasta and stick it into the microwave, hitting the popcorn button because the thing is too complicated. I tried to figure it out before, and at some point I thought I'd learn how to use all of the buttons instead of just one, but now I'm wondering why. I don't feel right about staying.

I guess that's why I'm angry. Ian is acting like he intends to be best friends with us for a long time, and my mom is eating this up. It's as if all my decisions are being made for me. Plus, I can't even protest without looking like an utter jackass.

I tug out the plate, cursing that it's so hot, and then carry the food into the dining room. Shoving aside the boxes, I fall into my food. I guess my surly mood is fairly evident because the laughter and chatter from the two magpies in the living room has shut down. I'll add "mood killer" to my list of sins.

Mom bustles over, showing more energy than I've seen out of her in weeks, and gives me a little hug. "Glad to see you're home safe, dear. I think I'll go into the bedroom and read before I turn in."

"'Kay," I mutter sullenly. She hesitates and then squeezes me again before disappearing down the hall.

"I think you've hurt your mom's feelings," observes Ian as he drops into a seat opposite me. It is the same chair where he asked me how much to suck his dick. And while no money was exchanged, the sum that he's spent on me in the form of clothes makes it seem like it is payment in kind. When I don't respond, he heaves a sigh and then kicks out his long legs.

Because I don't know what to say that would sound rational at the moment, I continue to eat my pasta until every last noodle and vegetable is gone. The popcorn setting is surprisingly good for heating up food so long as I take it out after the two-minute mark. Maybe I won't have to learn how to use the microwave.

I drop off the dirty plate in the dishwasher and then drain a bottle of water. I dispose of the plastic bottle in a recycling bin that I noticed under the sink this morning.

"Not talking to me?" Ian has followed me into the kitchen and is leaning against the island.

"Don't really know what to say," I tell him evenly. I grab another water and head down the hall, stepping inside the bedroom that is temporarily mine. The bed is made and Ian's blue T-shirt that I've been sleeping in is folded neatly and resting on the end. The white glove service apparently includes a daily maid. The comforter is like a cloud, and I wonder if I can take it with me when we move out.

"How much does this place really cost?" I ask Ian, who has followed me in and is leaning against the wall. He's closed the door behind him but hasn't made a move toward me.

"Five million, give or take a few hundred thousand."

I'm glad I'm lying down so I don't faint.

"Is it the money that bothers you, Tiny? Because I thought you said you were all about the money." He's mocking me now but it's gentle and without spite.

"I don't know what it is," I say slowly, staring up at the white ceiling. At least the ceiling looks normal here, if not a little higher than my old apartment. "I feel like I'm always playing catch-up with you. I said I'd do the Howe project for you and now it feels like I'm getting fired. You're spending money on me like . . ." I struggle for a comparison and use the clothing lady's version. "Like nothing is more than a latte from Starbucks, and it makes me feel like we'll never be equals."

"And being seen as an equal is important to you?" He's moved away from supporting the wall and is now sitting on the edge of the bed. I move over, not sure if I'm making room for him or getting away from him.

"Wouldn't it be for anyone?" I counter.

"I really only care what is important to you." He settles next to me but is careful about not touching me.

"It's so fast, Ian, and I'm not a plastics company. I'm a human and moving into this apartment, getting all those clothes, and now, having you say things that suggest you are interested in something serious when we don't even know each other confuses me." I figure there's no point in subterfuge, not when I want honesty in return. "I don't know how much is an act and what's real."

He shifts me closer and his implacable hand turns my head so that we are eyeball-to-eyeball. "That I want you? It's no act," he says harshly.

I can't hide my misery. "This game is too hard for me. I don't know the rules, and I'm afraid I'm going to get hurt in the process."

Ian releases my neck and cups my cheek. "Let me tell you what you need to know about me. I'm loyal, generous, and I like to have things my own way."

"The last one isn't really a plus," I mutter.

"Who said I was itemizing my attributes? This is who I am. I want you, Tiny. In my bed and in my life. You aren't being fired. We're reassessing the situation. Let's enjoy each other in the process."

"For how long?"

"For however long it lasts. Tell me what you want out of life, Tiny."

Did I know myself as well as Ian? He was able to lay out a very definitive description of himself.

"You should know that I'm loyal too," I say slowly. "I care a lot about my family and would like to have one of my own some day." A wave of longing hits me as I articulate something I didn't even realize was a necessity in my life. My mother's sickness and my relative personal isolation are part of why Ian's intense attention is filling me with confusion. I want what he's offering, but I realize that I want it too much and I want it to last forever. Ian is staring intently at me, as if everything I'm saying is of vital importance. I wish I could read his mind.

He says, "I won't deny that I was attracted to you from the first minute I saw you on the street. I love that you challenge me, but every minute I spend with you, it cements what I've already suspected. You, Victoria Corielli, were made for me. I'm not going to apologize for knowing what I want," he argues. "Why can't you take us one day at a time? Let me shoulder some of your burden?"

"Because I'm afraid."

"Be afraid then. It's my job to convince you that the fear is unnecessary." He utters these words with complete confidence, as if by saying them he can will away my anxiety. The bed dips as he climbs off and saunters into the bathroom.

"Gee, thanks." I listen as he runs water inside the bathroom. Could I go with the flow? What would be the harm? So what if my heart gets broken. Is that really something I can't recover from? I've had bad breakups before.

When he comes out, he's dressed in casual clothes, a pair of soft pants and a thin white T-shirt that clings to his hard frame.

"I'm going to work a bit." He lifts a bag that I hadn't noticed before. It's so worn that it looks like it's traveled twice around the world. The creases have creases. Noticing my stare, he pats the side with an affectionate hand. "This baby has been with me for over ten years. My first boss gave it to me. Said every man who aspired to prosperity owned one good leather bag. I couldn't afford one. One night I was working late and fell asleep at my desk. When I woke up, the bag was sitting next to me. I've never used another since. Never will either."

The words fall like rain on my greedy heart. He's telling me that his affections aren't so easily displaced. I give him a small smile and then rise up on an elbow to kiss his cheek. He turns so our lips meet and he gives me slow, wet kisses that make my toes curl. Drawing back, he cups my face with a gentle hand and rubs a thumb across my wet lip. "Get some sleep, bunny."

After Ian leaves, I tiptoe down the hall to my mom's bedroom. She's asleep, lying in the huge bed with her reading glasses on and a book beside her. I pull off the glasses and move the book to the nightstand. "Love you, Mommy," I whisper.

"Love you too, baby girl," she mumbles as I walk out.

It takes me a long time to go to sleep, but Ian remains out in the living room doing whatever it is that constitutes work for him. Even when I do fall asleep, I'm restless, missing his big, warm body. Later I feel him climb in beside me. A warm arm slides over my waist and a big hand cups my sex in a comforting rather than provocative manner, and I'm finally able to sink into a deep slumber.

Sometime in the night, he rouses me and makes love to me gently, moving my limbs and kissing me warmly all over. When he presses inside me, it's with tender intent. Our bodies move leisurely together and when my orgasm hits, it's a gentle wave instead of the pounding hurricane of our previous encounters.

He breathes out my name in a long rush of air against my ear as he jets into the condom. I fall asleep with his warm body tucked around me again.

Ian is gone by the time I wake up. The clothes that were lying in the living room last night are hung up in the closet. Some of the items are strange runway-types of clothes that I thought no real person ever wore, and I can't imagine putting on my body, but others—like a wispy dress with angled pumpkin and white stripes—are so lovely that my heart skips a beat.

The shoeboxes are stacked in a corner, and the felt bags rest like little dumplings in a row. My piles of T-shirts, tennis shoes, and bike shorts look incongruous and cheap next to the newly bought finery. Just seeing the juxtaposition of my clothes next to the ones that Ian has presumably bought for me highlights the differences in our worlds. We don't look like we belong together.

I rifle through the clothes and realize that many of the items he's purchased look very comfortable despite their expensive fabrics. There are several pants and longer skirts. The tops are loose fitting and made out of a knit fabric or stretchy lace. Even the dresses don't look like something that would be tight and super revealing, but rather fabrics that will skim my not-very-prominent curves. Maybe we can find common ground after all.

He returns around lunchtime with a satchel, which he unpacks in the closet where my new and old clothes hang. I watch him silently and remain quiet even after he raises a challenging eyebrow. I'm still trying to figure us both out. Having him around more isn't really a problem.

The next day, before Mom's chemo session, he has Steve drive us to the Bronx Zoo. Chemo seems easier this time around. Hallie arrives to read another chapter, and I take off to do the day route instead of the late afternoon and evening. Despite being worn out, the following day Mom is upright and sitting in a chair out on the small balcony. The city noise is loud, but the cool breeze from Central Park is almost refreshing.

Mom loves Ian and he is incredibly tender and caring with her. My heart swells larger than my body can contain when I see them together, but it's a sweet pain. The days go by swiftly as I look forward to going home and seeing Ian and a cheery mom. The nights are long and passionate. I've never been happier.

After a week of missing Ian in the morning because he gets up before the crack of dawn to go to work, I haul myself out of bed early, wearing my beater tank and a pair of panties that he bought. He's lathering his face with a brush, raising suds as he works his shaving soap in a circular motion. Shirtless, but wearing pants, he leans against the counter toward the mirror, pulling down on his skin and making funny O's with his mouth as he spreads the soap around.

His actions are mesmerizing, and I stumble into the bathroom for a closer look. Ian taps his brush against the sink and turns, lifting me onto the counter in a smooth movement. "Like what you see?"

"It looks like you have whipped cream on your face." I draw a finger down a soap-lathered cheek, watching the flesh appear underneath.

"Don't lick your finger. It doesn't taste like whipped cream." He flashes me a quick grin, his teeth gleaming whitely from between lips that look fuller and pinker in contrast to the shaving cream.

"May I?" I ask, picking up the brush. He clenches his jaw once, then nods and moves between my legs. The wooden soap dish is half-full, which seems to indicate that he's been using it for a while. I sniff the brush and it smells vaguely of lemons. Slowly I swirl the brush in the soap. "Are the bristles soft?" I ask as I smooth the soap on, trying to mimic his earlier circular motion.

His hands are on either side of my hips, and he's leaning so close to me that I can see the palpable beat of the artery in his neck. The air is thick around us and my mouth is inexplicably dry. I lick my lips and open my mouth to ease the ache in my chest, but the tension is choking me. Still, I keep rubbing the bristles along his taut skin.

The little bristles catch on his hair-roughened cheek and jaw. I swirl the brush in small circles, watching the soap lather up with each pass. My feelings for Ian are so intense and consuming. I want to do everything with him—even this small, intimate act. I wonder how many others have seen him like this. How many have run the brush across his jaw and traced the dip in his cheek?

"You're it," he says softly.

My eyes flick to his and all I can see is me. Me and sincerity. And because I'm tired of being alone, tired of battling by myself, tired of fighting, I give in. My hand creeps behind his neck and grips the nape, drawing him closer to me. From this distance I can smell the lemon and menthol. I can see the soft skin under his eyes, the hard line of his nose. His lids are at half-mast and his hands move restlessly along my outer thighs.

"Tiny," he groans and then pulls me hard against his erection. His eyes are blazing. "I have no control when it comes to you."

Without regard for the soap, his mouth finds mine. The suds smear across my cheeks and some even creeps between our lips, but I don't care. It tastes like Ian.

His lips break apart from mine and trace a path from my jaw down to my neck. He breathes my name repeatedly like it's a prayer. *Tiny, Tiny, Tiny.* I hook my legs around him, reveling in the feel of his hot, hard column of flesh rubbing up against my tender and wet parts.

My tank is pushed up and over my head, and then one breast is palmed and the other is taken into his mouth. Thank goodness for the wall that catches me as I fall backward. He sucks hard on my nipple, so hard I feel my pussy clenching with each long pull. I rub myself against him, wishing he wasn't wearing his pants. Wishing that we were both naked.

"I need inside your pussy so badly," he mouths against my breast.

"Yes."

With a growl, Ian attacks my other breast. The soap on his face is nearly all rubbed off into my skin, but apparently he doesn't mind the taste either.

My hands fumble at his waistband, but I manage to unbutton and then unzip his trousers. Delving inside his briefs, I release a moan of delight at the feel of his heavy cock in my hands. God, had it only been a few hours since I touched him last? It seems like months. As Ian lavishes attention on my breasts, I encircle his cock with both my hands. The wetness on the tip exhibits his desire. I want more of that. I want all of him.

His mouth is back on my neck, sucking hard. The suction sends a shudder throughout my body. Ian lifts me against him and walks into the bedroom, following me down onto the bed. With swift kicks, he rids himself of his pants. I can't stop touching him.

"Need to taste you," he grunts, and pushes down my body, ripping my panties down my legs. Without any preliminaries, his mouth is on me and his tongue is inside me. Bells sound in my head followed by the rasp of a heavy guitar. Wait, a guitar? I manage to roll my head toward my nightstand where my phone is ringing.

"Don't answer it," Ian orders. He's on his knees now, braced over me. His mouth is slick from my wetness, and he's replaced his tongue with two of his fingers. I turn away from the phone. Malcolm can wait. Reaching down between us, I pull out Ian's cock. Saliva pools in my mouth. I want his thick length in my mouth, down my throat. I want his balls in my hands. Tugging on him, I sidle downward and he reluctantly lets me. I can tell he's torn between wanting to be in my mouth and wanting to finger me, but it's my turn.

The phone rings again. And again. And then there's a knock on my door. "Tiny," I hear my mother say. "Malcolm's on the phone and he says it's urgent."

I drop my hands from Ian's body and he groans in dismay. "Jesus. I hate your brother."

"Me too," I sigh. If it weren't for my mom, I'd ignore the call and finish stripping Ian's clothes off. I pick up the phone and hit the call button. Immediately Malcolm starts yelling.

"Why aren't you picking up? I've got four fucking angry customers that need their deliveries. Are you going to get your ass in gear and make deliveries for me, or do I have to get someone else?"

"Get someone else," Ian barks because Malcolm is speaking so loudly that the people in the apartment next door can hear him.

"Is that fucking Kerr? Are you fucking him?" Malcolm is pissed off.

"None of your business, Malcolm," I shoot back, but I'm up and moving toward the closet. Ian curses and heaves himself out of bed. His cock bobs angrily in the air as he wrenches on his discarded boxers and then his pants.

"I'm sorry," I mouth to Ian, and he gives me a tight smile. His pants are tented out, and Ian grips himself and then heads into the bathroom.

"I'll be there in thirty," I say, and hang up before Malcolm can shout any more obscenities.

"I don't like that you do deliveries for Hedder," Ian grits out while he begins shaving once more. I intentionally keep my gaze away from him because he's angry and because he looks so goddamn sexy shaving. I kind of resent how intensely attractive I find him.

Ian stomps around some more, picking out a tie and then wrapping himself up tight. He picks up the same mother-of-pearl cufflinks that he wore the other day, which I find odd given that he has so much money one would think he'd have dozens of cufflinks. He seems to have a huge number of ties in my closet alone. Who knows what he has stored at his Bruce Wayne fuck pad.

"Yeah, well, I need the money."

"You work for me."

I ignore that and get dressed. Out of the bedroom, the living areas are empty. My mother has made herself scarce. Ian's right behind me.

"I can get you a different job. A permanent one. You wouldn't need to ride bikes in New York's insane traffic where any number of cabbies are hoping to knock you off the street."

"Like a made-up one?" I mock because there's no job in the financial sector where someone like me could work. "Tell me what company. What would I be doing?"

He shrugs, and I know it's a fake job. "I'm not sure. Let me look into it."

"I don't know." I'm reluctant to give up the income that Malcolm's drop provides. "I'll think about it." I grab my pack and make sure my headphones are inside of it.

"You do that." He gives me a hard kiss and then pats my butt.

When I get to Queens, I'm ten minutes past the thirty I'd promised and Malcolm is seething. He throws the packages at me when I cross the threshold. "You are so fucking dumb, Tiny." He paces in the living room as I unzip my bag and stuff the five envelopes inside. He recites the addresses to me, and I'm grateful that they are all grouped together over in Brooklyn. Park Slope moms who can't stand their kids, I think.

"I'm dumb because I overslept?" I ask. I hate being called dumb, and Malcolm knows it.

"If you're letting Kerr in your pants, it's the fucking stupidest thing you've ever done. And you've done a lot of stupid shit in your life."

The accusation stings because I rarely do stupid shit. I lived a quiet life with my mom before she got sick. I didn't start doing stupid stuff like working with Malcolm until I had no other recourse.

"Screw you, Malcolm. What's it matter who I sleep with?" I turn to go, but Malcolm grabs my arm.

"He likes to fuck around. I read up about him. He's thirty-two and never had a single solid relationship. He's the type who's always got some new piece in his bed. Guys like Kerr think that women are good for one thing only. And you're disposable to him. Like Kleenex. He'll blow you once and then throw you away."

I give him a tight smile, trying not to show how easily he's hurt me. "You get all that from the Internet?"

"*Page Six* has a dossier on him. If you could read, you'd know."

I gasp at his low blow. "You know nothing about us."

This generates a mean laugh from Malcolm. "If you think there is an 'us,' you're already done for. You want to be a toy for a rich man? Fine. Enjoy it, but know that you're one of a thousand plastic Barbies he's sticking his dick into."

"Jealous much?" I retort. Shouldering my pack, I roll my bike out the door. This time Malcolm doesn't stop me. When I turn back, his expression is unfathomable. For a moment I think I see pain and then worry, but a sneer and his next words erase that thought.

"Hope he's paying you well. Might as well get double time on your back." He slams the door in my face.

I don't get why Malcolm is being so hateful. Is it jealousy? Like, he wishes he could get paid the money to lure Richard to his demise? I want to tell him that it's no fun. The really disturbing thing is that Malcolm and Richard have both claimed that Ian is a lothario, but it doesn't match what I've seen of him or what he's told me.

There's no reason for Ian to tell me that he wants me, that he cares about me, because he's already gotten me into bed. I'm a *sure thing*. Yet he still keeps coming back. I can either buy into the negativity that Malcolm and Richard are selling or trust Ian.

Maybe it's stupid and foolish, but I'm going to trust Ian.

There are no bike lanes or paths from Queens to Brooklyn. Instead I have to take Atlantic Avenue, which is getting busy by the time I hit the road. Malcolm is right to be mad at me. It's far more dangerous to be biking now than it would be earlier in the morning, but the first three deliveries go fine.

The fourth delivery is in Brooklyn Heights. The address recited to me by Malcolm leads me to a five-story Greek Revival townhouse. Its gorgeous all-brick exterior is framed by bushes on either side that are starting to flower. The lower windows are grated, but the upper windows are large and sparklingly clear. Shaking my head, I wonder briefly why anyone who is able to live in such a gorgeous place would need anything Malcolm is selling. I lean my bike against the front stoop and head down a short flight of stairs to the basement entrance. Deliveries aren't usually made to the front door in homes like these. Not even the type of deliveries I'm making.

I knock and ring the doorbell but no one answers. I can't very well tuck this envelope in the mail slot, so I head to the main entrance. The door is big and painted black. There are no sidelights, so I can't even tell if anyone is home. I ring the bell and then try to lean over the side of the stoop to see if I can see any movement from the front windows. I wait what seems to be a long time but is likely only thirty seconds or so. Maybe I have the wrong address. I pull out my phone and am in the process of pulling up Malcolm's phone number when the front door opens, revealing a husky man of indeterminate age, dressed in boxers and a short robe that hangs open.

"What the fuck are you doing?" he snarls at me. I start to reach into my pack when he grabs my wrist. "Were you taking a picture?"

"No," I answer and try to wrest my wrist away. "I was calling Mr. Hedder to see if I had the right address."

"You can't take fucking pictures." he rants and squeezes my wrist a little tighter.

"Sir, you are hurting me. I promise I wasn't taking any pictures." But my words don't penetrate.

He repeats his claim, only this time there is white spittle forming at the sides of his mouth. He grabs my other hand and yells again, shaking me hard. "You shouldn't be taking pictures of my fucking house."

My heart is pounding, but I try to stay calm. "I wasn't, sir. Really. Let me get your package."

I should've noticed the wild, dilated pupils. Maybe the flushed skin was a warning, or his disheveled appearance, but none of it registered so when the slap comes across my face, I only respond with dazed surprise.

The first blow is followed by another and then another. I'm trying to pull from his grip, but he has both my wrists captured in one hand. My legs kick out, but he's unmoved. There's a ringing in my ears and my face is on fire. I try to hold my hands up to avoid more blows, but he's relentless. Suddenly he releases me, and I fall backwards down the stairs. I try to catch myself, but I'm so, so dizzy. The ground rises to meet me.

And then he's on me again, bludgeoning me with his fists on my face, my body. The pain is piercing and pulsating and I can't breathe. I curl up and try to avoid direct hits to tender organs and then suddenly he's gone. There's a shout and a scuffle. I hear thuds. He's away from me, so I try to crawl in the opposite direction of the noises. If only I can get to my bike. My hands scrape against the concrete, and I feel as if I'm leaving bits of me on the sidewalk, but I'm OK with that. I need to get to my bike.

Despite my blurred vision, I think I see the curved back tire maybe ten feet away. I pull myself up on my hands and knees and start forward until a big hand drops on my back. My immediate reaction is to collapse into another ball. Raising my hands to cover my head and drawing my knees up, I cower. "No more, please. I wasn't going to take a picture," I sob out.

"Victoria," I hear a deep male voice say. "It's Steve. You're going to be all right, sheila. Ian is on his way."

Steve's voice, so distinctly not American, is comforting in its familiarity.

"What's a sheila? Is that like a girl kangaroo?" I ask, catching my breath. My fingers run over my helmet, and I cringe at the long crack I feel on the top of the plastic. My bike helmet helped cushion my fall, but it obviously didn't make it through unscathed. I'll have to get a new one before I show up downtown at my job. Struggling to my feet, I fight back a wave of dizziness. In the back of my mind, the presence of Steve niggles at me, but I can't think about that. All of my concentration is on not puking my guts out. I try breathing through my nose.

"Nah, it's like the opposite of bloke," Steve answers. "Maybe you should sit down before you—"

My sudden retching interrupts his words of advice and I puke right into the front bushes I was admiring. Groaning, I lean forward and rest my hands on my thighs. Lying back down on the pavement seems like a good idea. My legs buckle, but Steve is there to catch me before I do a header into the plants. He presses a white cloth against my forehead.

"You hit your melon pretty hard falling down the stairs, so you need to stay awake, girl." He snaps his fingers in front of me. I decide that I no longer like Steve and his nasally accent. Jerking my head away is a mistake, though, and I close my eyes, hoping that the darkness will make the pounding go away. Wish he would let me go.

Is it OK for me to sleep on the sidewalk in Brooklyn Heights? There's probably a homeowner's association policy against that sort of thing, and really, I need to get to Neil's. I can't afford to be late.

Heaving a sigh, I try standing upright using Ian's driver for support. "What are you doing in Brooklyn Heights?" I ask, trying to figure out why there's two of him. "And stop moving," I order. He's swaying so much that the motion is creating a double vision.

A squealing of tires followed by the hard slam of a car door grabs my attention, but when I turn toward the sound, nausea rises up and I bend over to avoid another bout of vomiting. Heavy footsteps slap against the asphalt as if someone is running and then I feel Steve move aside and a new, familiar body settle next to me.

"Ian." It's funny how much being next to him makes me feel better. He strokes my back in sure, comforting movements.

He lifts the white cloth stuck to my forehead and hisses. "Oh, bunny, what have you got yourself into?"

The tender concern in his voice threatens to break the dam that's holding back my emotions. "I thought Batman and Robin traveled together," I joke lamely. "How come you and Steve aren't together?"

It doesn't make sense to me but not much does right now. I take a few more deep breaths and then straighten up so I can get on my bike and go—only the sudden movement makes me stumble and my knees buckle again. Before I can take another breath, Ian lifts me into his arms.

"Put me down," I say. "I have to get going. What time is it, anyway?"

I had it planned so that my last delivery would allow me to get to my job in time. I know I can't allow any more late arrivals or absences due to my mom's illness put my once secure courier position in further jeopardy. Ian's arms tighten around me as I struggle, but then the pounding in my head gets stronger so I give in. It's easier to lay my head against Ian's broad chest and close my eyes.

He curses softly. "What happened?"

"Guy attacked her. She fell down the stairs, and he hit her a few more times before I could get to her." Steve pauses. "Sorry, man. Parked too far away. She vomited when I tried to sit her upright. Probably has a small concussion."

"Where is he?" Ian growls, like a feral animal. The harshness in his voice is in direct contradiction to the tender way he's holding me. "I'm going to kill him."

"Mate, we need to move her soon."

He's silent for a moment. "Get his details. I'm coming back once I have Tiny squared away."

"Don't go to sleep, Tiny." Steve snaps his fingers in front of me again. When I have the energy I'm breaking those digits off so he can't snap them again.

Ian shifts me higher in his arms. "Where's the car?"

Steve must've gestured because I don't hear any verbal response. "What car today?" I ask because I don't feel like pulling my head out of the nice little nest on his shoulder. If I place my nose in the right spot, I get a whiff of lemon from his shaving cream. And the lemon scent makes me think of how great the morning started, with Ian heavy between my legs, before I came out here to this quiet family neighborhood and got the crap beaten out of me.

"Things went to hell in a hurry this morning," I murmur into his collarbone.

"Should never have left you," he replies tersely. When we're at the car, Ian settles me against the side of the vehicle as he opens the car door.

"We should get a minivan," I tell him. "In the commercials, the doors open and close with the push of a button."

"I don't think anyone in the city owns a minivan." He sounds amused.

"We'll need it for our kids."

He sucks in a breath and then hugs me tight as he puts me into the back of the Bentley. I stretch out on the soft leather and fall into a light sleep. It's not even sleep because I can hear Steve climb in and then another car door open and shut.

"Should we take her to the hospital?"

Ian replies, "We can't. They'd be bound to report an assault, and Tiny's got the packages on her. Let's go to the warehouse."

As Steve takes off smoothly, Ian plucks a phone out of his pocket with one free hand. The other is pressing me against his chest. "Roger, Ian Kerr here . . . Great. I'm glad that investment worked for you. Hey, I've got a friend who had a little run-in. Need her checked out . . . Yep, my place over on Hudson. See you in thirty minutes."

I doze in and out of consciousness on the ride to Ian's loft. "What were you thinking that day?" I ask during one of my lucid moments.

"Which day, bunny?" He's holding me on his lap with one hand propped against my head and the other running lightly over my outer thigh. It's really nice.

"When your snake camera was looking at me. It scared me."

"I was thinking that you looked regretful that you were leaving the box and about how much I'd enjoy bringing it back to you."

"You're always so sure of yourself," I whisper.

"Yes, but you are too, Tiny, or we wouldn't be in this mess."

"Right," I nod and then stop because that hurts. "You want to think for me. Sounds like a great plan."

"Let's wait to have this discussion when your head isn't banged up, because you're saying things right now that you might regret."

"You're big on the no regrets thing."

"When it matters."

I don't remember being carried up the stairs and into the loft, but a bright light in my eyes wakes me up.

"Ow." The pinpoint light is directed right at my eyeballs. I bat at it but someone takes my hands and folds them in his.

"Tiny," Ian says. "There's a doctor here. He's checking you out."

"Does he have to blind me while he's at it? I thought they took an oath to do no harm." He doesn't resist when I pull my hands down, but I don't try to hit the doctor either. Not even when he presses into my ribs, causing me to release a hiss of pain.

"OK, that hurts," I tell the doctor, whose face looks like a big, black dot. "You don't have to press so hard."

He continues his palpation of all my sore spots until I feel like I'm one big ache. *Thanks for nothing, doc.*

"I don't think she has any broken ribs. The swelling in her face should subside in a day, although if it doesn't you should take her in. The helmet did a good job of protecting her, but she might have a concussion since you said she was in and out of consciousness and had vomiting and nausea. Time is your best treatment. My recommendation is for her to stay in bed for a day and then take it easy for the next week."

"A week?" I yelp. "There's no way."

I struggle upright, fighting off the pain in my head and the nausea in my belly.

"Watch for increased head pain, drowsiness, or more vomiting. Anything like that."

"Do I need to wake her every two hours?" Ian asks, completely ignoring me.

"No. Monitor the symptoms. We're looking for a worsening condition and if that happens, we should bring her in for testing."

"Thanks, Roger." Ian shows him to the door.

I fall into a restless sleep, and when I wake up I see Steve leaning against a long, low console table snugged up against the wall.

"You got a phone?" I ask him. A giant television hangs behind him. The ticker at the bottom of the news channel he was watching says I've slept for three hours. He looks at me like I'm crazy, but I don't see a phone in here. There's got to be a landline in this joint someplace. Ever since 9/11 and the overwhelmed cell towers, people in the city scrambled to install landlines. I can't see Ian not having one.

I stagger toward the door where Ian and the doctor have disappeared. Outside runs a long hallway and a glass railing that overlooks the main floor where I first laid eyes on Ian Kerr. Steve trails behind me, not stopping me but not letting me out of his sight either. There appear to be other rooms on this level, so I wander down the hall. The next doorway opens into an office and in it is a phone. Bingo.

Swiftly I enter the room, barely making note of the floor-to-ceiling bookcases on one side and the multiple television monitors on the other showing stock tickers from all over the world. The phone at my work rings twice when my boss answers, "Neil's Delivery Service, timely and discreet courier services for all your city needs, can I help you?"

"Um, hey, Neil," I say, cringing because I know what's coming. "It's Tiny Corie—" I don't even get my whole name off before he starts yelling.

"Where the hell are you? I've had to reschedule five deliveries this morning!"

"I had an altercation, but I'll be there in like ten minutes." If I bike fast, I should be able to get to the downtown office in fifteen, but I figure ten sounds better. And then it occurs to me that I'm going to need a helmet because mine is cracked. Neil will not allow me to deliver anything without a helmet for insurance reasons. "I'll be there in thirty minutes."

"Guess what? You can take sixty minutes to get here because you're fired." He slams down the phone. I look at the receiver in my hand in dismay because I'm not sure what happened there. I press redial.

"Look, Neil," I rush to explain before he can answer. "I fell off my bike and hit my head, but I promise I'll be right there. I've got to stop and get a new helmet. I swear it won't be more than five, maybe ten extra minutes."

"Hey, Tiny, it's Sandra. Neil stomped out of here." This is better because Sandra can assign me some deliveries, and once I make them, Neil will cool off.

"Sorry about making your job more difficult this morning. Fell off my bike," I explain. "I'll be over in like thirty minutes. You can schedule me to work this evening and I'll cover whoever took up my morning route."

"No can do," Sandra replies. "Neil had me delete your name from the system this morning. I hate to tell you this, but he's been aching to let you go ever since your mom got cancer. He couldn't because everyone would think he's a jackass. And you know, we all think he's a jackass anyway, but since you missed a day the other week and now are a no-show this morning, he's feeling empowered. Sorry." I hear phones ring in the background. "I gotta run. Take care."

The buzzing dial tone turns to discordant beeps before I realize that there's no one else on the line any longer. Ian reaches and presses the disconnect button on the base and takes the handset from me.

"Cool phone," I comment lamely.

"Thanks, but I didn't pick it out." Ian shepherds me out of the office and down the hall back to his bedroom. Steve can't meet my eyes when I brush by him. Apparently watching someone get fired over the phone is off-putting.

"Don't pick out your clothes or your phones, huh?" There's no point in fighting him as he pushes me down on the bed. I sit passively as he bends down and pulls off my sneakers and socks.

"No. I like things to look good, but I don't want to put the effort into making that happen, so I hire people to do it for me."

Like me.

"But not everything," I counter, and twist away from his hands as they try to pull my shirt off. The motion makes me wince, which Ian catches.

"Let me look, Tiny," he commands.

"Your doctor already did." I slip under the covers and pull the downy soft comforter up to my chin. Ian sits down on the edge of the bed, and I notice for the first time he's still in the navy-blue suit that he donned this morning. Whoever dresses him does a very good job. The wool sits perfectly across his shoulders but hugs his waist. Underneath is a snowy white shirt that has smudges of blood on it. My blood? I feel my temple and find a bandage there. Must have been slapped on me while I was resting earlier.

Ian tugs on the blanket half-heartedly and then sighs. "You're in no position to argue so I'm going to let you sleep, but we're not done with this conversation."

Later I'll be gone, but I'm not telling Ian that. I'll close my eyes, take a brief rest, and then after he's gone, I'll take off. Maybe for the next week, I'll double my deliveries for Malcolm. *Oh shit, my last delivery.* I had five and made only four of them.

I shoot up in bed. "Where's my pack?" Kicking the covers back, I slide off the end of the bed before Ian can catch me. By the time he does, I'm halfway down the stairs but he's faster, stronger, and hasn't been knocked around like a piece of produce in a grocery basket.

"It's downstairs. Steve has already taken off to deliver the last package in your pack. I've called and left a message for Malcolm. The only person I haven't contacted is your mother," he says calmly, trying to redirect me up the stairs. "Figured you would want to talk to her yourself."

"Fine," I mutter ungraciously. The sooner I lie down, the sooner

I figure I can leave. At the bedroom door, I stop and push him backwards. "I need rest and quiet," I repeat the doctor's orders with a mocking tone. He gives me a shake of his head but allows me to shut him out. In his bathroom, I peel off my top and then my shorts. There's a big bruise on my right ribs and a scrape on my left shoulder. The left shoulder injury must have been from falling down the stairs, but the right side? That's the result of the stupid-ass druggie.

"I'm going to kill him."

Startled, I drop my hands to cover my naked chest, which is probably stupid since he's seen me naked, but Ian's presence is a surprise. "I told you to stay out."

He stalks over to a door and opens it to reveal a linen closet. From the back, he pulls out what looks to be a first aid kit and tosses it on the counter. "You said you needed rest and quiet, not for me to stay out."

"That's what the closed door meant." I start to pull on my discarded shirt, wincing as the fabric rubs against my scrapes and bruises.

"Put this on," he orders, throwing me a white cotton undershirt. It does look more comfortable than my bike shirt. Turning around, I set my work shirt on the counter and pull the T-shirt on. It's a V-neck, and given the large size on my small frame, the V dips rather low.

Ian must like it because he grunts in satisfaction.

"Really?" I give him an eye roll.

He gives me a shrug in return. "I'm intensely attracted to you, so even though you're beaten, bruised, and angry with me, I can still appreciate that you look sexy as hell in one of my shirts. Now pull the neck aside so I can apply some salve to your scrape."

I do as he says only because I can tell I'm not getting out of the bathroom until that scrape is covered. His fingers are light on my wound, working the balm in with tender brushes across my skin. The pads of his fingers move beyond my abrasion to run down my arm. He grabs my hand and places it on his left breast. Underneath the cotton cloth of his shirt, I feel the beat of his heart as it thuds against my palm. "Tiny." His gaze captures mine. "Let me take care of you. Just this once." A heavy, discomfiting silence fills the bathroom. The green in his eyes is intense and brilliant. I know what he wants is capitulation, but I can't give him that.

"Is that what you need, Ian? For me to completely give myself over to you? I can't do that." My words were whispered, but my hand doesn't move from under his—if anything, I've stepped closer. His free arm reaches around and closes the distance between our bodies, trapping my hand against his chest.

"I don't want to own you." His eyes search mine as if he can compel me to understand his true intentions. "I want to take care of you. Let me."

And under the pressure of his gaze, the heat of his body, and the trauma of the morning, my resistance turns to water.

"OK." I close my eyes. "But only for a little while."

Without another word, he lifts me into his arms and carries me to the bed. Settling me under the covers, Ian makes quick work of his clothes. He picks up his phone he tossed on the nightstand. "Steve, call the office and let them know I'm out for the day . . . No, cancel them all."

"Are you losing money when you're not working?" I ask as he settles his body in beside mine.

"No, and even if I was, I wouldn't care." He rolls onto one side, careful to avoid touching my bruised body. He brushes the hair off my forehead, and I close my eyes again. His gentle fingers trace my cheekbones and my jawline and down the sides of my neck. The light touches are somehow as erotic as his fierce ones, and I can feel my body stirring in response. Restlessly, I shift my legs underneath the blankets.

"Do you need something, bunny?" Ian's voice sounds like it's dropped two octaves and only serves to make me even more disturbed. His hand dips lower, until it's sliding underneath my panties where the wet evidence of my arousal is unmistakable. He releases an audible groan of satisfaction; I return the favor with a low whimper when his fingers slide into me.

"Yes," I whisper hoarsely.

"Then give yourself over to me. I'm going to take care of everything." His fingers thrust inside me in measured, slow strokes. Reaching down, I rub my clit in circles. He turns my face toward his and my eyes flutter open. His irises have darkened to a dense forest green, but the want in them is unmistakable. I rise halfway up to meet his mouth. He takes my lips softly but with possessive intent. And even though I was hurt this morning, the need between my legs will not be assuaged by his fingers.

I tug at his arm and try to hook my leg over his hips to draw him on top of me. Breaking away from my mouth, he growls, "Not while you're hurt." But his fingers don't stop their relentless strokes between my legs.

"I need you, Ian," I whimper. "You said you'd take care of everything."

At this he pauses—and then with a wry smile, he agrees. "I did."

He removes his hand, which causes me to cry out in dismay. Turning back to me, he presses a firmer kiss against my lips. "Condom," he says. He's not gone for long.

Kneeling down between my legs, he rubs his covered cock against my sex. "This what you want, bunny? A good fucking?"

I give a nod. Arousal has transformed Ian. He is no longer the half-amused, indolent businessman. The individual between my legs looks like a fierce warrior who's come ashore on a land he's been waiting to conquer for an age. There's strength in his every movement, from the hands that press my thighs upward to the slow push of his thick cock inside me. His mouth comes down to tease mine, but he doesn't settle in for a long kiss. Instead he strokes his lips across my entire face, feathering kisses on my forehead, jaw, cheeks, and eyes. And with each kiss, his cock moves deeper and deeper inside me until finally, finally he's fully seated and a cry of pleasure releases from my throat.

"Shh," he whispers as I moan and whimper. "I'm going to give you everything you need."

CHAPTER 25

Ian has intense command over his body and moves with surety. He knows how to use his body in innumerable pleasurable ways, but I didn't think he could be so tender or so gentle.

"You undo me," he says. The steady pressure of his hips is relentless, so my interest in exploring what he means takes a backseat to discovering how good he can make me feel. When he lowers his body over mine, the rub of his chest hair against my nipples is electric. "I shouldn't be doing this with you. Not now—but I want you too much."

"I want this too," I breathe.

I buck up against him, trying to get closer, but he's in charge of my body. As his one hand rests above my shoulder to brace his frame, he slowly glides in and out of me. He puts his right hand to work caressing the apple of my shoulder and tracing over the slight muscles in my biceps.

It's like he turns every inch of my body into an erogenous zone with his touch and my skin is hardly a barrier between his lips and my nerve endings. The pleasure he's delivering in this slow, measured fashion is indescribable. Even my eyelids feel prickles of sensation as the deep thrusts inside my body push tendrils of sweet delight to the surface.

And everywhere my hands touch I feel the power in his body— from the flex of his shoulders to the straining biceps that bulge next to my cheek. His ass clenches and releases with each downward drive of his hips. There's no urgency in his movements. It is as if he could fuck me forever. As if there is nothing more in this world he wants to do than enjoy the pleasure of dragging his cock along my engorged tissues.

All the while, his eyes bore into mine and everything in my vision is forest green. My whole world is his heavy, muscular body stretched and straining above mine. His eyes are all I see. And his scent is the only thing in my head.

"Your body is so beautiful," he whispers. "There will never be enough time in this life for me to do everything. I won't be done until I kiss every inch. Until I've touched every hollow and rise. All the public places and the secret spots. And then I want to do it all over again."

His words are as erotic as all his touches.

He doesn't allow me to touch him for long. Gathering my wrists in one hand, he pins them above my head.

"Let me give this to you," he whispers, and then covers my mouth with his. As his lips move languidly over mine and his tongue stokes inside my mouth, I shut my eyes and do as he orders. I let go.

I allow the stream of sensation to close over my head and sweep me away. And it *feels so good*.

He grasps my hip to pull me closer and the rhythm of our joining quickens and the spasms of my climax overtake me. My toes curl and my mind is empty of everything but what Ian has placed there. The release that overtakes me floats me onto an ocean of sensation as wave after wave of delirious joy buffets my body. I don't even know if he's come, I'm so wrapped up in what he's given me.

But his eyes have lost that fierce, hungry look and the flush in his cheeks has drained away. The tension of his body has been traded for loose-limbed satisfaction.

"Was it good for you?" I half-joke because it was so good for me that I think I'll cry if this is how it is for him with every woman. *Lie to me*, I think. *Let me believe.*

"Better than I'd ever imagined."

If it's a lie, I can't tell. His eyes are warm and full of affection. With careful hands he covers me with the comforter and strides into the bathroom, but his absence is quick. He returns with a warm washcloth and the bottle of antiseptic lotion. After sliding under the covers, he places the warm cloth between my legs, soothing my sensitive flesh. He tosses the cloth on the ground and spreads another thin layer of lotion on my abraded shoulder.

"I feel really good," I admit. It's like I've been drugged because I don't feel any pain, only the lingering happiness following a euphoric event.

"I'm telling myself that sex is good for you." He smiles and traces a finger down the side of my face. "I think I read somewhere that the endorphins released during orgasm boost the immune system when you're sick." He turns over to place the lotion on the nightstand and clean his fingers off with a tissue. "It's how I'm justifying my incredibly selfish actions."

"If that's you being selfish, I'm afraid that I will literally die if you become altruistic in bed." I stretch a little, letting the sheets and comforter slip down below my chest, and slide my legs along his hairy, masculine ones; the feel of his coarse hair reminds me of how wonderful it felt when his chest rubbed against mine. My nipples respond to the memory by tightening up. Ian growls in appreciation. His hand hovers over my breasts and then drops down to drag the blankets over me.

"I'll have to put that to the test in a few days," he says, tucking my head against his shoulder. I let myself sprawl across his body, my thigh thrown over his and my hand threading through the light sprinkling of chest hairs before moving lower.

"A few days?" I whine. That's not what my body wants to hear. "I thought you said sex was going to heal me quicker."

He chuckles and the sound vibrates inside my own body as if we are connected. "I said endorphins make you feel better, not that they make you heal faster. But I do know that you should be getting some rest, so sleep now."

"All right." My words are slurred because I am feeling drowsy. "But I'm not waiting a few days to feel like this again."

"Noted." And his hard body shakes with suppressed laughter next to mine. It's the most comforting feeling, and when I fall asleep I know it's with a big smile on my face.

◆ ◆ ◆

When I wake up later that day, it takes me a minute to orient myself. The surface I'm lying on isn't my sofa bed nor is it the bed in the Central Towers apartment. As I sit up, the aches and pains in my shoulder and side overtake the pleasant memory of how Ian made sure I went to sleep. On the foot of the bed is a silky robe with a blue geometric pattern; it's lined with burgundy velvet. When I put it on, I realize it must be Ian's robe—it's far too big for me in the arms and the belt can be wrapped around my waist twice. This puts a puzzled smile on my face because I really can't see Ian wearing something like this. If he's not dressed in his suits or jeans, he seems to prefer almost nothing.

I take a moment to check out my injuries in the bathroom. I'd avoided looking before because that made it easier to pretend nothing had happened, but the face in the mirror looks bad. My left eye is encircled by a ring of bruises and there is a swelling on my left temple. When I pull aside the robe collar, I can see my left shoulder is starting to scab over. Under my right breast, there's a purple, yellow, and black bruise that spreads from my side almost to my belly button. It's hard to believe that Ian looked at my body and called it beautiful, because right now I look like I belong in a horror show.

As I step out into the hall, still dressed in only Ian's robe, familiar voices drift up the stairs. My mother's voice stops me in my tracks. I don't want her to see me like this but she calls my name before I can run back into the bedroom and hide.

"Hey, Mom," I say weakly. I wonder if I can magically heal by the time I hit the floor or she'll get tired of waiting for me and leave. Both are fairy tales, but it doesn't stop me from slowing my descent. She gets up and comes to stand at the bottom of the steps, ready to chase me upstairs should I turn tail and flee. There's nothing like facing an angry momma—unless it's trying to explain yourself to a disappointed one.

When I get close, she gasps and covers her mouth. My feeling of dread gets worse when she starts to cry. "This is my fault. You wouldn't be doing stuff for Malcolm if I hadn't gotten sick."

"No, Mom." I fly down the stairs and gather her in my arms. Her bony shoulders and frail body shake against me. My stricken eyes meet Ian's sympathetic gaze and he comes over in response to my silent plea.

"Sophie, she's fine. I had her all checked out." Ian draws her away and sits her down on the sofa. Mom leans into him and instead of looking awkward and uncomfortable, he simply looks down at the top of her head with genuine affection. As I watch them, my heart turns over. Ian could make love to me a thousand times but nothing will ever mean more to me than his steady arm around my distraught mother.

Suddenly I want to cry, not in sadness but relief. So this is how it feels to share a burden with someone. My throat tight, I head for Ian's fancy kitchen to find something to drink. I'm going to need something to sedate myself so I don't fly into his arms and confess my undying love for him.

There's no doubt in my mind that I love him and, worse, I'm not ever going to get over him when he's done with me. But as with my mom, there's no sense in borrowing trouble. I resolve to take one day at a time and enjoy the sheer pleasure of letting him order my life around for a short while.

I can mourn when it's over.

I find a pitcher of water in Ian's refrigerator and white porcelain coffee mugs on an open shelf above a fancy-looking espresso machine mounted into the wall. I fill two mugs and carry them over to the living room, setting one down on the metal side table next to Ian. He gives me a nod and my mom a brisk rub on the back.

"I've a friend who's setting up a security business. He needs some-one to answer phones and keep track of his guys in the field. It's a dispatch-slash-receptionist position. I talked to him about your read-ing and writing issues, and he says that it's fine. Most of your contact will be over the phone. What you can't write, you can dictate—your voice messages will be transcribed by their computer software. He's got some ins with the defense department, so his software is a lot better than anything you're going to find on the market." Ian pins me with a sharp gaze. "It's a real job, Tiny. Not something I made up for you."

Talking about my learning deficiencies makes me uncomfortable. Most of the time it's no big deal because not that many people know about it, and the ones that do never really bring it up. Only Malcolm, and that's when he's trying to piss me off.

"I don't know—" I begin before my mom cuts me off.

"This is perfect." My mom breathes a sigh of relief, and I figure that I'll have any additional discussion about a potential job with Ian in private.

"Great." Ian gets to his feet and heads over to the kitchen as if the conversation is over and my new job is a done deal. "We'll go over to Jake Tanner's office in the morning. For now, I'm going to order some dinner."

My mom jumps up. "Oh no, let me make something. How about shrimp scampi?"

"I don't really have the ingredients for that," Ian replies ruefully. He opens his refrigerator door and even from my place on the sofa I can see it's mostly empty shelves and bottles of energy drinks.

Mom is already up, as if she's going to hit the streets and find a grocery store and drag all the ingredients back. I shoot a worried look at Ian, but he's already on it.

"Let me call Steve to take you over to Chelsea Market." Ian's got the phone in his hand before my mother can say another word. She makes a small face, and inwardly I smile because she's getting a tiny taste of his highness's *my way is the only way* attitude. And it's clear that Ian doesn't even realize what he's doing. This is who he is.

After pressing money into my mom's hands for the groceries, Ian wanders over to sit next to me. I notice that his hands are bruised.

"Boxing without your gloves?" I tease, running a finger lightly over the abrasions.

The side of his mouth quirks up. "Something like that."

"I didn't hear you working out down here." I look over to his gym area, but I don't see a bag. Only free weights, a few mats, and a wall of mirrors.

"I worked off my frustrations elsewhere." It's said glibly, but he won't look me in the eye.

"Your frustrations?" I ask slowly, and then it occurs to me that his knuckles might not be raw because of a gym workout. "Please don't tell me you went back to Brooklyn Heights."

Ian's evasiveness evaporates as he turns to me with a fierce look. "No one will ever raise a hand to you without suffering the consequences. You're mine now. You gave yourself to me, and in order to honor that gift, I protect it." He raises our joined hands and kisses our fingers. "Don't ask me not to because that's one promise I won't give."

I open my mouth to object, but he drags me onto his lap and crushes my protestations under his mouth.

CHAPTER 26

"I've got an appointment this morning, but I'll have Steve swing by after lunch and we can go see Tanner then."

Ian's voice is muffled by the blankets I have over my head. My body aches and there's a tiny man behind my temples bashing a hammer against my skull. After Steve took Mom home last night, Ian and I had gotten into a little tiff because he was stubbornly resistant to having sex again.

"You had no problems earlier," I'd pointed out.

"And I already feel like a heel. Roger'd have my dick in a vise if he knew that I didn't allow you to rest." Ian had shoved a hand through his hair, looking incredibly irritated. It was self-directed, but I still felt like I was somehow at fault. He'd stomped into the bathroom to get ready for bed. It didn't make me feel better that I'd rolled over on my side and was asleep so quickly I didn't even feel Ian climb back under the covers.

He shakes my shoulder lightly, but even that small movement generates a moan of pain. "Take two of these." When he pulls back the covers, I open only one eye. At least I'm not seeing double, only one impeccably dressed male in a pale-blue cotton shirt underneath a light-gray suit coat. His navy-striped tie is unknotted around his neck and his collar is flipped up, signaling that he's all but done with his morning routine.

"Did you shave without me?" I ask, reaching up a hand to stroke his cheek. It's smooth as butter. He rubs his face lightly against my hand

and then reaches down to lift my neck up slowly. He slides two pills into my mouth. Holding me semi-upright with one hand, he presses a glass of what I presume is water against my lips. I take a big gulp and wash down the pills. As soon as he sees me swallow, my head is lowered to the pillows and the covers are pulled up to my chin.

"Yes, but I'm sure I didn't do as good of a job lathering up." He bends close enough for me to smell his aftershave. "You can do me tomorrow."

I crack my eyes open to see him waggling his eyebrows at me with exaggerated lascivious intent. "I have plans for that shaving brush. I thought I'd see how your more sensitive parts respond to it," I say and am pleased when I see his eyes darken and his jaw clench.

"No more of that, or I'll be late and I'll have to whip myself again for taking advantage of you." He presses his lips to my temple and then, for good measure I guess, traces a path over my ear and down the side of my jaw.

"Please," I moan, half in pain and half in arousal, "take advantage of me."

"We'll see how you are after lunch" is his implacable response. Deciding that a retreat is in order so I can enjoy being ravished later, I burrow under the covers.

A ringing brings me out several hours later. It's my phone, and I can see by the display that it's nearing noon. I'm not able to unwrap myself in time to answer, but the missed call message reveals that it's Ian and it's followed thirty seconds later by a voice mail message.

Text me a smiley face if we're still on for the meeting with Tanner. There's an outfit for you in the bathroom.

Sending Ian an emoji isn't too difficult for me. He sends me a return image, one of a smiley face and one of a sandwich. I guess he wants me to eat. The idea of Ian hunting through dozens of little tiny pictures to find a way to remind me to have lunch puts a smile on my face and warmth in my belly. The way he's so easily adapted to my issues with reading and writing is pretty darn incredible. In the past, I'd always avoided telling guys I'd dated I had any problem. It was easy to see that they'd texted, so I'd pick up the phone and call them back, preferring to talk instead of respond with a written message.

The text messages remind me of the one that Richard had sent. I pull up his contact and see several messages, one with a picture attached of him lounging on a rooftop patio and making the "call me" sign with his fingers. I send him back a smiley face for lack of a better response and resolve to speak to Ian about it later.

In the bathroom, there are a pair of wide-legged navy-blue slacks and a white linen top with tiny white raised dots. Next to the clothes are white lace boy shorts and a lovely strapless white lace bra that is banded on the bottom with a one-inch strip of white silk that ends in a bow between my breasts. When I pull it on, I see the bow covers two hooks that hold the bra closed at the front. Again, I'm struck by Ian's thoughtfulness. My left shoulder is still sore and not having a bra strap riding on it all day will make it a lot easier on me.

The shirt has a lovely Peter Pan collar edged in navy and the small puff sleeves end in a cuff with the same trim. I can see my mother's impeccable taste in these clothes. The shoes are nude and have a fairly low heel, which is good for me today. Ian's even provided me with a small clutch. Or his personal shopper has. Either way, it's a nice touch. It's not the most professional outfit, but I've never been to an interview with a security consultant before.

On the counter, there is also an assortment of makeup, all unopened. I'm not as good at this as my mom would be, but I do my best to cover up the bruise around my eye. In the refrigerator in the kitchen I find a wrapped sandwich filled with roasted vegetables and a big portobello mushroom.

When Steve arrives, I'm washing down the last of the sandwich with a glass of water.

"Ready?" His tone is a little gentler today but not by much.

"You have a girlfriend, Steve?" I ask, picking up my clutch and phone to follow him down the stairs to the alley.

"Yeah." He sounds wary, as if I'm trying to trick him.

"Do you ever say more than two-word sentences to her?"

I pull open the front passenger door and slip in before Steve can even respond. Besides, he's busy engaging the lock and a dozen alarms.

He gives me a sour look when he sees where I'm situated. "Passengers ride in the back," he grunts, but I ignore him because I know that he's not going to forcibly remove me. I don't think Ian would like that very much.

"Not this passenger," I respond. Today, we're driving in the Bentley. "Why'd Ian buy this car?"

"Couldn't say," Steve says.

I tap a few of the dials to drive him crazy, but since I'm in no shape for a real fight, I retreat to my seat and let him deal with the Manhattan traffic in peace.

"Where's Tanner's office?"

"Upper West Side."

Again with the near monosyllabic responses. "What's Tanner's business?"

"Security."

I give up. We ride the rest of the trip in complete silence. Steve doesn't even turn the music on.

Jake Tanner's office is the bottom floor of a twenty-foot-wide townhome three blocks off the Hudson River on the Upper West Side near the Museum of Natural History. Steve illegally parks in front of a fire hydrant and tells me to stay put. Despite the fun I had earlier poking Steve, I decide to do what he says because Ian might be watching, and I don't want Steve to get in trouble with his boss. When he helps me out of the car, I thank him nicely, but he gives me an impassive stare in return. I wonder briefly who his girlfriend is and whether he ever smiles at her. Poor girl.

There's a low wrought iron gate that Steve opens, and I follow him down a short flight of stairs. The plaque reading "Tanner Security" is so discreet that I almost miss it. Ian opens the door as we approach. Steve brushes by him, but instead of allowing me through, Ian halts me in the little stone alcove outside the door.

"How are you feeling?" He tilts my head upward and examines my face, taking in my makeup job and my overall appearance.

"Not bad," I admit. "Thanks for the sandwich. And the clothes. My mom has excellent taste."

He smiles at this. "She does indeed."

Then he leans down and takes my mouth with his. I'm surprised by this but find the public affection endearing. There's no tongue involved, simply a firm and sensuous press of his lips against mine for a long minute. It's pleasurable, like being at the beach, the summer sun's rays heating my entire body.

"Mmm," he says, finally lifting his head. "We'll have more of that later."

Thoughtful, generous, but oh so autocratic.

"Is this really acceptable pre-interview behavior?" I ask, opening the door and entering the office. If I stay outside, I'll fall into his arms again.

"I don't really care," he responds. Taking my arm, he leads me past the front office and down a long, narrow hallway. Despite the length, there are only a few doors and no windows. I wonder if they're holding prisoners or something inside those closed-up rooms. Behind a door on the left at the end of the hallway, I can hear the murmurs of Steve and another man. I assume it's Jake Tanner.

Ian knocks and enters when a deep voice says, "It's open."

Jake Tanner is about as big as Steve. He's got dark-brown hair and deep-set brown eyes. Even though it's early afternoon, stubble is darkening his jawline and upper lip. The set of his shoulders is wide, and I have no doubt that people feel safer when he's standing near them.

"Jake Tanner, this is Victoria Corielli." Jake steps forward and offers me his right hand, which I shake firmly. He grips me a bit too tightly, but maybe he can't tell given that it's a prosthetic.

"Nice to meet you," he says.

"Same," I grin and let go of his hand. At his direction, I settle into a chair in front of the desk. Ian sits down beside me while Jake circles around behind the desk to his chair. Steve leans against the wall, arms folded across his chest. I'm not sure who he's guarding in this scenario.

"Do you always conduct interviews with Batman and Robin here?"

Jake looks like he's choking on something but manages to get out, "Does that make me Superman?"

"I don't know. Can you fly?"

"I've got the bionic hand and leg," he says, lifting up his foot and pulling back his pant leg to reveal another prosthetic.

"Then I think you're the Six Million Dollar Man," I answer.

At this he gives a shout of laughter, and Ian squeezes my hand. When I look at him, he's got a huge smile on his face. Even Steve looks a little less grim.

After he's done chuckling, Jake leans across the desk. His fingers entwine, making him look a little like Robocop or some futuristic badass. "Ian's explained you have a disability, and I'm fine with that." He raises his metal fingers and waves them at me. "All I'm looking for is someone who can, using her own methods or systems, keep track of all my guys in the field and what projects they're working on, along with making sure that the calls we get are properly screened. Ian says that you're quick and have a great memory."

"That's right." I nod. "Your reception desk has a black phone with a shoulder rest attached to the back of the handle. There are two modules attached to it with digital screens. I might have trouble reading those. There are two chairs in front of the desk, one is purple and one is blue. You must have bought them thinking that they were the same color. I'd call and have one of them hauled away and replaced with a true match.

Behind the desk, there are three art prints depicting a highly stylized U-boat split into three parts—"

He holds up his hand to stop my recitation. "OK, that's good enough for me. Ian vouches for you. Says that you were doing some stuff in the past that might not pass muster for security clearance but otherwise you're clean. That right?"

"Yes," I nod. I'll have to ask Ian later exactly what he divulged to Jake, but now is not the time.

"Then I'm ready to hire you—but given your face, you can't come back until you're fully healed or the customers are going to think I suck at security services."

With that, the interview is over. Jake stands up, and Steve pushes away from the wall and heads out.

"Thank you for seeing me, Mr. Tanner," I say, shaking his hand again.

"Jake, please." And he smiles at me, revealing perfect white teeth.

Ian cups my elbow and leads me back down the hall. Steve is nowhere to be seen.

"You've got a good one there," Jake says as we reach the front door.

"I know," Ian replies and then places an arm around me, subtly drawing me away from Jake. "And I intend to keep her."

"Don't blame you."

Embarrassed by the talk, I chirp, "Nice to meet you again," and then hastily exit. Combined male laughter follows me out. Outside, I can see that Steve is already in the car, ready to take me back home.

A touch on my elbow makes me turn, and Ian smiles down at me. "I thought you two would be a perfect fit." There's smugness in his voice, but I guess he's entitled.

"Because we both have disabilities?" I ask.

"Because you both understand that others place limitations on you that don't exist." He leads me to the car and opens the back door.

I crawl in and Ian climbs in behind me. "Do you wish I would have said something prior?"

Shaking my head, I say, "No, why would it matter?"

"Why, indeed." He leans forward. "Central Towers."

"Not back to the fuck pad?" I joke lightly, but I'm worried that means he doesn't intend to stay with me.

"No, I figured you would want to be with your mother. Besides, so long as you scream into the pillow, we should be fine."

His careless words are arousing, and I cross my legs to assuage the sudden ache. When I see Ian's dark gaze pinned to my chest, I think that those words weren't so careless after all. But I'm glad, too, that his first thought was to how we'll be managing to have scream-worthy sex again. I want that. Oh how I want it.

CHAPTER 27

"Howe texted me," I share that evening. "I meant to tell you, but I had the accident."

"Someone beating you up is no accident." Ian's face is grim. "An accident is when your bike wheel gets caught in a pothole and you fall down. Getting beat up is assault and battery."

"OK . . ." I can see that he isn't ever going to let this go. "Anyway, I can't read all the messages, but he did send a picture of himself. It's not really incriminating. Just a picture of him drinking. Does he really have a wife? He doesn't ever mention her."

Ian gives me a disbelieving look. "If you were trying to pick up a new girl, would you tell her about the one you have at home?"

"I don't know. I've never had two guys on a string before. Seems complicated." I hand him the phone. He proceeds to read the texts out loud.

Sorry for running off at the mouth about your friend Ian.

No doubt he's a good guy, but if you ever need to talk let me know.

Oh dear. If possible, Ian's grim face has gotten even darker. "What did he say? Is he responsible for your doubts?"

I rub my hand down his arm, a gesture meant to soothe his mood. He captures my hand and brings it to his mouth. But he doesn't kiss it softly. He opens his mouth and bites down on the fleshy bit right under my palm, which sends shock waves right to my core. I gasp and then moan when he licks the bite. "He's poison. Don't forget it."

There's nothing for me to do but nod. Ian presses another kiss to my palm and then returns to reading the rest of the messages.

Thought of you today when I got some flowers delivered to my mom. Realized how convenient bike couriers are. Bet your legs are super strong.

Checking out the rooftop bar at the Kimberly. Hit me up if you're interested in visiting.

After I sent the smiley face, he'd sent another reply.

Only a smiley face? You can do better than that.

Ian tosses the phone aside, looking agitated. He puts his hands on his hips. "I don't like this, Tiny."

"What do you mean?"

"I don't like that he's texting you, flirting with you. That he even knows your name."

"Isn't it a little late for that?"

He shakes his head. "I need to figure something else out."

"Why is it so important to you?" I've never pressed him before. It hasn't been important, but if we're going to build something together . . . there can't be secrets. Not of this magnitude.

He rubs the back of his neck and looks away. At least he's not going to lie to my face. "It's something I'm doing for someone else. Not for me. I don't want to say more."

Underneath his terseness, I sense a darker emotion. Anger, tinged with fear. It's the latter that makes me soften and give in. "Not tonight, then," I say.

He places his hand on my shoulder. "Not tonight." It's not quite a promise that he'll be divulging all his secrets another day, but it's not a closed door either. He releases a small, humorless laugh. "It's something that I haven't shared with another for so long, I'm not sure how to tell the story. Or that you'll still want me when you hear it."

Turning my head, I press my face against the top of his hand, feeling the knuckles against the softness of my cheek. "You can trust me."

"I do."

We allow the silence to absorb the words that we are too afraid to voice to each other—*I love you* and *I need you* and *I can't live without you*—but we feel them. The connection between us is real and we are bound by it even if we don't want to be. It started that day on the street which feels like a lifetime ago. A hook in my heart is attached to a string that winds tighter with each passing minute. I couldn't wriggle loose if I wanted to.

These moments of shared vulnerability are what make me believe that we are equals. That what Ian said before is true—underneath money, fame, class differences, we all bleed the same color. We all hurt the same. We all need, hate, love, cry, *want*.

He gives my shoulder a squeeze, a rueful smile on his face. "Let's go out to eat. I want to look at a restaurant. The owner wants to open another one and is looking for an investor. Come and evaluate it with me?"

My bruises are still visible, but I like that he doesn't want me to hide out inside his loft or the Central Towers apartments. I knock on the bedroom door where Mom is hiding to ask if she wants to accompany us, but she demurs. Despite her recent energy spike, she feels very lethargic and would rather stay inside and watch television. Ian helps her into the living room and settles her on the sofa, fetching a blanket and a cup of tea for her.

I give her a kiss and, to my surprise, so does he. Mom grips his arm to prevent him from straightening up. "Take care of my girl."

"Always."

Their affection and exchange make my throat tight, so I take myself off to get changed before I start weeping happy tears.

After taking a quick shower, I wrestle my hair into a slick ponytail and rub on foundation. I long for the crew at the Red Door Spa but manage to draw on eyeliner and slick on mascara and lipstick.

In the closet, I pull out a pair of wide-legged black silk pants with a lace inset up the outer seam. I pair them with a top that ties at the neck and leaves my entire back bare. Another day without a bra. Ian will either be thrilled or painfully turned on. I hope both.

I slip on a pair of black pumps with red soles, like the ones the saleswoman was wearing. The narrow points of the front pinch my toes, but they look so fantastic I decide a little pain isn't going to kill me. Besides, if my feet were to really hurt, I have an inkling Ian would carry me home.

When I step into the living room, my mother's eyes light up.

"You look gorgeous, doesn't she, Ian?"

I roll my eyes at Mom's obvious attempt to garner compliments. Ian, looking like a sexy beast stepping from the cover of a men's magazine in slim-fitting pants, a matching cream suit coat, and a black shirt unbuttoned so that I can see a tiny smattering of his chest hair, rises from the sofa. "Lovely."

In two strides, he's at my side. "Lickable," he whispers in my ear. His hand spreads on the bare skin of my back, nearly spanning the entire space. Turning me ever so slightly so that my back is out of my mother's view, Ian slides his fingers inside my shirt and presses the tips of them into the plump curve of my breast. "Fuckable."

I stiffen my legs to keep from collapsing. "Night, Mom," I call and walk toward the door and away from Ian's tempting fingers.

"Goodnight, Mom," Ian echoes.

She laughs and it's to that joyful sound that we begin our evening. When we get to the lobby, the gray car is at the curb.

"Hey, Steve," I call out in greeting as I climb in.

He grunts, apparently having used up all his words when he saved me from the crazy drug client. We drive to Catch, a restaurant not far from Ian's loft. It's situated on the second floor of a three-story brick building, and the only way I know that there is even a restaurant is the doorman standing outside. The entrance so unobtrusive it might as well have a secret door. An elevator takes us to the second floor, and the place is packed. I can barely see the bar because of the number of people, and I'm insanely grateful for the height the painful shoes are giving me because everyone in here is super tall or wearing six-inch heels.

Ian places his hand around my waist as we wait for the maître d' to seat us. His arm provides a protective cage, keeping other people out but stoking a slow fire within me. He's having a hard time of it as well. I can feel it in the tenseness of his body and the way his fingers play with the edge of my shirt.

"Did I forget to give you the bras that we bought together?" he mouths against my ear.

"No, you forgot to buy shirts with fabric in the back. Apparently your money isn't enough to buy a complete top—only half of one."

He chuckles and because he's so close to me I feel the puffs of air against my hair, and it's as warm as a caress.

"We'll have to get a new personal shopper who will buy you shirts that have both fronts and backs, because these backless shirts are adversely affecting my ability to be in public with you." He steps even closer, and I feel the hard line of his erection against my hip. I am tempted to drop my hand and grasp him over the wool trousers, but the maître d' approaches.

"Kerr for two," Ian instructs.

The maître d's hair is a mass of curls, and I can't stop staring at them as they bounce atop his head when he bends down to check his reservation book. "It'll be thirty minutes." He gestures us toward the crush at the bar. Ian doesn't move and stares at the Harry Styles impersonator with a raised eyebrow. The look is one that clearly says, "We aren't waiting thirty minutes," and it flusters the host. He brings up his hands but before another word or gesture is delivered, a loud voice from Ian's right interrupts.

"Ian Kerr, so thrilled to have you with us tonight." The voice belongs to a slender, bald man whose pants are so tight I wonder if he can actually sit. He's sockless and the shoes he's wearing are bright blue and pointy. "Travis, what do we have?"

He looks down at the screen and suggests, "Private room?"

Ian shakes his head. "No, I want to see how it runs."

The newcomer nods his head multiple times, so many that he looks like a bobblehead. "Of course, right this way."

He leads us to a corner booth that is big enough to seat several people. I slide in, stopping at the center, and Ian follows, settling right next to me. His arm stretches across the back of the banquette.

"I'm Donatello, and I'm the assistant manager. We were so excited when we received your reservation. The chef has prepared a special degustation for you tonight, and we have an assortment of wines to serve so that you can sample the extensive cellar we keep. Our sommelier will be here shortly to describe the sensory journey we will take you on—"

Ian holds up his hand and Donatello stops talking immediately. "The degustation is fine but, please, no other special treatment tonight. As I said, I want to see how this place runs."

Donatello squeezes his hands together, and his cheeriness seems a little forced. "Of course. Of course."

I want to lean forward and reassure Donatello that Ian's always this high-handed, but all I can do is offer the manager a sincere smile and thank-you.

"He's afraid. Be nice," I warn when the manager wanders off.

Ian looks taken aback. "I didn't realize you wanted a thirty-minute dissertation on the bouquets of wines and their interplay with each little course we'll be served." He raises his hand to bring Donatello back, but I drag it down.

"No, just be nicer. He's trying to impress you."

He sighs, but the next time the manager returns, Ian smiles and says he's doing a nice job. Donatello floats away. "Not so hard, is it?" I tease.

Ian tugs at my ponytail and runs a hand down the ridges of my spine. "I'm already impressed. Let's go home now."

"No way, I put on makeup. Besides, this place is amazing."

I have lived in the city my whole life and I have seen every street and alley, but tonight the whole of fashionable New York is on display. And I can't stop looking. Everyone looks amazing. Perhaps it is the dim light or the reflections of the copper plating on the wall, but there are people looking fabulous in tight suits and even tighter pants and that is just the men. A thin, tall brunette with hair down to her butt is wearing a ball gown skirt and a tube top. Two tables down, a man is wearing a leather vest and a collar.

"I wish you could see yourself right now. Your eyes are so big," he whispers into my ear, and the sound travels all the way to my belly.

"Tiny," he says, and I can sense that he wants me to look at him. His hand reaches out, strokes my jaw, and then turns my face so that we're looking at each other. We're so close on this banquette that I could lean forward and be kissing him. The thought makes me lick my lips, and Ian's gaze drops from my eyes to my lips. When he flicks his gaze back upward, it's filled with lust and tenderness. If it wasn't for the waiter, who coughs to get our attention, I would have grabbed Ian's head and dragged him under the table with me.

I try to interject some distance between us and gather some decorum. The waiter, in a white-buttoned coat and gray pants, sets down two porcelain soupspoons filled with tuna carpaccio, a sliver of potato, and a shitake mushroom.

"I don't even know your middle name," I blurt out.

"Ian Kincaid Kerr." A hand curls around the back of my neck while his other hand raises the spoon to my mouth. I swallow it down and try to hold back the moan of delight. "That good, eh?" He swallows his own bite and winks at me.

"Sounds really Scottish," I say faintly. Another dish comes by and Ian feeds that to me as well.

"Ach, dinnae ken, my wee lassie, by my accent?"

I giggle. "That's pretty terrible."

"Well, now you know I'm bad at accents. How about you?"

"I've never tried speaking in an accent, so let's assume I'm terrible too." His hand is so warm that I want to rub my face against his wrist. The way that his body is canted protectively around me makes me feel like we are in a private room, all alone. The whole of my body is liquefied by the way he's feeding me each bite of food, his hand never moving from behind my neck. Despite the crowded restaurant and the incessant chatter of the patrons, we are in a bubble of leather, delicious food, and heady wine. It's intoxicating.

"So I should have invited you to dinner rather than drinks."

We both look up to see Richard Howe standing there with a woman on his arm—an older woman. Her age is indeterminate. She's in that New York socialite age range between mid-30s and late 50s. Plastic surgery can create a façade of youth that masks one's true age for many years. However old she is, the woman is beautiful. She has a delicate, fragile air.

Her body is thin, and she wears a delicate lace sheath that emphasizes her fine bone structure. Around her face, expertly coiffed golden hair falls in soft waves. But the translucency of her hands reminds me of my mother and, ultimately, it is those that give her away. There are age spots, which she's tried to disguise with a multitude of rings, and the backs of her hands show prominent veins, thin skin, and dots of pigmentation.

Under my awkward gaze, her hands curl and she ducks them underneath the table. I give her a tentative smile, but my untoward attention to her hands has immediately marked me as the enemy.

"Wife." Ian mutters in my ear. Tossing his cloth napkin on the table, he half rises to shake Richard's hand and then his companion's.

I hide my disgruntlement at the interruption behind a big—but fake—smile for Richard and his wife.

Richard leans over the table. "It's hell getting a table here, isn't it? You don't mind if we join you?"

It's not a question because he's already sitting down, drawing his wife with him.

"Cecilia Montgomery Howe of the shipping Montgomerys." Richard introduces us, and he sounds very smug when he rattles off her familial business as if he is personally responsible for her family's success.

"Nice to meet you," I say and shake the limp hand that she extends toward me in greeting as if I'm supposed to kiss it.

Ian's body is stiff behind mine, but his response is all ease and smiles. "Hello, Cecilia." Apparently everyone knows everyone else. Except for me, of course. I'm the new element in the old-time social scene. I shift awkwardly. Ian settles back, drawing me with him and putting space between Richard and me. "Did your reservation fall through?"

Richard shakes his head mournfully. "Cecilia and I were going to have dinner at Prospero, but I heard the executive chef has been ill for a month so we thought we'd head down here and try something new."

"No reservation," Cecilia gripes spitefully.

At this complaint, Richard hangs his head. "I know. Stupid of me."

"My god, how can I even eat with *that* looking at me." Cecilia's whine of protest causes all of us to swivel toward a gorgeous woman whose ass is so fine in her spandex bandage dress that I'm envious. "It looks like she's stuffed cotton in her cheeks. Poor girl. Can you imagine sleeping with someone like that? You'd never be able to shut your eyes. It would be like having a horror show under your sheets."

"She's got an amazing body," I counter, but when I get the attention of the two I regret speaking up immediately.

"It's a hard body," Richard agrees, and Cecilia glares at him.

The rest of the evening is spent eating small bites of food brought to our table every ten minutes or so while Ian and I are treated to an unending critique of nearly everyone in the restaurant from Cecilia, who clearly thought that Richard would join her.

The foreign language–speaking table is too loud, she complains.

"Internationals, what can you do?" Richard grins at me as if we're sharing a secret laugh. Cecilia scowls again and then quickly rearranges her face as if emotions cause aging.

Cecilia remarks that the boobs on the model wearing the tank top are much too large. "She must be a prostitute," Cecilia says. "No runway is going to let her walk."

After a while even the delicious food loses its appeal under this wearying critique. Each time she makes a comment, she looks at Richard for support. He only gives her a pained smile and then, when he thinks she isn't looking, he shrugs at me as if to say he doesn't have any control over her attitude.

When she isn't talking and he isn't sneaking looks at me, his eyes are everywhere. On the stark expanse of skin that the model shows every time she stands up to adjust her tube top. On the nearly naked bottom of another patron who is wearing hot pants and high heels.

"Is the food not to your liking?" Ian eats his dishes and mine because my appetite is gone.

"Too rich," I say, but I see understanding in his eyes.

Finally, when the last item is served and coffee is being distributed to Ian and me, with two after-dinner port wines for Sissy—that's what they call her—and Richard, Ian asks Richard what he's doing at Catch. "It seems like such a coincidence."

He laughs. "Not at all. I heard you were interested in investing in Sean Price's new food venture and that you were down checking out his business. I guess eating at Le Cirque every night gets tiresome?"

Ian shrugs. "I live down here. I haven't eaten at Le Cirque for months. Too far uptown for me."

Richard makes a *tsking* sound. "Still in that warehouse. That seems so déclassé. But maybe you've always had a little of the commoner in you."

"Always," Ian replies dryly, but beside me he is vibrating like a speaker box turned too loud. His hand has a vise grip on my thigh. "Some would blame it on my mother. She wasn't even from the city."

Richard's eyes dart toward me and then Ian and back again. He laughs and wipes his mouth twice. Obviously nervous, he taps his fingers against the side of his bottle. "I didn't know your mother well. Most of my dealings were with your father."

Cecilia scrunches up her nose at Ian. "This type of conversation is very low class. Perhaps we could move on."

"Of course, Sissy," Ian says smoothly. Underneath the table, his fingers are almost bruising me. Whatever wrong Richard Howe has inflicted upon Ian, it is serious and powerful enough to cause him to lose his vaunted self-control, both at the Aquarium and then here. We're able to finish dinner together, but it might be the longest meal I've ever sat through. Despite the chef's culinary wizardry, I ate almost nothing.

CHAPTER 28

"That was unpleasant," I say when we get back to Central Towers. As expected, Mom is asleep. She can't make it past eight in the evening most nights. "I don't understand how he can make a play for me one night and then show up with his wife another."

"He's testing you. He wants to know if having a wife is going to be a problem. I bet in a couple of days, you'll get more texts."

He drums his fingers on the side of the sofa as he has a glass of wine to unwind. That was my suggestion. He's agitated, and I'm afraid he's not going to be able to sleep tonight.

"At least it's just texts."

"For now," he says sourly, his hand gripping tightly around the stem of the glass. A vision of him throwing the tumbler against the wall at the Aquarium flits through my mind. He catches me eying the glass and downs the contents in one swallow. Standing up, he pulls me to my feet.

"Let's table this for now. It's been far too long since I've had a taste of you."

He makes love to me as if the devil is riding him. His hands are rough and possessive. He's in the grip of some madness, but the need in his eyes is obvious and unmistakable. Whatever he needs, I want to give him.

"I want you," he growls.

"You have me," I say, "in whatever way you need me."

In the aftermath of the storm, with the sheets tossed on the floor and the pillow wet from stifling my cries of completion, we lie entangled with each other. The tension that started building from the minute Howe showed up still hasn't left him, even after the sex.

"Won't you tell me?" I ask, stroking the sweat-soaked skin of his back. "I want to understand. If this," I gesture between us, "is truly something that matters to you, then you can't leave me in the dark."

He's silent for so long that I believe he's fallen asleep. But his sex-roughened voice interrupts the quiet.

"Four old-moneyed families sent their sons to Harvard. My father was one of them. Richard's father, Edward Howe, was another. The two others aren't important for this story. They are friends, business partners. When Papa Howe's son Richard needs a job, he asks my dad for a favor. But Richard's expensive lifestyle—and I don't know if it was drugs, gambling, shitty investment decisions, prostitutes, or what—leads him to embezzle money.

"My father covers it up, but then the market crashes and he's leveraged to shit. The embezzlement is discovered and the blame is pinned on Dad. Howe won't come forward. My dad has a heart attack and dies which results in us losing all of our possessions from foreclosure and bankruptcy. My mom is unable to hold her head up, and even if she could, she didn't have the money to play. She takes us to New Jersey, where she hooks up with a gambler. He gets her addicted and soon . . ." His voice trails off.

"Like Malcolm's mother," I say softly.

"You know, then?"

I nod. "Yeah, for a while. I mean, that's why he deals, and I guess it's why he's in with the other stuff. He's always bailing her out, but the addiction is too strong."

"My mother was never meant to have to support herself. Addictions use you up fast. She was doing . . . stuff . . . to get money. Anything."

His voice is strained. "I was ashamed of her. Pretended I didn't know her. Then I hated her. Finally . . . I felt relief, and that was the most guilt-inducing emotion of all."

Curling my body around him, I stroke every inch of his body I can reach, as if to protect him from his memories.

He burrows his forehead into the side of my neck. His voice is muffled, but his words are clear. "She got arrested for solicitation when I was fifteen. By that time, I was working, hustling on the boardwalk, and then taking every cent I had and playing poker in the casinos. I easily passed for twenty-one because of my size, my scruff. I was earning money, not as fast as I would have liked and not in as big amounts as I had wanted, but I'd had to lie low, not draw attention to myself.

"I was saving money, socking it away, thinking that I'd buy us a nice beach house and send my mom to an expensive clinic and it'd all be good. But it was too late. She didn't last more than a night on the inside. She asked me to bring her something, a Hermès scarf my dad had given her on their fifteenth wedding anniversary. Like a dumb shit, I brought it. She kissed me and then I left. Later, I learned she'd bribed a guard with sex to let her bring the scarf into her cell."

He doesn't have to finish.

"I'm so, so sorry." I choke back the tears, knowing he won't welcome them.

"Yeah, me too," he sighs heavily and then, to my surprise, he turns into my embrace and allows me to give him comfort.

CHAPTER 29

Seeing me with Ian again only renews Richard's pursuit. He sends me text messages that I have voice transcribed or Ian reads to me. Afterward, the muscle in his jaw always clicks. And invariably, he feels the need to touch me, usually someplace very intimate.

But other than this texting game I'm playing with Richard, which hasn't progressed beyond mild flirtation, nothing truly scandalous, my life is pretty good.

Mom is doing really well these last couple of weeks, but her doctor has advised against going out too frequently. Her immune system is very low and he says that even a cold could be dangerous. Tonight Ian orders dinner from Le Cirque to be delivered to Central Towers in lieu of going out.

"Tiny says your parents have passed."

"Yes. My father died of a heart attack when I was thirteen, and my mother passed away when I was fifteen."

"I'm so sorry. You were required to assume responsibility far too early."

"It's what made me," Ian replies, shrugging as if having to spend the latter part of his teen years on his own was normal and easy.

"I hope you won't take this the wrong way, but I'd like to give you a bit of advice. Not about Tiny, of course. I wouldn't presume to go there. But life advice."

"Sure," he squeezes my hand to let me know that the inquisition and the advice don't bother him.

"Life is fleeting, ephemeral almost. Don't waste a minute, even a second, on anything that's not important. And if you do have something important, do everything to hang on to it. Don't assume that tomorrow will bring you something better. Treasure the now."

"I will, Sophie. Thank you for caring enough to share with me."

She flushes with pleasure at the compliment, and I glow inside at how he understands that it is because she loves me—and perhaps because she is beginning to care for him—that she is brave enough to voice her concerns.

On the Sunday before her chemo day, I take her to the Frick Museum. She says she wants to spend time with me. It is our favorite museum, and not because they have a policy of "paying what you wish" for admission on Sundays. Today, I drop in a fifty to cover all the other visits when we paid nothing. The Frick is a treasure chest of a museum, only two floors with everything from Fragonard—my mother's favorite—to Whistler. We walk around the museum, arms clasped around each other, and end our tour in the atrium.

The fountain is working, the water quietly gurgling over the stone bowls and into the pool below. The foliage helps to soften the stone walls and the tall pillars. The atmosphere and the glass ceiling are so calming that the stone benches actually feel comfortable despite their hard surfaces.

"It's hard to believe someone lived in this place. Can you even imagine having a reflecting pool in your living room?"

"I can't imagine the upkeep."

Then we smile at each other because this is the same conversation we have at the end of every visit.

"I'm so glad that you have Ian," she says.

"I'm not sure that I have him so much as I'm being dragged behind one of his fancy cars as he speeds toward some destination only he knows."

"I'll tell you one thing I've learned in the last three years, and that is you need to seize opportunities for happiness when they present themselves to you. Don't close this one out. Give him a chance." She squeezes my hands and glances out the window to the tops of the trees of Central Park. "I don't want you to end up alone."

"I won't." I lean over and kiss her on the cheek, ignoring the paper-thin feel of her skin. "I have you."

Steve is idling illegally on Fifth Avenue when we depart.

"Not having to wait for a taxi or bus is certainly worth extra effort." Mom winks at me. Steve gets out and helps Mom into the car, carefully propping up her feet on the extended leg rest. The venture out drained all her energy, and she's asleep before we hit Midtown. He must have called ahead because Ian greets us at the curb.

"Thanks, Steve. I'll see you in the morning."

It takes both of us to help my mother up to the apartment. He shoots me a worried look as he supports her slim weight, but I refuse to acknowledge the concern in his eyes.

"She's fine," I mouth to him.

"Lie down with me, Tiny," she says when we step into her bedroom. I ignore Ian's worry and help Mom into bed.

Using the remote, I shut the drapes and roll onto my side so I can cuddle with my mom as we did when I was a child. Because it was the two of us, we often slept together even as I grew older. Lying here with her now, though, I feel as if I'm the protector and she's my child.

"I love you, Mommy," I whisper, laying my hand on her chest.

"Love you too, dear. More than all the stars in the sky." Her cool hand covers mine, lightly gripping it as she drifts off into sleep. The steady, even sound of her breathing is comforting, and I let my cares drift away, cocooned in the expensive comforter inside this lush apartment and holding my mother's hand while my lover waits for me.

It is everything I could have hoped for.

But while I sleep, a chill settles over us, waking me. My mother's hand is ice-cold and there is blood coming out of her nose, dripping onto the pillowcase. There's a dark, ugly pool on the side of her face.

"Ian!" I scream, shaking my mother but she is non-responsive. "Iannnnn!"

He's at the doorway and then at my side.

"I already called 911." He has the phone in his hand.

He slides a finger into her mouth and then tips her head back to clear her airways. Then he blows into her mouth. Once. Twice. He pumps her chest, one hand folded over the other. Blowing and pumping over and over as I grip my hands to my mouth to keep the screams inside me.

I don't register the ambulance arriving or the EMTs' urgency as they prepare my mother for her trip to the hospital. I only notice the sounds. The shrill whistle of the sirens as we speed uptown toward the hospital. The digital beeps from the machine. The thud of the crash cart. It's a macabre symphony playing a funeral march. And the drumbeat that I want to hear never comes.

I know she is gone before anyone comes to the waiting room. I suppose I knew it when we were at Frick and she was telling me good-bye. I hadn't wanted to acknowledge it was good-bye, so I had shushed her. I wasn't ready to hear her talk of death, even though that was what she needed—whether it was to prepare herself or me, I'm not entirely sure.

She'd been ready to go as soon as she'd learned her remission state was over. She had told me so on the stairs after the first appointment with Dr. Chen.

I can't make it.

And maybe if Ian hadn't come along, she would have clung on longer for me, but she was ready and saw his entrance into our lives as a sign that I wouldn't be alone.

I can't really begrudge her that. Not when it was her suffering that would end. My pain is a selfish thing. I realize that now.

But oh, my heart is empty. The sun has been snuffed out, and inside me there are only vacant hallways and rooms through which the wind gusts endlessly from one barren corner to another. The frost is building up, the vortex of feeling being wiped away. And in the void, I am cold, but the piercing pain is gone. And for now, that is good enough.

I remain numb throughout the parade of nurses and doctors who have come to say they are sorry. For what? Not saving her? It's with little interest that I watch Malcolm and Ian pretend to get along while arranging for my mother's interment. I am able to tell Ian that my father is buried in Flushing Cemetery. He stops bothering me about the details after the third day. I dress myself for the funeral in a black knee-length shift that Ian must have bought for me. It's sunny out, which makes me weirdly offended—as if the clouds should be crying instead of smiling. But I'm not crying either. I can't. I'm afraid if I start, I'll never stop.

"I'm sorry, Victoria." Malcolm's mother has arrived. She looks worn-out and old—far older than her fifty-some years. The skin under her eyes is dark and wrinkled. Her face is heavily lined and she smells like a tar factory. I feel nothing but pity for her.

"Thank you," I say. It is the first of a thousand thank-yous I dispense that day in return for the thousand I'm sorrys given to me. Through it all, Ian stands by my side. He's my spine today. Without him, I wouldn't be upright.

I wish I had something inside myself to give to him. At the end of the service and after the burial is over, I find that even with Ian beside me, I cannot stand. He catches me before I collapse on the dirt. Cradling me in his arms, he carries me to the Bentley. I'm glad. I think of the Maybach and its little folded leg rests as my mother's car, and I wouldn't be able to ride in it today—maybe not ever.

"I can't help you with Richard anymore."

"Forget it. It's unimportant."

It's not, but I can't bring myself to care at the moment. I want to stop caring about everything right now.

CHAPTER 30

That night, Ian draws me into his arms but makes no effort to have sex with me. I wonder if he'll leave soon. If I conjured up my future mate, he'd be someone who drove a delivery truck like my dad. Or maybe he'd be a construction worker. Some kind of blue-collar guy who didn't make much money and spent his time watching the Mets and cursing the Jets. Someone like Malcolm, without the drug dealing and the pimping. Ordinary. And if I were asked what kind of woman Ian would end up with, I'd say rich, beautiful, smart. A lawyer or a banker. Or the daughter of some super-smart investor. Not a semi-illiterate, learning disabled bike courier.

It's not a reality I'm ready to face, so I sleep for a very long time where the painless void awaits me.

After we bury Mom, I don't want to get out of bed. I don't want to eat, dream, work. I especially do not want to make love to Ian. I think I don't want to be happy. I know I don't, because I feel mocked by the spring days of late April and May and their nonstop sunshine.

May. All around me there are advertisements for Mother's Day. It's best if I don't leave the apartment. On Sunday morning, Ian wants to take me out, but I refuse. Instead I lock myself in the bedroom and stare at the wall. I'm empty inside. I don't have anything to give him, not anymore.

When I hear the front door of the apartment open and then close with Ian's leaving, I get up. I pull on a pair of tennis shoes and shorts and a ratty T-shirt. Downstairs, the concierge produces my bike and I get on and ride. I ride down Fifth Avenue, swerving in and out of traffic as if the cars are traffic cones and I'm taking a road test. I give a cop the finger when he honks at me, but I'm able to speed away before he can catch me. His police car is stuck in Mother's Day traffic and my bike is too nimble for him. I ride north along Harlem River Drive and up the Saw Mill River Parkway until the city falls away and there's nothing but long stretches of pavement and forest. I cross over and head east toward North Street and then down south.

I keep riding until my legs feel like jelly and the sweat is soaking my shirt and shorts. The burn in my body is easing the ache in my chest, so I keep going until I'm not even conscious of what my body is doing. Until I can't see for the veil of mist or water sluicing down my face, obscuring my vision. Until I fall off my bike, crashing into the sidewalk. I collapse then puke up what little I have inside me.

I lose track of how long I lie there. Maybe it is only seconds before I feel the cool touch of his hand. Another moment and he's drawing a cloth across my face, wiping my mouth.

He pulls me into his lap and places the mouth of a bottle at my lips. I sip or he forces me to drink. It is all one and the same now. I allow him to cradle me like a baby because I'm too spent physically and emotionally to move.

We sit there on the edge of the road, a tall chain-link fence at our backs and squat brick apartment buildings facing us. The sound of our breathing—mine harsh and labored, his even but strained—is broken only by the occasional sound of tires crunching the asphalt. Out here, away from the core of the city, traffic is light this early Sunday morning.

"It's Mother's Day," I say finally.

"I know."

"How did you find me?"

"I followed you."

I roll my head to the side and see a shiny sports car parked on the side of the road.

"No Steve today?"

"No, just me."

Not ready to address the big issues, I continue to make small talk. "I didn't know you could drive. I can't."

"You could learn."

"Maybe." Driving sounds interesting. What would it be like to handle four wheels instead of just two? Then another thought occurs to me, and my brief spike of enthusiasm sputters out. "I wouldn't be able to pass a written test."

"They probably have oral versions," he says mildly. We sit like that for a few more minutes until I decide that our positions are too ridiculous for words. I'm not a child, but when I push away, I find I have little strength.

With a sigh, I ask, "Can you help me sit up?"

He does and I realize where I am. The Flushing Cemetery. Without prompting, Ian helps me to my feet. The entrance is just around the corner. He places an arm around my waist and slowly we walk into the cemetery. Ian and I aren't the only ones here. There are others leaving flowers for their mothers, and somehow even that makes me feel a little less alone. It takes us several minutes to walk toward the back, where I find the gravesite. A black granite headstone declares the dates of birth and death for both my parents. A shiver creeps up my spine. Is there room between the two of them for me? I want to lie down and pull the sod up like a blanket and just sleep forever.

But the arm around my waist is hard as iron and it is holding me back. I struggle, just slightly, but the arm doesn't move.

"You aren't alone."

His gruff words whisk across the surface and then hover there. Will I reject them or allow them in?

"Will you let me comfort you, Tiny?"

"I'm so sad." It's a non-answer, but the only truth I have right now.

"It's OK to be sad."

"I'm just afraid that I can't give you enough anymore."

He presses a soft kiss against my temple. "I'll take anything from you as long as it's something."

We stand there for a long time. I search the grave for signs of my mom, but I don't hear her in the wind. I rub my hand across my chest but I don't feel her there either.

"She's still there, even if you don't feel her today," he tells me. "One day, you'll realize how much of her you still carry with you."

He's speaking with a voice of experience and I want to trust him, to believe in everything he says, because what's the alternative? To feel empty forever?

I lay my head against his chest. "When will I be done grieving?"

"No matter how long it takes, I'll be with you."

CHAPTER 31

Two weeks after Mother's Day, Ian announces we are going out of the city.

"We're going on a field trip today," he says.

"Fine," I answer. There are plenty of people in the city who never learn to drive. It seems like an exotic task, and Ian is a master at it. I get a silly pleasure watching him control this big machine. "You look good behind the wheel."

He smiles and shifts into another gear when the engine begins to rev. His large hand rests on the manual shifting mechanism, the light glinting off the hairs on the back of his hand. A feeling stirs between my legs and I squirm, squeezing my thighs together. The motion causes Ian to give me a sharp look, one so full of hunger and desire I gasp.

The hollow space inside me begins to melt under that fierce glance. His hand drifts off the gearshift to my thigh. Giving me a slight squeeze, he says, "Driving will be one more thing I can teach you."

The warmth of his palm seeps through my jeans and spreads down my leg and up my thigh. My fingers begin to tingle at the thought of caressing his forearm and solid biceps. Unconsciously I begin to rub that forearm, and his fingers move up higher on my thigh until they are nearly resting against the center seam between my legs.

I had forgotten how warm he was, how big his hands were, how much I *want* him. "You've been very patient with me," I say softly.

"I'd wait forever for you, Tiny," he responds. "If you don't believe it now, you will in fifty years when you're still with me."

I suck in my breath at the meaning behind that declaration. Nothing more is said between us until we arrive in Connecticut. He drives toward Long Island Sound and stops at a long driveway that is blocked by a short gate—more for looks than security. A flick of a button and the gates begin to slowly open.

At the end of an alley of trees, a two-story white chateau-like structure with a blue roof appears.

"Fifteen thousand square feet of house. Eleven acres of land. Looks over the Sound. Has its own private beach. No boat landing, though. Water's too shallow." Ian begins to itemize the features of the property.

"Do I want to know how many properties you own in the city?"

"This isn't in the city."

With that, he climbs out of the car and comes around to open the door for me. I step out and into his arms.

"You're not the only one who is alone in this world. You're not the only one with dreams that include falling into bed at night with someone by their side. I want a family too, but I want it with you. I can't give you your mother back, but I can love you as fiercely. Tiny, I love you. Be my wife. Let's start our own family."

He doesn't wait for an answer.

"This place," he waves his hand. "I bought this because I wanted to settle down, to start a family. I saw it and knew I had to have it. When I saw you on the street that day, I was done for. Kicked in the gut. Whatever metaphor you want to use. I saw you and that was it. I had to have you."

"This house is huge. It's way too big for a bachelor," I say with wonder. I'm trying to process everything, but I feel winded . . . and almost joyful.

"Do you know why I was at the wig shop the day we first met?"

"No."

He snorts. "Her sister is a Realtor. Has been my Realtor for years.

She came to me and asked me to lend the owner a sum of money. I complied, it worked out. But on the day that we saw each other, I was meeting Margaret to put an offer in on this property. When I saw you, I knew right away that you belonged here and that you had to belong to me. I've wanted to bring you here for weeks but figured it would be too soon and you would be frightened off. Like a scared bunny. But you aren't anymore. Are you scared?"

"I am, a little." I press my hand against my heart. "How did you survive this at age fifteen? All alone?"

"Because I must have known that someday I'd meet you, fall in love with you, and you would need me."

He pulls me against him and kisses me then. Or I kiss him. We stand there, our bodies fused together and our mouths expressing all the words that are too scary and intimate to say out loud.

Breaking away, he says, "Your sorrow has weighted you down."

"But you're easing it. "

"This is our home. We'll fill it with happiness."

"What about Richard Howe?"

"Let it go," he answers.

"Easy as that? You've planned for this for almost two decades."

"Because I had nothing else, Tiny." He draws some of my hair back away from my face, dragging his fingers down to my jaw and tipping my face upward—willing me to understand.

Alone, parentless, friendless. The things that powered Ian to go from poor person to billionaire were revenge and hate, but somewhere along the line he was able to let them go.

"It was you, Tiny. Seeing you with Richard made me realize that there were things I could hate more than Howe. Like seeing another man's hands on you. Seeing you flirt, talk, engage with another man. I can't have a future if I'm always looking behind. Let's look forward together."

"Take me home, then."

We spend a couple of hours poking around the house. The interior furnishings are a weird mix of old world and ultra-modern. "It can all go," Ian says when I make a face at the black leather sofa situated in the middle of a sky-blue reading room.

Outside, the grounds are beautifully manicured, complete with a pool and tennis court. The lawn is so big that it takes us twenty minutes to get to the beach. The waves lap lightly against the coarse sand.

"Mom would have loved it here," I sigh.

He places an arm around me. "I know."

On the drive home, I don't have much to say. I'm drinking it all in. The house. Ian's declaration of love. His ringless proposal.

Before bed, Ian draws me into the bathroom.

"Let's take a steam shower," he suggests. "You can make it smell good. There's a little thing down here where you pour something in and then the heat makes it aromatic."

"Aromatherapy."

"Right." He rummages around looking for something in the vanity. Triumphantly, he holds up a small brown bottle that looks about five years old. The letters on the label have started to rub off. "Eucalyptus."

He pours a few drops onto a tiny metal dish only about two feet off the floor and then taps the LCD screen inside the shower. A low humming noise starts and steam pours into the shower space. Soon, the entire bathroom is redolent with eucalyptus. He sits me on the vanity and leans between my legs as we wait for the shower to fill up with steam.

"What do you think?"

"I can't believe you still have that bottle. It looks like it was sold during the Stone Age."

"I'm a big collector of things."

"Am I a thing?"

"No, you're my heart."

Right there in the steam-filled bathroom, we make love. I kiss, stroke, and lick his every available body part. In his embrace, I try to show through each touch the truth of my love and that he holds my heart too, although it is bruised. The words I can't say just yet, I try to express through my touch. Those words are weighted with too much sorrow.

As he carries me, damp and worn out, to the bed, I whisper, "Yes, I'll marry you and be your wife."

"Oh, Tiny." He kisses me again. "You'll never regret it."

When I get up, the bed is empty. I hear music downstairs, a woman singing in Italian. Opera. Shrugging on a blue silk robe from the bottom of the bed, I float out. I find Ian leaning against the unlit fireplace with a drink in his hand. His eyes are fixed on a leather box with a big silver clasp on the table.

I settle onto the sofa, tucking my legs underneath me, and stare at the box.

"My mother's things are in there. Her wedding rings, a few pieces of jewelry she hadn't sold. The clothes and other things I walked away from, but I packed this all up and haven't ever looked at it again."

"Do you want me to open it?"

"Would you? Or is it too painful?"

"No." Even if it is painful, I'd do this for him. After all he's done for me.

The box is lined in a beautiful white silk with a classic chain pattern. There are a few cards—anniversary mementos—and an envelope labeled "Ian."

"It's for you," The envelope is yellowed and the ink is faded but still visible. The letters aren't perfectly formed, as if the hand that drew them out wasn't stable.

"I can't read it." He shakes his head and pushes away from the fireplace. There is only one sheet of notebook paper in the envelope; it's soft in my grip. Because he's not ready, I read it to myself. It takes me awhile to decipher all the letters. It might be the most reading I've done since high school.

Dear Ian,

I'm so sorry. For everything. I failed you time and

again because I'm weak. Already at fifteen, you are the man your father and I had hoped you would become. No, you are something else. Something better. And if I remain with you, tainted and tarnished, it would only diminish you.

I bite my lip to prevent my scoff. Selfish is what this is. I don't want Ian reading it, but I must finish.

I tried to redeem us. I tried so hard, but he laughed. He laughed at your father. He laughed at me. He said that your father shouldn't have been so soft. That he did him a favor by taking him out as early as he did before someone else ate him up.

When I asked him to help us, even after he turned your father down, I hadn't realized what I was giving up. One night was all. One night. But the help never arrived and the one night was for naught and it has haunted me ever since.

I saw him then at the Casino Grand. Flush and ruddy-faced. He apologized. Said that he had been young and brash. He offered to make amends. All I needed to do was give him one more night. This time he did pay me. But he laughed again, and I hear him still, every time I close my eyes.

You will be alone, but it is better this way. Better for both of us. I am no longer an anchor but a heavy weight dragging you into the dark depths. Be free. Live for all of us.

Your loving mother,
Joanna

Carefully, I fold the letter and place it back into the envelope. My hands are shaking with the effort not to rip it into a million shreds so that Ian will never be able to piece it together. Across the room, he is grim-faced. His glass is full once more. He must have filled it while I was reading. He tosses back half of it, his face marked by utter despair.

"You know," I croak.

He nods, drinks the rest of the whiskey. In two strides, he's at the sofa, pulling the letter out of my hands. "It was with the scarf when I went to pick up her things."

I don't say "I'm sorry" because those are the two most ineffectual words in the English language. They won't take his pain away or bring back his mother. When he said he was alone in this world, I didn't realize how deeply the ache of isolation went for him.

I am overwhelmed by the extent of his devotion to me and his willingness to sacrifice to make me happy.

But it is too much.

Far too much.

The scales will never be even.

I reach out my hand and pull his head into my lap.

"Turn out the light, Tiny." The words are tight and clipped.

I reach over and the light is swallowed by the shadows. Hugging him against me, I cry the tears he won't release. This matter with Richard Howe is not finished. For all the times that Ian has said he wants to look forward, this horrible truth will always hold him back. Hold us back.

"Don't leave me," Ian shudders, soundless emotion shaking his frame.

"I won't. Not ever." And then I'm finally able to say the words. "I love you, Ian Kerr. More than anything."

TO BE CONTINUED . . .

ACKNOWLEDGMENTS

After finishing up with *Last Breath*, I sat down to write a completely different book than *Losing Control*, but when I typed, Ian Kerr and Tiny Corielli were what appeared on the page rather than the other characters I had planned. But even as I wrote out the first chapter, it was more just for fun than anything. It wasn't ever going to be a book.

Instead, I emailed the story, chapter by chapter, to a couple of friends. Three, to be exact. And after every chapter, each one of those people—Daphne, Michelle, and Katy—kept emailing me back wanting more. And if I missed a day without emailing an update about what was happening with Ian and Tiny, I would get impatient responses.

So I kept writing it until there was a somewhat complete story. But then it had to be put together into a book, and I suffered some anxiety over whether it was good enough. During that period of indecision and uncertainty, there were two people who kept me sane and read the story in several incarnations, multiple times.

Cece Carroll and Michelle Kannan, your endless patience with me can never be thanked enough.

Then there are my writer friends, Meljean Brook, Jessica Clare, Katy Evans, and Elyssa Patrick. They deserve a special thank-you because they listen to me moan on a near daily basis about how I'm not going to finish my project or how I'm going to meet my writing goal only to end the day with an email about how I spent the entire day online looking at cat GIFs.

Daphne is a true treasure of a friend. I love our weekly chats and our passion for food. I appreciate her willingness to listen to my crazy ideas and her levelheaded responses, particularly when I'm going down the wrong path.

I love that I'm surrounded by amazing women, and Lisa Schilling Hintz of The Rock Stars of Romance is one of those incredible people. She has seemingly endless energy and is an amazing promoter of good books. I count myself very lucky to be able to send her a Facebook message at any time of the day or night. What's even better is that we can chat about important things other than books, like which pair of shoes with the red soles she's buying next.

Lastly and most importantly, I have to give thanks to my dear family. My loving husband, who doesn't seem to mind when I lock myself away for hours to write, and my sweet daughter, who patiently waits until I stumble out on the weekends, just before bed, to hear about her day. I love you both so much.

ABOUT THE AUTHOR

Jen Frederick is the *USA Today* bestselling author of *Unspoken*, part of the Woodlands series. She is also the author of the Charlotte Chronicles, which appeared on the Kindle Top 100 list. She lives in the Midwest with her husband, who keeps track of life's details while she's writing; a daughter, who understands when Mom disappears into her office for hours at a time; and a rambunctious dog who does neither.